PARIAH

a Terran Shift novel

JAMIE ALAN BELANGER

To my parents

and all those who believed in me

Special thanks to Paul for helping with editing

To my parents
and all those who believed in me

Special thanks to Paul for helping with editing

CHAPTER
1

NEW TAMPA, FLORIDA
JULY 18, 2030 9:30 PM EDT

Lisa plopped herself down on the dingy bar stool, red leather pants sticking to patches of freshly dried alcohol. She fiddled with a zipper on her shirt with one hand while pushing locks of her light brown hair from her face with the other. She watched the bartender intently, waiting for him to acknowledge her presence. He pushed a glass of bright green liquid in front of someone down the counter and nodded enthusiastically while pocketing a bill. Lisa tapped her foot on the stool while pulling out some money. The bartender glanced in her direction and nodded as she pushed a folded bill across the counter toward him.

"Whiskey," she said in monotone.

The bartender nodded his head as he reached beneath the counter. Lisa shifted on her stool and frowned as she realized how sticky it was. The bar was dark, a little damp, and reeked of stale beer. A few people were scattered around the room, some standing and some seated at various tables. A group in one corner was talking loudly at each other while drinking their beer and giggling like the drunken fools they were. The windows had been painted black to keep the sunlight out and a heavy blanket draped in front of the entrance foyer. Music drifted in from speakers set in the ceiling, a constant pounding of bass that gave the floor a slight tremble. Just loud enough to barely hear the instruments, but not loud enough to disrupt talking completely. Some kind of new wave techno from South America, judging by the sound of the instruments she could pick out. As she glanced around the place, a tired looking man in a black raincoat awkwardly pushed his way through the entrance blanket. He looked around at the people in the place, then started toward the bar. He was dressed for work, not a bar, complete with a wage slave's button-down shirt and tie. He didn't look like he belonged here. Neither did she.

"Whiskey," the bartender said as he placed the shot glass on the counter behind her. He took the folded hundred-dollar bill from the counter and put it in his pocket. Lisa turned around, slammed the drink, and returned the glass to the counter. The bartender promptly refilled the glass. "You wanna run a tab, or you want some change now?"

"I'll run a tab." She took the glass from the counter as he nodded.

"Got anything to eat here?" the man in the black raincoat asked. The tone of his voice made his question sound more like an apology.

"Appetizers mostly. Chicken fingers, cheese sticks, stuff like that."

"Chicken. Sounds good."

The bartender opened a sliding portion of the wall behind him and relayed the order. The man in the raincoat looked at Lisa and smiled. Not a flirtatious smile, just a friendly one. Lisa smiled back involuntarily, caught herself, and immediately refocused her attention on the shot glass in front of her. He unfastened his raincoat and sat on the stool next to her. He didn't say anything to her; he just glanced over every few moments and then turned away. And then his food arrived and he left with it. By then, Lisa was on her fourth shot.

"Drinking alone?" another man asked while sliding onto the same stool. He was taller than the last, unshaven and more shabbily dressed. He had a slight tan and a more muscular build than the first man. He looked her over with an odd grin on his face.

"Like it that way," she informed him.

"Why's that?"

"Quieter."

"Quiet? In this place? First time here, huh?"

"Seems quiet so far."

"Yeah, until the dog sisters over there get drunker." He pointed out the "dog sisters" as he called them - a pair of exceptionally unattractive girls sitting at a table near one of the windows. One of them noticed him pointing at them and promptly flipped him off. He smiled and winked at her, which only seemed to infuriate her more.

"Ah, rowdy place then."

"Yeah, not your kind of scene, huh? You look more upscale. Manhattan material."

"Never been to New York." She downed another shot.

"Nah, I mean the club down the street. Manhattan. Real classy place. They charge a cover and everything. Buncha rich kids drinking themselves silly and dancing till the next day and such."

"Sounds like Hell."

"Totally, but I'd be there in a second if I could afford the cover. Bastards." He turned to the bartender and slapped his hands on the counter like an impromptu drum set until he turned around. "Heya Sammy, how bout them Rays?"

The bartender just stared at the guy for a few seconds, then scratched his chin. "Dunno man, I hate football."

"*Baseball*, Sammy, *baseball*."

"Whatever. Look buddy, not everyone in New Tampa knows shit about them sports teams. You gonna order something or what? I got work to do."

"I'll just have a beer."

Lisa motioned for Sammy the bartender to fill her glass again, then glanced over to her right. The guy in the black raincoat was sitting at a table under a red neon EXIT sign, staring right back at her. When he noticed her looking, his face turned slightly crimson and he looked back down at his chicken fingers. He picked up the fork and knife, hands shaking, and cut off a bite. She turned back to the bar as Sammy handed the other man a beer. He got up from the stool, nodded to her, and left.

"Who is that guy?"

"Huh? What guy? That one just here?"

"No, the chicken guy."

"Dunno, never seen him before."

"Oh." She glanced back at the black raincoat man and studied him a bit. About six feet tall, she guessed, and maybe two hundred pounds. A little overweight, but not anything out of the ordinary these days. He had short black hair, tired looking eyes, and a smoothly shaved chin. Khaki pants, light blue shirt, navy tie. Typical cubicle monkey most likely in a dead end job. The other man with the beer approached the table and sat down as she watched. She turned back to Sammy. "What about the other one?"

"No clue."

"But he seemed to know you."

"Look lady, I said I ain't got no clue. Everyone seems to know me. Hell, place is called Sammy's if ya hadn't noticed."

She hadn't. She had just picked the place at random. She wanted a drink. Several, in fact. Anything to get away from the daily grind of dealing with her father and his lawyer friends. She cringed involuntarily at the thought of all those lawyers. Greedy bastards who did everything they could to get as much money for the corporation (and themselves) as they could. The body-guards had been harder to shake, but she was sure she was going to get at least a few moments of relative peace here. She grabbed the shot glass and drained its contents.

"Bathroom?" she asked. Sammy pointed over her shoulder to the other side of the room. She got up, feeling a little wobbly. The room was spinning a little too much for her comfort. She leaned back and felt the stool press into the backs of her thighs. She looked up and saw the signs for the bathrooms ahead of her. Not a very far walk, perhaps thirty feet at the most, but it was far enough to pose a problem to her in her current state. She wasn't entirely sure she wanted to pee in a place like this, but she was sure she didn't have much of a choice. When the room stopped spinning around her, she took a step forward and stood there for a few moments to make sure that she wasn't going to fall on the floor. She decided to count to ten. She took a step forward, then another. A few more steps and she decided she was okay to get to the bathroom.

"Hey, Lisa!" called a voice off to her left. She whirled around, almost losing her balance. She saw a blur of movement, a flash of steel. And then she heard a sickening crunch, the clear sound of metal piercing flesh very close to her. She took a step backward and looked down. A steak knife handle was sticking out of her chest, stuck somewhere in her left breast. She looked up, her vision starting to get cloudy. She saw a man sitting at a table underneath a red neon EXIT sign. Black raincoat.

And then she felt herself falling.

CHAPTER
2

NEW TAMPA, FLORIDA
JULY 18, 2030 9:17 PM EDT

N eil leaned back in his chair, stretching his arms and cracking his knuckles in one smooth, calculated movement. He took off his optic interface glasses, pinched his nose, and squinted his eyes. He'd been staring at the same source code for over ten hours straight and his eyes were beginning to ache. He knew he was close to fixing his latest issue, he just needed to look at the problem sideways. He concentrated on the problem and tried to analyze it in his mind. When the solution finally did come to him, he sighed and shook his head at the sheer simplicity of it.

Just as he was putting the glasses back on, he heard footsteps approaching from outside his cubicle. He knew the footsteps were his boss and that the deliberate heavy walking was usually a warning that translated roughly into *our client wants the software, you're the only one who can do it, and so I need you to work this weekend.* There was only one way around that last bit, and that was to work extra hours before the weekend and pass the code off to the testing department early. Neil hated doing that, but he'd rather skip some of his own quality assurance testing than skip his weekend.

The footsteps halted and his boss cleared his throat dramatically. "Hey, Neil."

"Bob. What's going on?"

"I need that code done tomorrow. Can you do it?"

Neil sat up straight in his chair and sighed heavily. "Should be able to. I'm almost done now, actually. Just have to fix the last issue and do some more testing."

"Good, glad to hear it. Looking forward to seeing it in action."

"It'll be done tomorrow."

Bob nodded and left. Neil turned back toward his desk and sighed again. Four years of school. Four years of his life spent learning not a damn thing that he didn't already know from his own time spent exploring the Net. And he'd spend the rest of his life paying off those four years. He stared at his desk, a barren table before him with plush cubicle walls on three sides. Fluorescent lighting above provided inadequate illumination and a barely audible humming. Three partially filled cups of coffee, gone cold with age, and a two foot stack of specification printouts shoved into a corner.

Neil shook his head and looked down at the optic interface glasses he held. They were an older technology, resembling over-sized sunglasses, with a long thin cable running to the computer stored under his desk. There were newer models on the market, but his boss insisted on purchasing these because of the special deal he got. The glasses worked, which Neil appreciated, they just didn't have all the features and comfort of newer models. They weren't even equipped with a wireless connection option. The inside of the glasses held tiny display screens that filled the user's field of vision when worn. The technology resembled solutions that came out of the virtual reality experiments in the 1990s, but in a much more portable package.

He put the optic interface glasses back on and held out his hands. Images of the Net flowed toward him, gradually slowing as they got closer. His user interface scrolled into view, every widget placed just so. Bright orange gradients against a steel blue sky. He moved his left hand to type out a command, gloved fingers punching virtual keys in the air above his desk. He moved his right hand down a bit, then typed out a password with both. Goliath Incorporated's private datastore opened up to let him in.

Goliath wasn't a bad company, generally speaking, but Neil hated them simply because he knew he'd spend the rest of his life working for them. As soon as he got out of college, he was offered a full time job as a programmer there. Neil was always good at dealing with computers, much more so than with people. When tested in high school, he placed abnormally low in communications but showed an aptitude for mathematics and logic. He took an introductory programming course after those tests and within a week he was teaching the teacher. He typed so fast that he broke their antiquated typing tutor. Then he took out loans for college, Computer Science classes mostly. And now here he was, twenty-seven years old and still so far in debt that there was no ending in sight.

Neil opened his latest project, a government-sponsored firewall called Shield 4. The project modules unfolded before him like brightly colored origami, wings of a crane stretching to fill his field of view with someone else's idea of the best way to organize three million lines of code. He leaned back in his chair, scrolled to the module he was currently trying to finish, and stared at the lines of code that floated in front of him. The clock in his status bar widget ticked minutes away as he contemplated how to implement his latest fix. He reached into the code, moved a piece, then started typing into the gap left over. He used his right hand to scroll the code block up to see the next section, where he had left one of his infamous "TODO: Fix this crap!" comments that *used* to make his co-workers chuckle. Now they just groaned and rolled their eyes at him. He replaced the comment with a few lines of code to help with the debugging he knew he would have to finish the next day. He stretched his arm to the right, triggering a hidden menu to open with some of his favorite blocks of common code. Neil reviewed the list and selected one he'd used dozens of times - a small utility he wrote for monitoring incoming connection attempts. It was widely believed that the Shield line of firewalls was uncrackable, but that didn't lessen Neil's paranoia. Internet security was an arms race from day one.

There. He thought. *Done.* He issued the compilation command and waited. A few seconds later, it finished with no errors or warnings. Few programmers bothered trying to clean up all the warnings that seemed to be inevitable with modern compilers, but Neil was a stickler for details. He smirked as he logged out and took off the glasses.

"Time enough to test that tomorrow," he said out loud while taking off his gloves and shutting down the computer. His chair creaked in protest as he stood up and stretched one last time. Neil grabbed his black raincoat from the hook in his cubicle and headed for the door.

*   *   *

Night. Neil had barely stepped out of his office building before he realized that it was already dark out. He turned up the collar of his raincoat out of habit and started walking toward home. His apartment was only a few blocks away, but after a long day of typing, the last thing he wanted was to walk twenty minutes to get home. He knew the path well from his years of service to Goliath. He walked to work because he couldn't afford a car. The car he had while in college was forcibly removed from him the year after he graduated when the American government declared all gasoline powered vehicles illegal. Some last-ditch misguided effort to combat the growing global warming problem. He couldn't afford to get one of the new electric cars, so he walked. He could barely afford to live these days, which was rather ironic considering the size of his paycheck. At first he didn't mind it at all. He needed the exercise, and it wasn't that far unless it was June. It always rained in June. The summer heat didn't matter since he rarely left work when there was still light out.

He inhaled deeply, enjoying the fresh, warm air. It had been a long time since he'd been able to breathe so comfortably. Something odd had happened to the area after New Tampa was built, several years after most of the surrounding bay area had been flattened in 2015 when the war against terrorism had turned nuclear. Neil was too young to remember that day well, and luckily he had been out of state visiting his grandparents. His parents had been less lucky. Tampa, Los Angeles, New York City, Chicago, and Dallas were all attacked simultaneously by a terrorist group whose name Neil could barely remember let alone pronounce or spell properly. Nobody saw it coming. Or at least, nobody admitted that they saw it coming. There were scandals, and accusations, and a couple thousand pages of government studies and reports; but in the end the bottom line was that the people in charge were more interested in blamethrowing and in the economic impact than in the people. More than thirty million people had died instantly, and another fifty million died over the next few years from the fallout. His parents had been among the latter group.

A few years after the area was declared safe for living and was built up again, he decided to move back. The college tuition in New Tampa was only slightly less outrageous than the tuition near where his grandparents lived, and he had gotten an offer through his high school to work part time at Goliath while he attended classes. He had grown up watching the Internet transform from a series of two-dimensional pages with little blue hyperlinks into a three-dimensional consensual silicon dream world. And now that he was at Goliath, he was writing the software that made it work, the software that made it safer.

Neil turned the corner onto a side street and saw a light up ahead. Sammy's. He'd passed that bar every day, twice a day, for years. For some reason, the yellow and blue neon sign seemed to call him in. It was either that or he'd eat yet another peanut butter sandwich when he got home. He dipped a hand into his pocket and looked at the contents. Seven dollars and some change. He figured it might be enough. He opened the door and stepped inside.

The entrance to the bar was unusually clean. "No Smoking" was painted in tall black letters on the plain white wall across from the entrance. Beneath that, someone had written "unless you share" in blue magic marker. A dark green blanket hung from ceiling to floor in front of the only other exit from the entryway to shield sensitive drunk eyes from the sunlight outside. Neil pushed it aside and entered the bar.

The place wasn't as full as it could have been. It smelled funny, like stale alcohol, and there was a constant pounding of a techno song's bass track that made Neil's stomach a little uneasy. There were only a few people here, scattered around at the various tables. A rather attractive brunette wearing a white shirt and red leather pants was sitting on a stool by the bar, looking in his direction. He saw the bartender put a glass on the counter by her. She turned her attention to the glass as Neil walked over to the counter.

"Got anything to eat here?" Neil asked the man behind the counter.

"Appetizers mostly. Chicken fingers, cheese sticks, stuff like that."

"Chicken. Sounds good."

Neil figured he could always pay with his ATM card if he didn't have enough cash to cover the food. The bartender turned around, opened a sliding wall panel, and relayed the order to someone on the other side. Neil looked at the girl again, and she smiled. He wasn't sure if she was trying to flirt with him or just being polite. He opened his raincoat and sat down on the stool beside her. He had never had much luck with women, so he decided to let her make the first move. She sat there, hands folded protectively around a shot of some kind of hard liquor. He looked up at her face, studying the features, her smooth skin, cute little nose, light brown eyes. She turned her head a bit and he immediately turned away. *Damn*, he thought, *caught again*.

A few minutes later, she still hadn't made the move. Then the bartender set the chicken down in front of him along with a fork, steel steak knife, and the bill. He looked at the bill and placed a five-dollar coin on the counter. Neil shrugged, gathered up the food and utensils, and left the bar area. He found a quiet little table in the back area of the room, next to the exit door. He sat facing the bar, facing the girl, and watched as a man sat down on the same stool and started talking with her.

"Oh well, lost another chance." Neil said, mostly to himself but loud enough for the people at the next table to hear. He shrugged at them and cut into the first piece of chicken. It looked like chicken, but was almost as tough as a steak. Now he understood what the hefty steel knife was for. He set down the utensils and stretched his hands, cracked his knuckles, and pulled a napkin from the dispenser on the table. He looked back up toward the girl at the bar, just in time for her to turn around and stare back at him. He flushed, could feel his face turn bright red, could feel his cheeks burning. He quickly shifted his gaze back to the chicken. He picked up his knife and fork, hands shaking, and started to cut into it again. "Bar food," he said between mouthfuls. "Should have stuck with the sandwiches."

"No shit buddy, that's why I only eat at home."

Neil looked up to see the man who had been at the bar talking with the girl. He held a Bud Light bottle in his hand. He looked a little like Neil's old college roommate, except with a little less facial hair and a lot less alcohol in his system. Add a few days' growth and a dozen beers and the resemblance would be uncanny.

"Mind if I join you?" he asked.

Neil swallowed the chunk of chicken he was trying to chew and nodded.

"Cool, thanks man. Saw you lookin' over there toward the bar. That chick ain't worth it, some kinda weirdo."

"Right." Neil glanced at her. She was talking to the bartender and pointing a thumb in his direction. He felt his face flush again. "She's just a cute one."

"Cute my ass, she's a major hottie. I'm gonna do her tonight."

"Ah, cool." Neil couldn't think of anything more intelligent to respond with, so he took another bite and looked up. The girl had stood and was slowly wobbling toward the bathrooms. Neil put down his fork and knife and grabbed another napkin from the dispenser on the table.

"Nice, thanks." The man put his beer down, picked up Neil's knife, fiddled with it a bit, and stood up. "Hey, Lisa!" he called out.

The girl turned toward where Neil was sitting, her eyes half closed and her arms limp at her sides. A flash of light from his right caught Neil's attention. He dropped his napkin and watched in horror as his steel steak knife hurtled through the air and embedded itself into the girl's chest. She stood there for a few seconds, took a step backward, then looked down at the knife sticking out of her chest. She looked up, looked right at Neil, and then fell forward onto the floor.

Some girls at a table by one of the painted-over windows screamed. Neil looked to his right. The guy was gone. He turned back to see everyone in the bar staring at him. Someone killed the music, the sudden stop of the bass beat leaving only startled cries of confusion.

Run.

Neil shook his head, feeling the grip of mental fog he usually associated with alcohol. He hadn't had a drink in years. The bartender had a phone receiver in his hand and was talking into it with a very concerned look on his face. The curtain pulled back and two men in black suits walked in. They glanced around, saw the girl on the floor, and pushed past some of the people and made their way quickly to her. Some officers in uniform walked in after them. One of the men by the girl's side looked at the officers and shook his head. He lifted his arm and spoke into his sleeve.

Run.

The voice came to him again, rolling slowly through his head as it repeated the same word in a soothing tone.

Run.

One of the officers stepped up behind the two men and raised his hands. "Everyone stay where you are and remain calm."

Another man entered the bar, wearing black pants and a plain white shirt and tie. He had a gold police badge attached to his belt at one hip and a holster with a gun on the other. He moved toward the two men crouching over the girl's body. "That her?"

Run.

"Yeah. He won't be pleased."

"Wait a second," Sammy spoke up from behind the bar. "How the hell did you get here so fast? I'm still on hold."

"We were..." the plain-clothed policeman started to say, but stopped when one of the black-suited men placed a meaty hand on his shoulder. "That is, we were nearby." He turned away from Sammy to address the rest of the bar. "Everyone stay where you are. We have several officers here and several questions to ask about this incident. You," he addressed Sammy again, "what happened here? To her?"

Run.

Neil's head was swimming. Murder. He just saw that girl get murdered. The thought made him want to vomit. His hearing seemed to fade out, like he was watching a movie where the sound suddenly cut out, the only sound the pounding of his own heart as his pulse quickened. Sammy was talking to the officer, his arms telling the story Neil had just watched, complete with the motions of throwing and an accusing thumb pointed in his direction. Neil looked down at her body, white T-shirt stained a rusty crimson from the blood pouring out of her chest. Her body seemed to twitch, her mouth seemed to quiver as a fresh spot of blood poured out. Neil gagged and looked away, turned his head and saw the exit door.

Run.

His head pounded, an ache that made his ears vibrate and his vision blur. Where was this throbbing coming from? Was the music still on? He put his hands flat on the table and inhaled deeply, shook his head to clear his vision.

Run.

He had no idea where that thought came from, but there it was: *run.* He didn't kill her, but everyone saw him sitting there with a goofy look on his face as the girl keeled over with *his* steak knife sticking out of her chest. Where was the guy that *did* kill her? The mysterious former roommate doppelganger who grabbed his knife before he had even realized what was happening. It had all happened so fast that Neil hadn't had time to look to find out. He cursed himself for not being more alert. A few officers with notepads started talking to the other bar patrons.

Run.

What would he miss anyway? Anything was better than spending the next forty years of life working for the same company, scraping through life and never having a chance to pay off anything. He envisioned himself in his sixties, still living in the same crappy apartment, still working at the same crappy job, still trying to pay off his loans. He pictured his cabinets filled with jars of peanut butter and his kitchen table with the loaf of three-day old bread. He mentally counted out his month's entertainment budget. He looked down at what was left of the chicken - two months' worth of entertainment budget. He felt sick to his stomach.

Run.

"I can't keep living like this," he mumbled, talking to himself again. He waited until the police officer closest to him was busy writing, and then he stood up and headed for the exit door. "Screw my life."

The alarm's wail pierced his eardrums as he pushed open the emergency exit door. Every officer in the building turned to watch him leave.

"After him!"

Neil turned and started running down the alleyway.

"Stop! Stop him!"

He ducked to his left, the sound of pounding footsteps close behind him. Rain-soaked cardboard boxes were stacked several high at irregular intervals along the sides of the buildings. He weaved his way past them as he ran down the alley. A few piles of trash moved, whether from rats or bums he couldn't tell, and he sure didn't have time to stop and check. The sky lit up bright as daylight. A few drops of water struck him in the head, chilled droplets that snaked their way into his shirt and sent shivers down his back. He ducked to the right into another alley. A loud blast of thunder rolled off into the distance. Neil slipped into an open doorway to his left and stopped, holding his breath. He listened as several pairs of boots pounded the pavement outside the doorway.

He was in some kind of house long since abandoned. Rats scurried around the floor as he walked deeper into the building. He stepped carefully around them, trying hard to not disturb the rodents. Furniture and shattered pieces of former furniture were lying around the rooms, mildewed and long forgotten by even the most desperate members of society. The windows were boarded up, graffiti all over the boards and walls around them. Neil pushed on the wood but it wouldn't give. The sounds of shouting outside intensified. Neil ducked behind a wall as a flashlight pierced the darkness around him. He held his breath again and glanced around the alcove, immediately noticing a staircase that led upward. Neil started up the stairs, hoping that the steps wouldn't creak and give him away. Halfway up, the pressure from his weight invoked a creak, the sound immediately drowned out by another loud crack of thunder. He breathed a silent thanks and bounded up the last few steps. He went up two more flights of stairs until he reached a door at the top, which opened out onto the roof of the building. He stepped out and closed it softly behind him.

The sound of police officers yelling orders to each other carried up to where he was. He walked to the edge and peered over. Several flashlight beams danced around the alleyway. Figures darted around, shouting to each other. He turned and sat down, propping his back against the roof wall. He leaned his head back and stared into the sky, trying to mentally recap his day. He had followed the same routine as always. By all accounts, the day should have turned out the same, but now his life was going to be different. He tried to reconcile that notion, to figure out what the hell had gone wrong. The only answer he could conjure was Sammy's, that somehow the seedy little bar he walked past twice a day had been responsible for this. But it wasn't the bar, it was *he* that had run. Maybe if he had explained things to the officers, maybe if he had told them a man that looked like his former roommate had thrown the knife. Maybe he'd be back at home right now, sating his hunger with slightly stale bread and peanut butter. He had a lot of maybes floating around in his head. He needed something definitive.

He reached into his raincoat's inner pocket and pulled out his computer, lifted the protective flap, and pressed in the power button with one thumb while running his other thumb over the security panel. It beeped softly as it started to boot up. This was the most definitive thing he knew - computers were pure logic. Something about the small box comforted him in a way he could rarely put into words. He kept an audio journal on it, one that even he never listened to. There was just something reassuring about telling his thoughts to his computer. When his computer was done booting, he hit a few keys to start the voice recorder.

"Today," he whispered into the microphone with the most authoritative sounding voice he could muster. "Today I ran. I don't know why. I just... did. Maybe I wanted to, maybe I've always wanted to. I guess I finally snapped. I threw my life away. My stupid, stupid life." He paused a moment to listen to the police officers shouting orders to each other in the alley below him. The graphic equalizer on the sound recorder showed that it was registering some of them. Neil took a deep breath and then continued. "Good riddance. Hope the new one's better."

He closed the application, shut down the computer, and returned it to its pocket. Neil leaned his head back and smiled as the rain started to fall.

CHAPTER
3

NEW TAMPA, FLORIDA
JULY 18, 2030 9:43 PM EDT

H e leaned against the wall in the dark corner, trying to hide from prying eyes while swearing under his breath. He hadn't expected that many police to show up that soon. "Come on man. Just do it," he mumbled as he watched the man in the black raincoat fidget in his seat, obviously trying to fight the urge. He was a strong one, but not strong enough. Nobody was. It was only a matter of time. He pleaded with the figure, chanting a mantra of, "come on, come on, come on." Sammy had yelled for the music to be turned off and the whole place was still in a confused near-silence. One of the police officers bellowed out a standard everyone-stay-put type of order. The guy in the black raincoat stared at the corpse a while then shook his head. Sammy loudly recounted what he had seen to the officer.

The other officers wandered around, taking notes, and the man in the shadows grinned as he saw several patrons pointing toward the guy in the black raincoat. Finally the guy caved, stood up, glanced around nervously, then headed for the exit door. The alarm sounded as he pushed on the bar and the door popped open. "Hell yeah," the man in the corner announced a little too loudly. When he realized that his exclamation had been drowned out by the alarm, he relaxed and added, "like a charm."

The sound of the alarm caused every head in the place to turn. The police officers started yelling and running for the door. When the last of them had exited the building, he slipped out into the alley. He could hear people yelling off in the distance, heard the sounds of someone being chased, and could see flashlight beams bouncing off the brick walls. The sounds were receding. He'd done it. He'd done the job and gotten away without anyone noticing him. He'd been counting on people being shocked and not paying attention, and it appeared to have paid off.

He looked up and down the street, surveying the local area. He saw a public phone kiosk off to his left about a hundred yards away. Headlights from a passing car illuminated the street as he walked to the phone, cautiously glancing over his shoulder to ensure he wasn't being followed. The sound of police sirens in the distance echoing off the buildings brought a goofy smirk to his face. He had expected this job to be the toughest of them all, but it turned out to be the easiest so far. When he got to the phone, he saw it was one of the older kiosks that didn't support video, only voice. He slipped a small plastic card into the slot and dialed a memorized number. He was greeted with silence, just the sound of a phone being picked up.

"It's done," he said into the receiver. "Primary target, and all that jazz. Shoulda seen the look on her face, heh. And I think I might have pinned the thing on some other guy there too."

"The money has been transferred into your account," the oddly familiar female voice informed him.

"Thirty mil, right?"

"Ten. The balance will be paid when the job is complete."

"And my bus pass?"

"Greyhound lines in New Tampa. It leaves at 8:30 AM tomorrow morning. You can pick up the ticket in the terminal. Your next target will be in the Orlando station at precisely the same time you arrive there. You will have to act fast."

"Got it."

He replaced the phone receiver in its holder and looked up the street both ways. It started to rain.

CHAPTER
4

NEW TAMPA, FLORIDA
JULY 19, 2030 8:14 AM EDT

W hat've we got, Roen?" Jim Donners asked as he leaned against the wall of his office. He was in his late fifties, the twilight years of his career, and in no mood for the amount of trouble that this case was starting to pose. His tired eyes looked over to his partner while he reached up to idly smooth out his curly white hair. He just wanted to get this case solved so he could go back to expanding his waistline while poring over a stack of Key West promotional fliers he had stashed in the bottom drawer of his desk. He'd been working cases like this for almost forty years and he was long overdue for a vacation.

His partner, Steve Roen, was a young man with a toned body, short brown hair, and bright green eyes that had turned many a lady's head. He was sometimes too dedicated, and his persistence had gotten him into trouble more times than their captain could count. Donners was assigned as his partner in an attempt to tone him down and get him used to playing things by the book. "Fourteen witnesses," he responded to his partner's question. "Ten saw nothing, of course."

"The other four?"

"Two saw the knife thrown from the vicinity of the table of that guy that pulled the disappearing act. Then we have Sammy."

"Who?"

"Bartender. Says there was another guy at that table."

"Anyone else see this guy?"

"Nope."

Donners scratched his head. "Steve, this isn't much to go on."

"I know, I know. But then there's witness number fourteen. She says that the disappearing guy and his friend were both hitting on the girl before going to that table."

"Two guys hitting on a girl in a bar sounds suspicious to you? Think you need to get out more."

"Yeah, probably, but get this - one guy comes in, right? He goes up to the bar, orders the chicken, then sits down without saying a *word* to the girl. Then his friend comes in, chats her up a bit, then joins the first guy at the table. The only table, mind you, that was out of the view of the security cameras."

"You gotta be shitting me. Please tell me you already cited that bartender."

"Oh yeah, way ahead of ya," Roen said while sitting down heavily in his chair. "I got something else too."

"What's that?"

"This second guy, he talks to the first guy, then vanishes."

"So they were working together?"

"Could be. But after the murder, this other guy is *gone*. Just plain gone. Nobody saw him leave."

"What about these two guys?" Donners opened the blinds on his office window and nodded toward two large men in black suits. They had bodies that belonged on the beach, slightly tanned skin and rippling muscles that the suits could never hope to hide. Clean cut hair, no stubble on their chins, dark sunglasses. And neither officer had seen either of them crack a smile. They were sitting side by side on the hallway bench, each staring straight ahead without flinching. The one on the left was speaking into his sleeve at a low volume.

"I ran a check on them. Turns out they're bodyguards with some firm in Miami. Just like they said."

"Bodyguards. Who *was* this girl?"

"No word yet. Captain said he was gonna handle finding out."

Donners let the blinds fall back down into place as he turned around. He inhaled sharply, held his breath for a moment, then let it out with an exasperated sigh. "So... we got witnesses that saw two guys at the table, then the girl is dead, and there's just one guy at the table."

"Same guy that ran as soon as we showed up."

"That's still not much to go on. We still don't know who the guy is, Roen. Either of 'em."

"I know, but I got the guys down in the lab already running the prints on the knife and a beer bottle we found on that table. Maybe for that box we found under the table too but they weren't even sure what the hell it was. Should get word on the prints any time now."

Donners walked over to his desk and looked at the phone. He put his hands on his waist and tapped his finely polished shoe on the floor. The phone rang as if on cue. He pressed the speakerphone button. "Donners, homicide."

A voice crackled over the speaker. "Sir, we have some of the data that Detective Roen requested."

"Good," Donners said. "Fax it up." He pressed the button again to sever the connection and walked over to the fax machine. It started to print out something.

"I can't believe you're still using that old piece of shit."

"It works," Donners replied while the machine struggled with the page it was trying to print. When it finished, he pulled the page out and looked it over.

"Yeah, barely. Damn thing was obsolete three decades ago. So what's the deal?" Steve Roen stood up and tried to peek over Jim Donners' shoulder.

"Page one of five. That's promising. Let's see..." he scanned the first page. "Knife had four sets of prints. Bottle had two."

"And that other thing we found stuck under the table?"

"No mention. They're probably still testing it."

"Okay, then whose prints were on the bottle and knife?"

"Hang on, that's the other four pages." He grabbed the next page from the machine and looked at it. "Suspect number one, prints on the bottle and the knife. Sam Holsen."

"The bartender."

"Right, I expected that one. Suspect number two has prints on the knife. James Tanners."

Roen pulled a small notepad from his shirt pocket and flipped through a few pages. "Tanners... Tanners... Ah, the cook."

"Probably handed the knife to the bartender. Either way, if he was the cook then he was in the kitchen." Donners took the next page and looked it over. "Suspect three, prints on the knife only. Neil Roberts."

Roen turned a few more pages in his notebook, got to the end and closed it. "One of our mystery guys. No record of him in here at all."

"Last one, prints on knife and bottle... Huh."

"What?"

"Identity unknown."

"What the hell? Who doesn't have their prints on file?"

"Criminals. Good ones. Or diplomats maybe."

"True, but that guy's just one of the two at the table. Who's this Roberts guy?" He took the page from Donners and looked it over. "Neil Eric Roberts, born July 14, 2003 in Clearwater, Florida. Graduated high school in May 2021 at some place up in Ohio. Probably moved up there to avoid the war zone and reconstruction."

"What? Not with that birth date. He was like twelve when they nuked

MacDill."

"Well, anyway... Next record is a Bachelor's degree in Computer Science, Florida Cybertech College, June 2025. Been working at Goliath Incorporated here in New Tampa ever since he got out of high school on some internship program."

"Criminal record?"

"None."

Donners rubbed his eyes with his thumbs and sighed. "Okay Roen, scenario. Roberts and the mystery criminal guy meet at this bar. One of them orders food to get a free weapon that can't be traced back to him. The other distracts the girl and buys her drinks..."

"Bartender said she bought her own."

"Whatever. Anyway, they work together to get her drunk and distracted, then wham."

"I don't buy it. First of all, who was this girl anyway? Must be important or rich to afford two bodyguards."

"Yeah, bodyguards that did a sweet ass job in letting her get killed."

Roen sat down and leaned back in his chair. "Another scenario. This guy Roberts, straight and narrow, upstanding citizen type. He goes to work, pays his taxes, and lives a normal life. He meets this girl and she shuns him, right? Then he hires this other guy to have her killed. Only problem is he doesn't have a picture, so he shows up at the place to point her out. The other guy does the crime and splits. Then maybe this guy Roberts realizes what he did and runs when we showed up."

"Dunno about that one. Why would he have run and risked getting caught? He could have just sat there and played dumb."

"Scared shitless, maybe. Maybe he did want to stay and chat with us to provide some kind of alibi, then got spooked and ran."

"Could be. No way to know for sure until we find him."

"We should check out his place."

"Exactly what I was thinking. Let's go."

Roen and Donners left the office and headed for the stairs, past the two men on the bench who still hadn't moved. When they reached the lobby,

Donners walked over to the front counter.

"Hey," Donners said to the officer behind the counter. "Make sure those two suits outside my office are taken care of. I still have questions for them."

"Yes, sir."

"And have Baxter call me on my cell when he gets back from that thing he was doing this morning. I got stuff for him to do."

"Yes, sir." The officer pulled over a notepad and scribbled some things down.

Donners headed toward the front door to join Roen, who was already standing outside, smoking a cigarette. They walked down the stairs to the parking lot beneath the police station and got into Roen's car. He started the engine and pulled out of the garage, pausing at the exit for a break in the traffic.

It was a typical morning in New Tampa. The air was warm and heavy, the ground slightly damp from the previous night's rain but quickly drying in the summer heat. The sidewalks were already swarming with people heading for work. Some were trudging along out of sheer routine, bored looks on their faces and briefcases clasped in their hands. Others looked less bored, and walked briskly with rolled up umbrellas tucked under their arms, glancing nervously toward the sky every few seconds. Roen's beat-up old Ford pulled out onto the street and started to head eastward, small chunks of rust falling from the undercarriage as he went over the speed bump at the parking garage's exit.

"Friday."

Roen turned his head slightly and glanced in the rearview mirror. "What was that?"

"It's Friday, he's probably at work."

"Possibly, but it's worth checking out either way." Roen saw the light in front of them turn yellow and pressed his foot down softly on the brake pedal, bringing the car to a halt as slowly as possible. Someone behind honked and swerved past them, running the red light. Roen pulled out his notepad and wrote down the car's license plate number.

Donners sighed, nodded in silent agreement, and turned his head to look out the passenger window. A dozen children were playing hopscotch on the sidewalk, bouncing up and down, their feet landing with precision thrusts into the pale blue chalk outlines. A young couple was standing nearby, pointing at the children and smiling, the woman nodding vigorously as the young man with her whispered into her ear. Sunlight glinted off the ground near them, a green glass bottle broken into shards by the side of the street. And then the light changed and the car lurched forward, shaking violently as the electric motor attempted a gear shift, and then continued on its way. They passed a tattoo parlor, a quasi-legal remnant of earlier days that had a large sign in their window stating that they no longer offered piercings of any kind. Piercings weren't technically illegal, there were just too many laws regarding safety procedures in recent years and nobody wanted to risk breaking them. Further down the street was a stereo and video store, a greeting card shop, and a small bank where a man in a black raincoat was using the ATM.

"It should be up here on the right," Roen informed Donners. "Look for Grandiose Boulevard. Number four-sixteen, apartment nine."

They found the street and turned onto it. Low rent apartment buildings lined the street on both sides, interspersed with the occasional palm tree grove or mailbox cluster. The buildings themselves looked like they had been around since the turn of the century, possibly longer. Some windows were boarded up, but the boards were mildewed and crumbling. Building 416 was the nicest of the lot but not by much. The grass on the lawn surrounding it was brown, and in some places had been completely replaced with small rocks or patches of dirt. The driveway leading to the small parking area in the center of the building was wide enough for one car to get through. On the side of the building someone had spray painted "WELCOME TO HELL" in large letters using just about every color in a standard box of Crayolas. An old woman was sitting in a rocking chair on the front porch, singing a song the rest of the world had long forgotten while knitting what appeared to be either a sweater for a really large person or an afghan.

Roen pulled his car up to the curb and set the parking brake. They got out and approached the building, recently dried grass crunching under their feet. Donners waved to the woman when they were closer, but she ignored him.

Her attention was focused on her knitting, arthritic hands weaving the yarn together with impressive precision.

"Good morning ma'am."

She stopped singing, set down the needles and yarn onto the makeshift table created by her stretched skirt, and looked up at them. She squinted, then reached for her glasses. "Good morning."

Donners pulled out his badge and showed it to the woman, who inspected it with squinting eyes. "I'm Detective Jim Donners with the New Tampa Police, and this is Detective Steve Roen. We're looking for the man living in apartment nine, Neil Roberts. Do you know him?"

She shrugged and picked up her needles again. "Met him once or twice, sure. Lived here nine years. Met a lot of people in that time."

"Yeah, I bet you have." Donners stepped onto the porch and leaned against the wall. "Can you tell me what kind of man this Roberts is?"

"Quiet... It's always the quiet ones, isn't it?"

"Pardon?"

She leaned in closer to Donners, and he winced as he smelled the Southern Comfort on her breath. "The *quiet* ones. It's always them. You boys are with homicide, aren't you?"

"Uh... well, yes ma'am, we are," Roen replied as he looked over the rest of the building.

"See? The quiet ones. It's always them." She nodded and leaned back in her chair. She lifted her feet and let the chair tilt forward, then resumed her knitting and singing as soon as the chair had returned to its previous rocking motion.

Donners thanked her and joined Roen on the front lawn. They walked around to the back parking lot of the building. The building was built around a small courtyard with a few parking spaces in the interior. Three cars were parked in the lot, only one of which looked like it might actually work, if it wasn't propped up on cinder blocks with two tires missing. On the opposite side of the courtyard was a clean white door with a large iron "9" hung in its center. Roen and Donners walked across the lot to the door. Donners knocked. They waited for less than a minute before knocking again.

"Doesn't look like he's home." Roen picked at something in his teeth and looked around at the other apartments. "Doesn't look like much of anybody's home."

"Give it a little more time. He might be on the can."

"Sure, I got some time."

A muffled ringing sound emanated from Donners' left pants pocket. He pulled out the small cellular phone and held it up to his ear. "Donners, homicide. Yup. Hey Baxter."

Roen stifled a laugh. "I can't believe you're still using that old ass phone. Hey, ask him how that thing with his niece went, that school play or whatever it was."

Donners put his hand over the mouthpiece. "Yeah, you keep trying the door." He removed his hand and spoke into the phone. "How'd that thing with your niece go? What was she, in a play or something? Uh huh... ouch... oh man..."

Roen knocked on the door again, then tried to peer in through the grimy window but it was too dark inside to see anything. He tried the doorknob. "Damn, locked."

"Baxter, I need you to do something for me. Monitor credit and bank transactions on a Neil Eric Roberts, social..." He pulled the folded paper from his pocket and opened it. "Social is one-one-four-six-niner-niner-zero-two-five-six-three. Oh and make sure that officer at the front desk took care of the two guys outside my office. They should be in protective custody so I can finish questioning them later. Oh and Baxter, one more thing. Get me the number for Goliath Incorporated. It's a company here in New Tampa, not sure what they do but hopefully they're in the book. Thanks." He clicked the mouthpiece closed.

"Door doesn't seem that solid." Roen was pushing on the door, listening to the wood creak.

"Don't even think about it. Three years. *Three years* man, and I retire with pension. So don't even think about that. We get a warrant, you can break that door down no problem. Without a warrant..."

"Yeah, I know, just messin' with ya."

"Let's get out of here. He's obviously not here. Baxter should call back soon with the number of his employer."

"Okay Jim. Hey, how'd that thing with his niece go? What was it, anyway?"

"School play. She did okay until one of the other kids tripped and spilled some drink on her, then she ran off stage crying."

"Comedy?"

"Not intentionally, apparently."

"Damn. Poor girl."

They walked along the edge of the driveway and out into the front yard. The old woman was still rocking back and forth in her chair, humming the same familiar tune and knitting away. Roen's car was still parked in the same place, and he was quite thankful to see it still in one piece. Donners' phone rang as they got closer to the car.

"Donners, homicide. Hey Baxter." He snapped his fingers and made writing motions. Roen handed over his pen and notepad. Donners laid the notepad on the car, flipped to the back page, and scribbled down a phone number. "Uh huh. Got it. What about the guys outside my office? What? What do you mean they left? Who authorized that?" He kicked the front tire of Roen's car, which shook a bit in response and dropped a few ounces of rust onto the pavement. "Shit. Okay, okay. What about the monitoring on Roberts?" Long pause as Donners stared up at the sky. Then he looked back to Roen. "I see. Thanks Baxter." He hung up and got into the car.

"Well, what's going on?"

"Got the phone number for that Goliath place. And those two bodyguards left shortly after we did."

"Someone let them out?"

"Yeah, some guys showed up, nice suits apparently, flashed government ID badges and took them away. Not sure who they were with, but they signed for the release so we'll find that out back at the station."

"Damn. And the credit monitoring?"

"Apparently, Roberts withdrew almost all his cash from his bank this morning."

"Probably not even worth calling his job then."

"Yeah, well, I'll do it anyway, just to be thorough. It's procedure, just in case he does go or does contact his employer, then we might get a lead. Then I'll call Judge Hammond and see about getting a search warrant for his place here."

"All right Jim, I'll take us back to the station then."

Donners pulled out his phone and dialed the number that Baxter had read to him over the phone. Two rings later, a youthful sounding woman answered and transferred him to another extension. The phone rang twice more before being picked up.

"Good morning, this is Detective Jim Donners with the New Tampa Police Department. Are you the supervisor of Neil Roberts? Good. Did he come into work today? I see. Well, if he does contact you, can you please let me know immediately? No sir, I'm not allowed to discuss the case at this time, but we just need to ask him a few questions. Yes, you can contact me through the New Tampa Police Station, Precinct Twenty-Seven. If I'm not there, just leave a message and I will get it. Thank you." He hung up the phone.

"Yup, dead end."

"Just drive, Roen. Just drive."

CHAPTER
5

NEW TAMPA, FLORIDA
JULY 19, 2030 7:55 AM EDT

Neil opened his eyes to a cloudless sky, solid shades of blue and still air. It was early in the morning but already quite warm, which was usually an indication that it was going to be a very hot day. Puddles of water from the night's rain were scattered around the roof. He ran his hands through his damp hair and leaned forward.

The previous night was mostly a blur. He thought back over the events and tried to convince himself it was a dream. *I'm gonna do her tonight.* The voice echoed in Neil's head. He cradled his head in his hands and stared at his reflection in the puddle at his feet. The scene started replaying in his head again. *I'm gonna do her tonight... Nice, thanks... Hey, Lisa!* And then the distinct sound of metal piercing flesh and the eerie silence that followed, his mind having edited out the music and replaced the bass beat with the thumping of his heart. He could see the look of shock evident in her pretty brown eyes, her lips parted in a silent scream as the blood flowed down the front of her shirt. And then she looked down at the knife in her trance, and slowly raised her eyes to look directly at him. Her final action in this world was accusing him, not with words but with a piercing gaze, an eternal sadness echoed in her eyes. The thought turned his stomach, made the air feel thinner. Neil leaned forward a little further and threw up into the puddle between his feet. When he was reasonably sure he had finished, he stood and staggered toward the door to the staircase. He leaned against the door frame and inhaled deeply.

Why? He asked himself. *Why the hell did I run?*

He tried to focus, to recall what motivation had driven him to do something so stupid. He should have stayed, should have talked to the police. He'd probably be home right now. But that voice, like a confused siren calling out and telling him to run, offering salvation from his current dead-end life. Running was the worst thing he could have done. Part of him wanted to run right now, straight to the police station, to tell them everything he knew. They should understand, right? Or would they lock him up for murder? Running was stupid, and continuing to run was just plain insane. And yet there was a part of him that *wanted* to keep running, to leave his life as far behind him as possible. Start over with a clean slate. The thought was both revolting and invigorating at the same time. Even the notion of running away from his life made his blood pressure rise. It was a huge shift from the normal, sensible decisions he made. He thought of his apartment, and of his job, and the decision to run from it all was just too attractive.

Neil entered the building and started down the stairs. All was quiet in the building except occasional snoring from some people who were sleeping on the floor at the ground level. He stepped over one of the occupants as he made his way to the door. In the alley, he took a quick inventory. He was wearing his trusty raincoat, which had mostly dried. It felt a little warm for the raincoat, but he knew from experience that the sky could open without warning in Florida. Better dry than drenched. He used to carry an umbrella for that reason, but wearing a raincoat was easier, and access to dry inner pockets sealed the deal for him. In one inner pocket he had his computer, with the optic interface glasses and data gloves wrapped in a tight bundle in their carrying case. In the other was his wallet, but there wasn't much of anything of note in it. He'd spent most of his cash the previous night, but still had his ATM card in his wallet and some loose change at the bottom of his pocket. He returned his wallet to his inner pocket and headed toward the main road at the end of the alley. A sign attached to the street light in front of him gave him a good indication of where he was. He was very close to home, only a few streets away. *Home,* he thought. *Can't ever go back there.* He turned and headed down the street away from his home.

He shambled his way along the concrete sidewalk while trying to sort out his thoughts. He needed a plan, something, anything. He always came up with a plan while programming, why was his mind blank now? All he had to do was figure out a way to approach what was going on scientifically, methodically. He glanced up and saw an ATM for his bank on the other side of the road. Just then a thought struck him.

Neil glanced over his shoulder. He saw normal daytime traffic in the road, pedestrians walking along the sidewalk, and some kid playing acoustic guitar outside a small café. Nobody was looking at him. Nobody cared. He walked right up to the ATM and pulled out his wallet. The machine accepted his card with a barely audible beeping sound. He typed in his PIN number and selected the option labeled "English". When a few choices printed out on the screen, Neil pushed the button next to one and a slip of paper printed out. He had some money in the bank that would be gone in a day or two when his automatically paid bills were subtracted. A little over six hundred dollars. The machine only let him take out five hundred a day. When his card was ejected, he grabbed it and his cash, then immediately pushed the card back into the ATM machine. When it asked for his PIN, he hit the "1" button a few times. The machine paused, stupidly blinked a few lights in protest, and then promptly printed a message on the screen informing Neil that his card had been confiscated. He smiled and started walking up the street.

Not far from the bank he saw some children playing hopscotch by the side of the road. A young couple was standing in the middle of the sidewalk, pointing at the children and talking quietly to each other. Neil skirted past them and the children. He knew where he needed to go. There was a bus station up ahead somewhere, off the main road a short distance from the next intersection. A sign ahead confirmed that it was off to the left and closer than he had anticipated. He turned around the corner and could see the blue and green logo of the station's sign. Several buses were parked in front of the building with names of various destinations printed in large letters above their windshields. One of the buses marked "Atlanta" pulled away from its parking spot as he got closer to the building.

The bus station's interior was much larger than it appeared from the outside. The whole place smelled of booze and urine. A single ticket counter lined most of one wall, flanked on both sides with a bathroom. The entrance was in the center of one wall that was lined with windows at regular intervals. Directly across the room from the entrance were a few shops that sold typical bus station fare: stale bagels, lukewarm coffee, yesterday's newspapers, and seedy magazines wrapped in brown paper. The center of the building was filled with rows of molded plastic chairs welded to the floor.

Neil walked up to the counter and glanced over their destination board, which consisted of various city names that each had a short list of numbers after them. There was no index, no indication whatsoever of any kind of order. An older man behind the counter coughed dramatically and flashed a forced smile at Neil.

"Need help, young man?"

"Uh, when's the next bus out?"

"Where to?"

"Anywhere."

The man scratched his chin and looked Neil over. "You don't care where?"

"No."

"Just as long as it leaves soon, right?"

"Yeah, you got it."

"You in some kind of trouble, son?"

Neil felt the hairs on the back of his neck stand up and could feel himself start to sweat. "Uh... uh, no sir. Just need to get out of town for the weekend, clear my head and stuff." The man frowned and ground his teeth. Neil drummed his fingers on the counter, then forced himself to look more relaxed. He leaned forward and said in a softer voice, "Girlfriend. Bad breakup."

"I see." The old man sat on a stool behind the counter and stared at Neil for several terrifying seconds before his mouth broke into a smile. "Women, can't live with em, eh?"

"Yeah, they drive me nuts."

The man nodded and looked down at a monitor under the counter. "Let's see here... got a bus leavin' in ten minutes. Stops in Orlando for half an hour, then continues on to Miami."

"Okay, sounds good."

"You want round trip, or is this ex of yours some kind of psychopath?"

"One-way ticket is fine."

"Right. Maybe stay out there, find yourself some girl that doesn't expect the world. Like my ex-wife. Man what a psycho she turned out to be." He shook his head side to side while typing on the keyboard in front of him. "My fault though, I guess. I should have known when I met her father. What a miserable bastard, could see the pain written on his face. Not a pleasant bunch of memories. I used to live in Austin." He sighed, then turned and plucked a ticket from the printer. "Here you go. That'll be fifty-five dollars. Oh, and I need ID."

Neil pulled out three twenty-dollar bills and handed them and his ID to the man. The ticket agent slid the ID card through a card reader, pressed a few keys, and handed Neil the ID, the ticket, and a five-dollar coin. He pointed behind Neil toward the entrance. "Out there. Just look for the bus with the number on your ticket."

Neil nodded and headed outside. The bus he was looking for was next in line to leave. The bus driver took his ticket, ripped it in half, and handed the stub back. Neil found a seat in the rear of the bus away from everyone else and sat down by the window. *What the hell am I doing?* He wondered to himself. He propped his knees against the seat in front of him and leaned his head back. Before the bus driver even got back on the bus to start the engine, Neil was already fast asleep.

*   *   *

"Welcome to Orlando," said a synthetic female voice over the bus intercom system. "Those passengers who are continuing on to Miami are welcome to stay on the bus. If you decide to leave the bus, please return within thirty minutes and make sure that you keep your ticket stub."

Neil sat up and looked around. Most of the passengers had already gotten off the bus. The driver was outside helping an older woman get her bag from the baggage compartment on the side of the bus. The man who was in the seat across the aisle had left his newspaper behind. Neil grabbed the thin plastic sheet and started to flip through the virtual pages. He spent most of the thirty-minute stopover looking over every page for any news at all of the previous night. There was nothing. Not even a cursory mention in the police log, which he examined with the built in zoom function several times. He tossed the paper back on its seat. The bus started to shake as people boarded, handed their tickets to the driver, and then found a seat.

"This seat taken?"

Neil looked up at the young man standing in the aisle in front of him. He was maybe eighteen, five and a half feet tall, head shaved bare, and there was a shiny metal bar installed in his nostrils. A pair of earphones were wrapped around his neck, thin plastic wires running from them into a T-shirt that bore a logo for some music band Neil had never heard of. He was gesturing with one tattooed hand at the seat with the newspaper on it. Neil shrugged. "No, he just left the paper behind."

"Cool. I like the funnies." The kid sat down and grabbed the paper. He tapped his finger on the touchscreen a few times and then threw the paper onto the seat in front of him. "Shit, forgot the weekday editions stopped carrying them. You'd think they'd put all sorts of shit in these since they stopped using paper. Fucking cheapskates. I'm Chad." He held out his hand and Neil shook it.

"Neil."

"You got business in Miami? You look kinda suited up."

Neil looked down at himself and noticed that he was still dressed for work - black raincoat, dress slacks, shirt and a tie. He thought again of home and shook his head. "No, just heading out of town. Need a break."

"No shit, you look like you slept *and* showered in that suit."

"Something like that."

Chad fiddled with the metal bar in his nose. "Damn thing itches."

"What are you heading to Miami for?"

"You kidding? Orlando outlawed piercings years ago and nobody in Tampa wants to deal with all the new safety laws. Gotta go to Miami to get shit done these days. I'm gonna get my tongue pierced this time."

Neil winced. "Doesn't that hurt?"

"Yeah, but the chicks dig it man." Chad stuck his tongue out and wiggled it suggestively.

"What other kind of stuff can get done in Miami?"

"Shit man, anything you want. *Anything.* Tattoos, piercings, weird sex clubs. You seem cool. Despite the clothes. We gotta do somethin' bout that. I can hook you up man. I *know* people."

Neil turned to look out his window. The bus started moving forward, slowed to a stop, and then continued out of the parking lot. He turned back to Chad. "Anything?" Chad nodded. Neil leaned closer and lowered his voice. "I want to travel somewhere without using my damn ID card."

Chad smirked. "Not many people wanna travel that way man. Why?"

"I have my reasons."

"You got money? It ain't gonna be cheap."

"I can probably pay it."

"Then I got ya covered, man. You stick with me bro, I can get ya places."

Neil nodded and turned back to the window. Chad pulled the earphones up to his ears and started banging his head to the beat. Neil closed his eyes. *I'm gonna do her tonight.* He saw himself put the knife down. He saw the other man pick it up. He saw the look on her face, heard the sound of the knife. He tried to tell himself it was all a dream, that he was really just fast asleep in his cubicle at work.

The bus hit a bump in the road and Neil opened his eyes. His cubicle was nowhere near. His important work - the job he just *had* to do today - would never get done. He was done, gone, and never going back. His electronic check payments would bounce. If he hadn't withdrawn any money from his bank, his bills would have been paid and he would have been left with his monthly entertainment budget of twenty-three dollars. That was also his food and transportation budget. He had no idea how his paycheck was reduced to that paltry sum every month, and he had done well in mathematics and economics classes. But that no longer mattered. Life as he knew it was now over.

Neil looked out his window at the green mileage sign that read "Miami 162 mi" and smiled as he felt the anxiety seep from his shoulders. He closed his eyes and felt himself sink into the seat.

CHAPTER
6

ORLANDO, FLORIDA
JULY 19, 2030 9:30 AM EDT

He stepped off of the bus onto the pavement and glanced at his watch. He had thirty minutes to find a way to do this job, but first he had to find his target. He reviewed the schedule board posted outside the entry and saw that the bus with his target was delayed. It wouldn't even be here for at least another ten minutes. He pulled out a worn pack of cigarettes, took one out and stuck the butt end in his mouth. He fished around in his other pocket for a lighter and lit the cigarette. He leaned against the side of the bus and watched the people walk by. Most of the bus he was leaning against unloaded, some passengers taking luggage from underneath the bus and wandering off in different directions. He waited patiently, watching the driveway for oncoming vehicles while slowly smoking his cigarette.

Fifteen minutes later, two more buses pulled into the driveway. He saw his quarry exit one and walk into the station. He followed, studying the man as he went. His target was in his mid-fifties, had light gray hair, glasses, and walked like he really had to relieve himself. He dropped his cigarette onto the pavement and ground it out with his shoe, exhaling the last of the smoke while keeping an eye on his target. He was sure that this man was the target. He remembered the pictures that had been provided. He always got the job done right.

He followed as the man walked into the bathroom, facilities that were just barely big enough for two people to use them simultaneously. It reeked of alcohol and urine, even worse than the main lobby. The ceiling tiles were stained dark yellow from cigarette smoke. The bathroom was empty except for the two men.

The situation could not have been better if he had planned it this way.

His right hand removed a six-inch railroad spike from his coat pocket. The left wrapped around the man's face as he used the urinal, covering his mouth. The old man didn't even try to scream as he felt the spike pierce his kidney, warm blood trickling down the tails of his coat and spilling onto the tile floor. He let go of the spike and let the old man's corpse collapse to the floor, careful not to let any of the blood splash onto him. He stepped away from the small river of blood that was twisting its way along a crack toward the drain. He hurried out of the bathroom and sprinted for the terminal exit.

When he was outside, he headed straight for his bus and got on board. He flashed the bus ticket stub to the driver and took a step toward his seat. Before he turned to sit, he noticed someone sitting near the back of the bus that looked somewhat familiar. He sat down and stared openly at the man, trying to place the face, trying to remember who it was. When the man leaned over to toss a newspaper across the aisle, he saw the black raincoat and remembered.

"Well, I'll be damned."

He turned around and smirked, shaking his head lightly from side to side. He figured it was probably a bad sign that this guy was running away in the same direction as him, but he couldn't help but laugh at the situation he had created. He slouched in his seat and slowly peeled off his gloves, pushing them into his pocket as the last few people boarded. The driver reached over and pulled the lever to close the doors, and the bus moved forward.

CHAPTER
7

NEW TAMPA, FLORIDA
JULY 19, 2030 10:43 AM EDT

Donners opened the door to his office and stepped in. Roen followed him closely, closed the door, and leaned against it. Two men were behind his desk, one sitting in Donners' chair and the other standing behind. Both wore finely tailored suits, silk shirts, and gold colored tie clips. They were looking over some papers and speaking softly to each other. The seated one played idly with his mustache as the other spoke. They looked up when they heard the door close.

"And who are you?" the one seated at the desk asked.

"Donners. This is my office. So who the hell are you?"

"Inspector Ferez from Interpol." He pulled a badge out of an inner pocket and showed it to Donners. "This is my partner, Inspector Johnson. We understand you have been investigating this night club murder, correct?"

"Yes, myself and Detective Roen here. Had some guys outside on that bench we were going to question. You see what happened to them?"

"We let them go."

"You *what*?"

"Let them go. They don't concern this investigation."

"This is my case. I'll decide who..."

"This is not your case anymore. The girl's bodyguards were not needed for questioning."

Donners bit his tongue, tasted a bit of blood. "This... is... my... case..."

"Not anymore," Ferez said. "This is an international matter now, quite out of your jurisdiction. We understand that you have a list of the people that were at the club last night. I'd like to see that list."

"International matter my ass. Looks like a murder in my neighborhood. That's local. That's *my* case."

"Have you identified the girl yet, Detective?" Johnson asked.

"No," Donners admitted. "Not yet. We have people working on it."

"Want us to save you the trouble?"

"Sure, why not."

"Lisa Anderton."

Roen gasped audibly. "Oh shit."

"Damn right," Ferez replied while standing. "Lisa Anderton, only daughter of Roger Anderton, media mogul, multi-billionaire, former United States Senator, and owner of the largest empire of companies the world has ever seen. Lisa, well she was a brilliant scientist of one sort or another. I don't really understand computer stuff but that has something to do with her forte. She was the head of some think-tank subsidiary in the Miami area."

Roen stumbled further into the office and plopped down in one of the guest chairs. "Oh shit," he repeated.

"Yes. Oh shit indeed. Anyway, I'd imagine that her bodyguards are quite unreachable by now. More than likely swimming, if you know what I mean."

Donners leaned against the wall for support. He felt like the wind was just sucked out of him. "What the hell was someone like *her* doing in a place like *that*?"

"That's one of the questions we would like answered. Another is where have you two been all morning? Out searching for clues?" Ferez walked around to the front of the desk and sat on it. "And where is that list?"

Roen handed his notepad to Ferez. He told Ferez about the fingerprints of the two suspects and about their morning's trip to Neil's apartment. While he was going over all of the known details of the investigation so far, Johnson and Ferez listened patiently. When he was done, they looked to each other.

Ferez nodded and turned to face Roen. "I doubt this Roberts guy did it. It's possible he did, sure, but I'm more interested in the mystery guy. It's rare that we get a case where a murderer leaves such an easy paper trail. I have a feeling that we'll have to track them both down to piece this whole thing together."

"Well, we went after Roberts because he was the only missing witness we had a record for. We don't even know if he was the one sitting at the table or not. And without a record on the other guy, we can't even begin to figure out whether or not they were working together."

"I doubt they were working together, considering the circumstances." Ferez reached behind him to pick up one of the pages he had been perusing earlier. "You recognize this?" He held the paper up for the two detectives to see. Centered on the page was a photograph of a small, black mechanical device.

Donners nodded. "Yeah, looks like that thing we found stuck under the table they were sitting at."

"Do you know what it is?"

Donners and Roen glanced at each other, then both shook their heads in unison.

"It's called a Geas Box. Some geek invented it around six years ago. Named it after a spell in that Dungeons and Dragons game, a spell that would force someone to perform an action or submit to orders that they normally would reject. Kind of like a suggestion that you can't really refuse. You see, this guy made the Geas Box so that he could meet women at clubs."

"Rape women, you mean." Johnson interjected.

"Right." Ferez shrugged. "Anyway, we've only seen three of them before. Quite rare, and very expensive. Not everyone can afford a multi-million dollar device like this. It's designed to attach to the bottom of a table, then the guy sits down and starts chatting with the girl. He aims this end of the box at her, and it starts giving her orders or suggestions using microwaves. You can't even hear the thing in a quiet room because it's talking to you outside of the range of what people can hear. But you *feel* the thing, and very few people can resist."

Donners scratched the top of his head. "So, this thing was used on the guy who was sitting at the table?"

"Precisely. We've already analyzed the device and we know what it was saying to him."

"What?"

"Run." Ferez stood up and stretched his back before continuing. "But anyway, we'll track down this Roberts guy. Maybe he knew about the box and knew the other guy and this whole setup is just a plan to throw us off track. Or maybe Roberts was the one that planted this device and the other unknown guy is the perp. Or maybe he's just one more loose end that is going to get tied up. We won't know for sure until we get a chance to talk with them. And we'll see what we can find out about the other guy. You still have the prints for him?"

"Yeah," Donners replied, "but the database couldn't find him." He walked over to his desk and sifted through some of the papers there. He found the fax, pulled it out of the pile, and handed it to Ferez.

"The database you use isn't complete. Ours is. Thank you for your cooperation."

Donners sat on the desk. Roen stared blankly at the floor, still trying to piece it all together. Johnson and Ferez headed for the door.

"Gentlemen." Ferez stopped at the door and turned back to speak to Donners and Roen. "I hope I don't need to remind you that this conversation must stay private. I'm sure you've noticed both your own and the media's inability to figure out Lisa's identity. It needs to stay that way for as long as possible."

Both officers nodded, stunned.

"Good. Let's go, Johnson."

*   *   *

"You think they'll keep quiet?" Johnson asked as they walked down the hallway.

Ferez frowned. "I'm more worried they'll try to continue their investigation than talk to anyone about it."

"What should we do then? Get Ramirez to keep an eye on them?"

"No. Hell no. We need Ramirez in the field doing real work. Get an intern to do it. Maybe Jones or Hirosha."

"Hirosha, definitely." Johnson pulled a phone out of his pocket and flipped it open. The phone beeped three times in rapid succession. "This is Johnson. We need a one-fourteen. Detectives Roen and Donners, New Tampa PD. Put Hirosha on it. Uh huh. Thanks." He closed the phone.

"Good. Let's head back to home base and see what we can find on this Roberts."

The two agents left the police station and got into their rented Honda at the curb. Ferez pulled out into the light traffic and headed east toward their hotel. Johnson flipped through the notepad and read the contents out loud to Ferez. When he got to the fax with the fingerprints on it, he reached into his suit's inner pocket and pulled out his computer. It was a brand new Mitsumi, custom chrome casing and every option he could ever need in the field and a few that he still didn't even know how to use. Strictly top-of-the-line hardware. He flipped open a panel on the side, exposing a four-inch wide optical lens. He tapped a button inside the panel and a light came on. He ran the lens over the paper slowly, grimacing habitually with every bump that Ferez hit. But he knew the optics were able to compensate for much worse than these little bumps. When he was done, the computer beeped three times and the light turned off. He snapped the panel back in place and returned the computer to his inner pocket. He folded the fax and put that and the notepad into his other inner pocket. Ferez turned into the hotel parking lot and picked a space as close to their room as he could find. They got out without saying a word and went into their room.

Ferez locked the door and turned on their makeshift security system, a loose network of hardware he set up to alert them of people walking by their door and some sonic emitters designed to prevent eavesdropping.

Johnson took off his tie and sat at the table while undoing the first two buttons on his shirt. "This would be so much faster if I had one of those T-Jacks."

Ferez watched him as he opened a panel in the side of the computer and connected a power cable. "You know those are illegal."

"So? We're the government."

"They're also not safe."

"Yeah, yeah, I know," Johnson added with a note of disappointment.

Ferez plugged a data cable into the wall and ran that to the computer. Johnson leaned back in his chair, stretched his arms over his head, and cracked his knuckles. He pulled on skin-tight gray gloves and pressed his palms together to activate their connection with his computer.

"Get ready to record this," he told Ferez as he put on his optic interface glasses and pressed his computer's ON button.

*   *   *

Light flickered on the panels inside Johnson's glasses. He closed his eyes, waiting for the initial synchronization to complete. He heard a soft ding in his left ear and opened his eyes. Stretched out before him were stacks of data nodes like buildings reaching up toward the sky. Other people's avatars floated around the stacks, poking into them and withdrawing information. Off to his left was the central node for New Tampa, a directory kiosk that looked like something from a shopping mall. A woman appeared before him, hazy and wavering in the virtual light.

"Please log in," she said to him as she held out her hands. He placed his hands in hers and moved his fingers in a certain pattern he had memorized. She blinked a few times when he finished and then nodded. "Good day, Inspector Johnson. Welcome to New Tampa."

She removed her hands from his and generated a list of options in the air in front of him. She turned and looked to him expectantly. He waved the menu away. "Interpol," he said.

"Thank you Inspector Johnson. Transferring to the New Tampa office of the International Criminal Police Organization."

He sucked in his breath and prepared for the transfer. The digital skyline in front of him dissipated and was replaced by a virtual ceiling. The data nodes vanished and were replaced with a large Interpol logo. The logo spun on a vertical axis, an animation that had probably cost taxpayers a few million dollars. The woman morphed into a calm looking black man in a neatly pressed Armani suit with closely trimmed hair, bright blue eyes, and a goatee. The whole process took less than a nanosecond.

"Welcome to the New Tampa office, Inspector Johnson. How can I help you?"

"Give me all of the information we have on Neil Eric Roberts of New Tampa."

"Processing." The man looked toward the ceiling and his eyelids fluttered. Three seconds later he stopped and looked at Johnson. "Here you are, sir. Please let me know if you need any further assistance. My name is Markus."

Johnson reached for the file and grasped it with both hands. He placed it face up in the air in front of him and opened it. Strings of text leaped from the file and organized themselves in the air space in front of him. A scrollbar dropped from the ceiling and positioned itself to the right of the text.

"Privacy mode."

Large slabs of what appeared to be opaque plastic flew at him from all directions and encased him completely, sealing off his avatar and the file from any observing eyes. He watched as the last of the walls clicked into place and then waited as the firewall configured itself. "Encryption mode activated," the wall's synthetic voice announced. "Please determine strength." Johnson looked at the scrollbar that had superimposed itself in the middle of the wall in front of him. It was set to BASIC. He slid the bar all the way to the right. "Paranoid encryption activated." The program informed him.

"You ready Ferez?"

"Go ahead." He heard the familiar voice off in the distance somewhere.

"Neil Eric Roberts. Basic information that we already knew. Looking at his recent transactions. He withdrew five hundred dollars from an ATM this morning, then his card was confiscated." He watched the embedded ATM video feed for a few moments, then grabbed the scrollbar and moved it downward. "Not an accident, he forced it to be confiscated. He bought a bus ticket this morning. Greyhound. Headed for Miami, but he could also have gotten off at the Orlando stop. The bus was there for half an hour." He got to the bottom and read off some other numbers for Ferez to copy down.

"Any link to the girl?"

"None that I saw. He works with computers, programming stuff for Goliath. Mostly business apps and security programs. Nothing really related to Lisa's research, even though it is technically in the same line of work."

"Criminal record?"

"None of note."

"Too clean?"

"Eh. Two parking tickets six years ago. No current driving record at all. No registration on file. He either doesn't own a car or he drives it illegally."

"That's it?"

"That's all that's here."

"Okay. Look up the prints."

"Gotcha." Johnson closed the file and watched as all of the papers he was looking at flipped back into the folder. When it had finished, he reached out with his right arm and punched a hole in the side of the firewall. "Hey, Markus."

Markus appeared in front of Johnson and glanced at his arm sticking out of the side of the firewall. He smiled. "How can I be of assistance, sir?"

"I'm going to upload a file to you. Scan of some fingerprints."

"Yes, sir." Markus reached forward and grasped Johnson's other hand. "Proceed. File received. Standard virus scanning. File passed and certified. Checking database." Markus let go of his hand and closed his eyes. Ten seconds later, he opened his eyes and smiled. "I have an exact match." He handed a file to Johnson. "Is there anything else I can assist you with, sir?"

"Not at this time."

Markus nodded and vanished. Johnson pulled his hand in from the wall and the hole sealed itself. He placed the file in the air to the left of Neil's file and opened it. "Got it. Ready?"

"Go ahead."

"Jules Trionis. Also known as 'The June Goon'. Also known as 'The Midnight Express'. Residence unknown. Age thirty-four. Current whereabouts unknown."

"Record?"

"Where do I start? Convicted on one count of involuntary manslaughter at age nineteen. Served four years in state prison before being released for good behavior. Ridiculous. Several other murders attributed to him but nothing ever went to court. Nicknamed 'The June Goon' for a series of broad daylight murders he allegedly committed in Montreal in June 2026. A body count of over three dozen in a four day time span. No known motive, no evidence, nothing. Just some rumors and shaky eyewitness reports that it was him. The rumor section of his file attributes to him a list of about two dozen girls that were raped and murdered, all between the ages of fifteen and twenty-three. Also says he was nicknamed 'The Midnight Express' by a crime syndicate in Thailand for his reputation of getting any job done in less than twelve hours, if the price was right."

"So, it's a good bet that he's the perp. And a good chance whoever hired him to kill Lisa did so within a day of her murder."

"I'd say so."

"Is there anything else in his file?"

"Yeah, it's about two miles long. Lots of speculation, assumed links to various crime families, a few hundred murders attributed to him but nothing ever went to trial. He did pay a fine last year for..." Johnson chuckled.

"For what?"

"Um, playing with himself in public."

"Great, what a nice guy. Of all the things to catch him doing," Ferez said. "Guess it's too much to ask for someone to catch him doing something more than a misdemeanor."

"I'd say all the circumstantial evidence points to this guy. Someone who could afford to pay him for this kind of murder would probably also have the money and connections to get him a Geas Box."

"So then who's Roberts?"

Johnson closed the file, watching as all the strings of text worked their way back into the small yellow folder in his hands. He opened his virtual pocket and stuffed the file into it. A small progress bar appeared in the bottom portion of his vision to inform him that the file was being written to his computer's storage area. "Just some guy. Maybe hired Jules and wanted to watch to make sure the job was done right."

"With a reputation like that? I'd assume he was professional enough to get the job done."

"Yeah, you maybe. Maybe this Roberts guy didn't believe all the hype. Either way, that Geas Box may make him look innocent, but are you willing to risk the investigation on that assumption? I mean, if he was innocent, why's he still running? Geas Box effects don't last that long, maybe five hours at the most. You willing to let someone who keeps running get away?"

"Of course not. We'll have to find both him and Jules Trionis if we're ever going to figure this all out."

Johnson closed down the firewall and watched the panels fade away. Markus appeared in front of him. "Yes, sir?" Johnson waved him away. Markus nodded, said "Good day, sir" and vanished. The Interpol office faded away and was replaced with the general New Tampa node. The woman from the New Tampa login script appeared before him again. She re-opened the menu and looked at him.

"Check the newswire?" Ferez offered.

Johnson nodded. "Today's news," he said to the woman. She smiled and reached out to a data node that looked like it was a few hundred yards away. Her arm stretched out, selected a small yellow folder, and shrunk back. She handed the file to Johnson and curtsied. He smirked at the ridiculous gesture, placed the folder in the air in front of him, and opened it. He scrolled right until he saw the header for the national newswire.

"What's there?"

"Average gas price in Europe tops fifteen Euros per liter. Oil shortage blamed on Middle East war. United Kingdom considers gasoline engine ban. National survey shows over sixty percent of US population owns electric vehicles now. Diesel and gasoline based trucks to be phased out by 2037. UN Secretary General Abu Kanafari's murder last week is still unsolved, and no replacement chosen yet. Girl murdered in New Tampa bar."

"Shit."

Johnson double-tapped on that article and turned to the new window. He scanned through the text quickly. When he reached the bottom of the article, he sighed audibly. "No mention. They didn't name her."

"Good. Not the kind of thing you want anyone to know about until we've already got someone charged with the murder."

Johnson closed the window and looked down at the rest of the articles. One near the bottom caught his attention. "Murder reported in Orlando bus station." He double-tapped that article and turned to its window. "Earlier this morning, a man was found dead in the bathroom of a Greyhound bus station in Orlando, Florida. The man was identified as Richard Wilson, age fifty-four. Wilson was employed as a computer scientist at Anderton Enterprises' Computer Research Center in Miami."

"Lisa was the head of that branch... get the bus schedule for Greyhound. I want to know what bus Roberts was on and when he was in Orlando and for how long."

"I'm on it."

Johnson moved his hands in a circular motion, closing the newswire. He scrolled the list that the woman was holding and selected Transportation. She folded the list and opened a new one. "Bus Schedules" was printed on the top. Johnson pushed on the text with his hand and the woman smiled. She closed the menu and reached behind her again. When her arm came back, it was holding a block of text that resembled a small telephone book. She handed the book to Johnson.

Johnson reached inside himself and rooted around, grasped and released several programs until he found the one he was searching for. He inserted the tail end of the program into the bus schedule and opened up the other end of it. He placed his fingers into the program and moved them around, typing out the words "Orlando" and "Greyhound". The program beeped and printed the word "Processing..." beneath his search terms. After a few seconds, the book shrunk to the size of a few sheets of paper. Johnson grabbed the papers and flipped through them until he found the page with the current day's schedule on it. He held the papers tightly and looked up to the woman, who was still watching him and smiling vacantly.

"Greyhound bus terminal."

She nodded and disappeared. The world around him dissolved into a pristine representation of a bus terminal. All four walls were lined with glass and the floors reflected almost as well as any mirror. There was a soft pinging of Japanese elevator music from somewhere above. A menu program designed to look like a young woman greeted him from behind the counter.

"Welcome to the New Tampa Greyhound terminal. Where would you like to travel to?"

"Inspector Johnson, Interpol." He flashed his digital badge.

The girl's eyes blinked a few times and she nodded. "Credentials recognized and verified. How can I be of assistance, Inspector Johnson?"

"I want the travel schedule of Neil Eric Roberts. He purchased a ticket from New Tampa to Miami this morning."

"Yes sir. Processing." She stared at the ceiling for a few moments. "He purchased a ticket with cash money this morning and was reported to have reached his destination in Miami earlier this afternoon."

"When was his bus in Orlando? How long was it there?"

"That bus arrived in Orlando at 9:29 AM Eastern Daylight Time. It departed the terminal to continue on to Miami at 10:00 AM Eastern Daylight Time."

"Nine-thirty to ten. What time was the murder, Ferez?"

Ferez cleared his throat. "Body was found about five minutes after ten."

"Damn. What was the name?"

"Richard Wilson."

Johnson moved forward, causing his avatar to lean on the digital counter automatically. "Okay, Richard Wilson. What about his bus?"

"Processing. Richard Wilson was on bus number ninety-three. The bus arrived from Miami at 9:45 AM Eastern Daylight Time. The bus departed at 10:00 AM Eastern Daylight Time for Daytona Beach."

"Damn, some vacation that was. Poor bastard." Johnson shook his head.

"Mister Wilson was not on board the bus for the second half of his trip. The Daytona Beach terminal did not register his arrival."

"Yeah, he got murdered in the bus station bathroom during a fifteen minute stopover in Orlando."

The girl looked saddened and a bit confused. "We assure you, that is not a service that Greyhound offers."

Johnson waved her away. She nodded, and the station dissolved. The host woman for New Tampa appeared in front of him again. Behind her, the data nodes were swarming with avatars surfing around and visiting various friends and businesses. Traffic was unusually high. Johnson pressed his palms together. The woman nodded and closed her menu. The virtual world wavered and flickered in front of his eyes. He waited until the inside of the glasses turned black before closing his eyes. He removed the glasses, then reached up to rub his nose while keeping his eyes closed.

"So," Ferez said, "Wilson went to take a leak and got killed in the bathroom?"

"Looks like it. And with that kind of time window, the guy that did it must have been a pro."

"Trionis again? But why?"

"With his reputation? I'd guess someone found the right price for disposing of Anderton employees."

"Well, Roberts' ID was scanned in Miami, so I guess we go that way."

"No." Johnson opened his eyes and started to undo the Velcro straps on his gloves. "No, I think we should hit the bus station in Orlando, question the people there, and view the surveillance vids. Maybe one of their cameras has an angle that will show us for sure who was in the bathroom with Wilson. Maybe we can get lucky and find out what name Trionis is traveling under."

"Okay. Makes sense. I'll get the car started."

CHAPTER
8

MIAMI, FLORIDA
JULY 19, 2030 12:05 PM EDT

T he bus station in Miami was almost an exact duplicate of the one in New Tampa. The company that built it had latched on to the same concept that fast food restaurants had: build your establishments the same way no matter where they are, and all of your customers will feel at home there. They had the same counter placement, the same molded plastic chairs, the same lighting. It even had the same booze-and-urine stench.

Chad patted Neil on the back and motioned for him to follow. He led the way through the bus station and out the other side. The air outside was slightly warmer than New Tampa, with a tinge of saltwater smell to it. Neil breathed deeply as he kept pace behind Chad. The street back here was completely devoid of cars. There were a few people milling around, all of them looking straight down at the ground and hurrying past the two men whenever they got close. They turned onto another street and Chad pointed at an older man thirty yards from them. He was wearing a torn altar robe and was holding a Bible above his head, shouting misquoted passages at random as people walked near him.

"Street preacher. He's a nutty one, man. Always telling people they're sinners cause they ain't like him. See, you'd probably be fine walkin' by him, but me? Shit no, he'd call me the devil or some shit. He goes nuts when he sees tattoos and piercings." Chad hurried his pace and pointed toward an alleyway on the right. "We're headin' in there. Anyway, last time I was here, I saw that guy yellin' at some girl, sayin' she was a whore just cause she had a miniskirt on. Looked damn fine in it too. Poor girl."

They turned down the alleyway and weaved in and out of the garbage littered around. They approached an over-sized metal door at the end. Chad looked over his shoulder toward the street, raised his hand, and knocked three times, two sharp raps followed a few seconds later with a third.

"Don't say nothin' Neil. Let me do all the talkin'."

A panel in the door five feet up slid to the side and a puff of smoke filtered out into the alley. "What you want?" barked a gruff voice from the other side of the door.

"It's me, man. Chad."

"Who's the suit?"

"Friend of mine, open up."

"What's he want?"

"A travel agent. Open the *door*, man."

The panel slid shut. A loud banging sound echoed behind the door and the sound of steel scraping against steel reverberated through the alley as the door swung inward. Chad stepped into the building and motioned for Neil to follow. Someone closed the door behind them. A dim blue light illuminated a small room ahead, shadows playing off the wall and stretching out along the floor toward the entrance. Chad headed for the light and stopped at the opening to the room. He turned to make sure Neil was following him, then walked into the room. He opened a door and motioned for Neil to step in. Stairs led up from here. There was light upstairs, and voices from some people talking. Someone screamed, their voice soon drowned out by the sound of raucous laughter. Chad bounded up the stairs, taking two at a time until he reached the top. Neil heard Chad call out a greeting to someone named Gino.

"Chad! Welcome back buddy."

Neil got to the top of the stairs and watched Chad embrace a large man whose bare chest was covered with brightly colored tattoos. Every orifice on Gino's face had at least one piercing, and a chain hung from one ear through his nose to the other ear. He said something to Chad, but his lip and tongue piercings gave him a lisp that was so bad he had to use a crude form of sign language to get his point across. Neil wasn't sure what he was trying to say, but Chad appeared to understand. Gino was a balding man in his late forties, and despite the tattoos and piercings on his body, there was a kindness in his eyes that Neil never expected would be there. He paused mid-sentence as he noticed Neil.

"What you want?"

"He's with me Gino. Name's Neil."

"I thee. Tho what you doin' in town Chad?"

"Tongue pierce." Chad stuck out his tongue.

Gino smiled and nodded. "The ladieth do love that one." Someone in the room ahead screeched in pain, followed by a few people laughing. Gino saw the look on Neil's face and laughed. "Jackath wanted hith privath pierthed." He reached down and grabbed his crotch, twisting his face into an expression of extreme pain. He straightened up, removed his hand, and shook his head. "Dumbath. Tho what you want?"

"Travel," Neil said. "Anywhere."

Gino shrugged. "Buth thtathun." He pointed toward the bus station.

"Don't want to use ID."

Gino looked Neil up and down. "You got cath?" Neil nodded slowly. Gino considered him for a moment, then turned and headed into the room. He pointed toward a side room. "Travel goeth there." Then he pointed to Chad. "You come over here."

Neil headed into the side room. A young woman looked up from the desk and frowned when she saw him. She had lightly tanned skin, Latino heritage. Her gaze pierced right through him in a way that might be disconcerting if not tempered with her obvious boredom. She leaned back in her chair and ran her fingers through her short spiked hair. A little of the purple dye came off on her hands. She wiped it off on her T-shirt, which might have been white at some point but was now just a messy tie dye.

"You need to go somewhere?" she asked.

"Yeah."

"Have a seat."

"Thanks."

"Where to?"

"Don't care." He sat down on the metal folding chair and glanced around the small office. Posters of various famous cities were nailed to the wood paneled walls. Someone had drawn a stick figure leaping off the top of the Eiffel Tower in black marker. Next to that was a picture of the Taj Mahal with an orange mushroom cloud drawn in the background. The desk and the two chairs were the only furniture in the room, all three badly abused. The desk was covered in papers and empty fast food containers which gave the room a distinct odor. The room was a mess of proportions that would stun most college students.

"Well if you got the money, we got a ride leaving in five minutes. Hundred bucks."

Neil stopped examining the office and looked the girl in the face. She had beautiful sparkling blue eyes. A real shame considering that he would probably have considered her to be pretty if not for the pierced eyebrow and purple hair. "And no ID."

"Honey, I don't give a shit who you are if you can pay the price."

Neil reached into his pocket, counted out five twenties, and handed them over. She counted the bills and pulled out a pink slip of paper, scribbled something down, and handed it to him. "Go downstairs. Look for the pickup truck. Hand this to the driver."

"Thanks... er..."

She pointed toward the door. "Better hurry. I don't give refunds."

He nodded and walked out. On the stairwell, he unfolded the paper and looked at what she had written. He had paid enough attention in high school to know that it was Spanish, but not enough attention to have any idea what it said. All he could make out from the scribbling was the girl's name at the bottom, Kayla. He headed down the stairs, refolding the paper as he entered the room with the blue lighting. The panel in the door slid open as he approached, letting in a little bit of light around the profile of someone's head. The panel slid shut and the door opened.

"See ya."

"Yeah," Neil said to the outline he could barely see. "Take care."

He stepped out into the alley, heard the door slam shut behind him. He tried his best to step around the filth in the alley as he made his way to the street. He paused several feet from the alley's exit and leaned against the cleanest spot on the cold bricks he could find. Not a minute went by before a beat up pickup truck screeched to a halt in the street before him. Several men sat in the back, holding what appeared to be a heated conversation. The driver's door opened and an aged Mexican man stood up, looking into the alley. Neil started walking to the truck, holding up the pink note in his hand. The driver relaxed noticeably. When he got to the truck, Neil handed the note to the man, who unfolded it carefully and read.

The man looked up, nodded, and said something in Spanish. Neil stared blankly at the man, who sighed and pointed toward the back of the truck. Neil nodded and climbed in. The driver returned to his seat and the truck took off down the street.

Neil studied the other men in the back of the truck, who stared back at him. "Uh, hey," he said to them. "Where are we going anyway?"

The other men in the back of the truck nodded and started to speak excitedly in Spanish. One of them asked him a question, he judged by the inflection of the man's voice. The men stared at him expectantly. After a few moments one in the back started laughing. He said something to the other men in the truck, then looked up to Neil and added in English, "You no speak the Spanish."

"No," Neil admitted. "Not a word."

The man laughed again. "You have mucho trouble where we go, amigo."

"Where the heck *are* we going, anyway?"

"Cuba."

The other men in the truck nodded and started repeating the name. "Cuba."

"Cuba. Great."

Neil leaned against the side of the truck and closed his eyes, enjoying the feeling of the warm air rushing by as the truck hurtled down the middle lane of the road. Cuba. He'd read about it, but couldn't recall much about the country except that it used to have a Communist government. He vaguely recalled reading about a revolution and the overturning of the government a few years back. It was now an American territory, but still largely a Spanish speaking one. There should be English speaking people there. Maybe it was a good place to settle down and disappear. Maybe just a stepping stone on his way. Either way, it didn't much matter to him as long as he didn't have to deal with his former life anymore.

CHAPTER
9

ORLANDO, FLORIDA
JULY 19, 2030 11:40 AM EDT

J ohnson and Ferez drove along the highway toward Orlando at almost twice the speed limit, with their magnetic red police light firmly attached to the top of their car and siren blaring all the way. Every other car on the road swerved away from them, rubber tires squealing on the asphalt as their car roared past. They reached Orlando in record time but spent almost ten minutes trying to get their GPS unit to tell them where the bus station was. Several police cars were parked outside of the station by the time they got there. Ferez slammed on the brakes and the car skidded to a halt outside the front entrance. They got out and approached the building, holding their ID badges in front of them.

"Gentlemen," one officer addressed them as they entered the building.

"We have a forensics team in the bathroom looking for fingerprints and DNA at the moment. Sorry, but can't let anyone else in there until they've dug around for whatever clues they can find."

"Well, what about surveillance videos?" Ferez asked.

"Go into the office back there." The officer pointed to the other side of the counter at a single door in the middle of the wall that had the word "Office" in small black letters on it.

Ferez and Johnson headed for the door. Ferez knocked twice and opened it. Two detectives sat in front of a security system, going over a tape. One of them turned as they entered.

"I'm Inspector Ferez. This is Inspector Johnson. We're with Interpol." They showed the officers their badges. "What have we got?"

The officer facing them looked at the badges, sighed, and scratched behind his ear. He was a wiry man in his thirties with bags under his eyes and a few gray hairs on his head. "I'm Capshaw, Orlando homicide. Got two men entering the bathroom. One leaving. Few minutes later, another entered and then ran out and threw up on the floor." He shrugged. "That first guy out left in a hurry too."

"Any ID on him?"

"No prints on the murder weapon. We're running a face scan right now on a partial view we got while he was leaving. What's your interest in this case anyway?"

Ferez sat down on a folding chair in the corner of the office. "I think the perp killed a girl in New Tampa last night. Name Jules Trionis mean anything to you?"

The other officer whistled. "Shit, ain't that the June Goon? Killed a buncha people in Montana or something."

Ferez nodded. "Montreal. That's the guy."

A muffled ringing noise interrupted Johnson as he tried to cut into the conversation. Capshaw reached into his pocket and pulled out a phone. He opened it up and held it to the side of his face. "This is Capshaw, go ahead. Uh huh." He poked Ferez in the arm and nodded. "Jules Trionis. Got it. Yeah, I know, well out of my jurisdiction. Got some Interpol guys already here. Yes sir, I'll do what I can to assist them. I'll update you when I get a chance." He closed the phone.

"Trionis," Ferez said. "Damn, hate it when I'm right."

Johnson turned to Ferez. "Now what? Miami?"

"Yeah, as fast as we can get there." He turned to Capshaw. "Thanks, time for us to go." He reached into his pocket and pulled out a business card. "You find out anything else from this scene, let me know."

"Sure thing," Capshaw replied, taking the card from Ferez. "Need any-thing else? I'm s'posed to help you guys out with what I can. Department relations and all that."

"Not unless you can find out where this guy is headed."

"I'll give it a shot."

Ferez shook Capshaw's hand before heading outside with Johnson. They hopped in their car and started driving, leaving Orlando and heading south toward Miami. The road was nearly empty, with only a few cars heading in the same direction they were. Johnson waited until they were on the highway before flooring the accelerator. The car bucked wildly as it accelerated down the highway. Johnson kept one hand on the wheel and the other on the horn as he shot past the day's light traffic. Half an hour later, Ferez felt his phone vibrate. He pulled it out and clicked the speakerphone button.

"Inspector Ferez."

"This is Capshaw, Orlando Homicide. That Trionis guy is registered for a flight at Miami International Airport. Never would have caught him if we hadn't specifically asked them to try to match his face. He's traveling under the name Ben Rogers."

"Where's he going to?"

"Havana. Concourse E, gate 14. Leaves at three o'clock."

"Thanks Capshaw."

"No problem. I'll call ahead and let security know you're coming. They're already working on finding Trionis so they can keep an eye on him."

"Great, thanks again."

CHAPTER
10

HAVANA, CUBA
JULY 19, 2030 2:14 PM EDT

P alm trees swayed in the gentle afternoon breeze. Neil stepped off the boat into the damp sand on the beach, immediately sinking two inches into the soil. The other passengers from the dingy little boat followed him onto the sand. The captain waved, called out something in Spanish, and the boat slipped away from the shore.

"Now what?" Neil said.

One of the other passengers spoke to him for a while in Spanish, arms flapping in sync with his lips. Neil watched him for a short time, then sighed and looked around. The beach stretched off into the distance around him. Ahead and slightly to the east he could see what appeared to be a large city. Maybe not as large as New Tampa, but sizable nonetheless. He pointed to the city and shrugged.

The man standing next to him who had been chatting finally stopped, looked at the city, then looked back to Neil. "Havana?" he asked.

"There an airport there?" Neil asked.

"Airport, sure," said another man from behind him, the one who had spoken to him on the truck. "You not stay in this part of Cuba. It no good for man like you."

"Oh? Why's that?"

"You no speak the Spanish, remember?"

"Yeah, right. So where's the airport?"

"Ten kilometers," the main said, pointing toward the city. "That way."

Neil thanked both men and started walking. He heard some Spanish and muffled laughing behind him, but chose to ignore it as he trudged through the sand. He wasn't quite sure how far ten kilometers was, but he knew he couldn't stay in this area all day. He still had some money in his pocket, and a pretty good notion that he couldn't return home anytime soon. He concentrated on putting one foot in front of the other instead of focusing his attention on the city that was still quite far away and the constant ache in his thighs from the rough boat ride. Maybe he could find another ride somewhere else. Maybe he could find a place here and learn Spanish. He could always find work as a programmer, but that might call attention to himself, lead people to find him. All sorts of ideas floated into his head.

He stepped over a fallen branch and started making his way up the side of a sand dune. At the top, the ground was harder and there were patches of grass. The trees were more dense up here, but he could make out a clear path that led in the direction of Havana. He removed his raincoat and slung it over his arm, wiped some sweat from his brow, and continued trudging along the path.

*   *   *

By the time he saw the airport in the distance, he had already heard several dozen planes taking off or coming in for a landing, and his feet and lower back ached from the distance he had traveled. His mind ached from all the thoughts he was trying to process, all the potential plans he was trying to evaluate. He paused beside a palm tree, took off his shoes one at a time and shook the sand from them. He'd have fallen asleep while leaning against that tree if not for the near-constant roar of passing airplanes. After he replaced his second shoe, he turned around and relieved himself on the tree. Neil leaned his head back and stared up at the sky. *A Cuban sky,* he thought. *What the fuck am I doing in Cuba?* When he finished, he zipped up his pants and started walking toward the airport again.

By some strange stroke of luck, his path from the beach led him directly to the front entrance of the airport. Rental car buses continually pulled up to the terminal entrances, slowed down, then left little black puffs of smoke as they drove away. It had been several years since Neil had seen black exhaust. Cuba, being only a territory, was not yet subject to all American laws. Several people on the curbside tried in vain to hail passing taxis. Guards with American flags on their arms and automatic weapons wandered around, occasionally pausing to stare at the people as they passed by. Neil smiled amicably at one as he moved closer to the terminal.

The inside of the terminal was air-conditioned, a refreshing change from the mid-afternoon Caribbean hike that Neil had just taken. He paused inside the entrance and stood beneath an air vent, enjoying the frigid air washing over his face. After more than a minute of this, he surveyed the inside of the terminal for the closest restaurant. He saw a generic bar-and-grill type place, and stumbled toward it. He sat at the first table he found and relaxed, closing his eyes and listening to the people chatter in Spanish as they walked by the restaurant.

"What can I get ya?"

"Ah, English!" Neil opened his eyes and saw a mid-twenties man with a bushy red beard looking down at him with large gray eyes.

"Yeah, thought you looked American."

"I am."

"Well, you want something?" He held a pen close to a little pad in his other hand and watched Neil intently.

"Er, I... Well, I..."

"Look, if you sit here, you have to buy something." He shrugged. "Rules are rules." He handed Neil one of the small laminated menus that was wedged between napkin holders in the center of the table. "Coke? I'll get you a Coke while you decide."

"Sure, thanks." Neil looked down at the menu. It had small pictures of various foods with descriptions in both English and Spanish. There were too many choices for him to decide on anything in particular. After his boat ride and hike, he was almost hungry enough to eat the menu itself.

When the waiter returned with his soda, Neil pointed at random to a honey mustard chicken sandwich. The waiter scribbled on his pad and left. Neil took a sip from the Coke and shuddered as he felt the chilled liquid move down his throat. He turned and watched the crowd pass by. Hundreds of people filled the airport, walking to and fro, slow lines at the ticket counters. A group of young girls with pictures of soccer balls on their shirts stood around a man and nodded enthusiastically as he wagged a finger at them and spoke. An unkempt older man wearing baggy jeans and a ratty T-shirt smoked a cigar, with eyes focused on the group of young girls. Off to his left, three teenage boys with bright green hair and dog collars around their necks smoked cigarettes and laughed incessantly. They weren't wearing shirts, and their oversized jeans had no belts to keep their boxer shorts from showing. One of them had monochrome tattoos on his forearms. An obese man in drag walked by wearing bright purple makeup to match his dress, pulling a wheeled suitcase behind him as he scratched at the beard he wasn't supposed to have.

"Just a regular freak show, eh?"

Neil turned back to face his table and saw an attractive woman sitting across from him. She had short auburn hair, straight and cut off at the shoulders. Her eyes were mint green, her smile wide and inviting. She wore a low cut pink shirt, slightly wrinkled but clean. Her pale white skin looked silky smooth, freckles spread sporadically over her face and arms. Her brightly painted fingernails tapped out a steady rhythm on the table. She leaned back in her chair and nodded toward the crowd.

"Yeah," Neil said, "just like back home."

"Where's home?" She leaned forward to grab Neil's Coke.

"Florida."

"Ah." She took a sip of his Coke, let go of the glass and returned to her chair. "I'm from Kansas originally, do a lot of traveling though."

The waiter returned and set a plate in front of Neil. He looked at the girl and asked her if she wanted anything. She shrugged. "No money. Been stranded here for a week and ran out yesterday."

"Get whatever you want," Neil offered, not quite sure what prompted him to do so. It just seemed polite. Plus she was attractive, and was talking to him. This was already the closest he'd been to a date in years.

She tapped her fingernails on the table again while eying Neil's lunch. "I'll have the same thing then. Thanks." The waiter nodded and wandered off toward the kitchen. She smiled and stole one of Neil's fries. He pushed the plate to her as the waiter returned with a Coke. She tilted her head to the side and peered at him. "Not that hungry?" she asked.

"Starving. I just walked ten kilometers from the beach, whatever that means."

"Six miles, give or take." She picked up the sandwich and took a bite, chewed quickly, and swallowed. Neil watched as she ate the entire contents of the plate, drank both of their Cokes, and then settled back in her chair to nurse a third. Shortly after she finished, the waiter returned with Neil's lunch and the check.

"Here," Neil handed the waiter two twenty-dollar bills. "Keep the change."

"Thanks. Let me know if you need anything else."

"So," Neil turned back to the girl and picked up his sandwich. "I'm Neil."

"Trixie. Well, that's what people call me anyway."

He took a small bite from the sandwich, chewed it, and swallowed before attempting a reply. "What are you doing in Cuba?"

"Traveling. On my way back to England in an hour or so. Was supposed to meet someone here but he never showed. Where you heading?"

"Don't know." He shrugged. "Don't care."

"You in trouble or something?" She reached across the table and stole a fry from his plate. He took a bite and chewed it slowly, looking around the restaurant. "Ah. What'd you do?"

He shook his head. "Just got fed up with life, had to leave. So who's this person you said you were meeting here? Old friend?"

"Just supposed to pick some guy up for my boss. He called a couple days ago, said something came up and he should be here by yesterday. Guess he got caught up even longer than expected."

"So now what are you going to do?"

"Well..." she leaned back in her chair, stretching her arms behind her. "That's the problem. I can't use just my ticket. Special deal. Have to use both. You really don't care where you end up?"

"Nope." He took another bite.

She bit her lower lip while considering Neil. "You wanna come to England? You could use my second ticket."

Neil put down the sandwich, chewed the bite he had taken and swallowed it. "Can't do that. They check ID. It's not my ticket."

"They won't check ID for these tickets. First class. They'd be afraid to offend anyone who could afford these seats."

"How'd someone with no money come across two first class tickets?"

"I told you I was here to pick this guy up. He never showed, so I'm stuck, and I've been stuck here for *days*. Was supposed to be a milk run. 'Just a quick flight over the pond and back' my boss said. Now it's been a week and he's screaming like *I* did something wrong. Look, the plane leaves at 5:30, boards in a little under half an hour. I have to head back but can't without someone else. So you wanna go to England or what? Come on, it'll be fun."

"Why me?"

Trixie sighed and rolled her eyes. "I saw you walk in the front door over there with no luggage. I guessed you had no real destination in mind and took a chance. So?"

Neil picked up his sandwich again, and stared at his plate as Trixie stole another fry. He considered the options, and quickly realized that he didn't really have any others. Running off with some random girl he just met was a far more interesting prospect than any others he had considered on his walk to the airport. He shrugged and stared into her eyes. "Sure, I'll go. Why not."

*   *   *

Neil and Trixie hurried toward the terminal after leaving the restaurant. He made a quick stop in an airport restroom while she glanced at her watch and kept mumbling about the flight's departure time. He glanced at her tight blue jeans and kept trying to concentrate on not tripping over anything because he really wasn't paying attention to where he was going. They arrived at the ticket counter ten minutes before the flight was supposed to leave. She reached into her pocket and pulled out a credit card, shoved it into the slot of the kiosk and tapped her fingernails on the side of the machine while it processed.

"Thought you had no money," Neil said.

Trixie cast a mischievous grin his way. "None that I can spend. Disposable card. Tickets were already paid for."

A menu came on the screen. She clicked one of the options before Neil had a chance to read any of them. Two tickets printed and were ejected from the machine into a small metal sleeve at waist level. She took them and the credit card and walked to the gate.

"We have no luggage," Trixie said, "so this should be quick."

"You've been living here for a week with no luggage at all?"

"Yeah, why?"

"You look great. I'd never have guessed." Neil glanced down and took a quick inventory. His pants and shirt were wrinkled and he was reasonably sure he had bed hair. He had merely gone overnight without luggage or toiletries and he was already halfway to looking like his alcoholic uncle.

She caught him checking himself out and smiled, stifling a laugh. She took a step forward and handed the boarding passes to the security guard. He looked at them, did a double take, then handed them back. "Thank you Mister and Missus Rogers. Please proceed to your left to gate twelve."

Once Neil figured they were out of earshot, he gently grabbed Trixie's forearm. "Trixie Rogers?"

"Karen Tyler, actually. Friends call me Trixie. Some Korean guy I met online said I was very tricky, but it sounded more like 'Trixie' when he said it. The name stuck."

"So who's Rogers?"

"Don't know. Some guy I was supposed to meet here and fly back to England with. Security here tends to ignore married couples traveling in first class. But damn do they question the hell out of unmarried couples traveling together. Especially in Havana. There's still a conservative majority here."

Neil nodded as he let his hand move down her forearm until they were holding hands. She handed the boarding passes to the girl behind the counter outside the jetway, who scanned the bar codes, ripped off the receipt ends, and handed them to Trixie. Neil and Trixie walked down the jetway to the plane, hand in hand. A stewardess inside the plane looked at their boarding pass receipts and pointed to two empty seats in the first class section. They sat down and buckled their seat belts.

"Next stop, jolly old England," Trixie whispered to Neil in a thick and obviously faked accent.

"Sounds good to me."

Neil closed his eyes and soon felt the plane begin to move backward as his perception of time started to skew, exhaustion finally overtaking him. The plane turned one way, then the other, then lurched forward. As it picked up speed while rolling down the runway, he drifted into sleep.

Trixie looked over at him as the plane lifted into the air and smiled, studying his features in the afternoon light. She had picked him at random, not knowing a thing except that he didn't seem to fit. At first she had thought he might be the one she was supposed to meet there, but his demeanor shot down that thought almost immediately. Far too kind, far too trusting to be *that* man. But he wasn't opposed to traveling on a whim, and at this point she just wanted to get home. She began shaking her head slightly from side to side when she realized he was already fast asleep.

She looked down and saw her hand still firmly clasped in his.

CHAPTER
11

MIAMI, FLORIDA
JULY 19, 2030 2:00 PM EDT

J ules drummed his fingers on the countertop while watching the young man type his last name into the computer with painstaking precision. The man stopped typing, stared blankly at the screen in front of him for a few moments, then nodded. He smiled, obviously pleased with himself. The machine next to him started printing out a boarding pass. When it finished, he took the pass and handed it to Jules.

"Here you are, sir."

"Thanks." Jules grabbed the pass and walked to the security station. Dozens of people were in line to get through security, dozens more in lines at the ticket counters. Jules sighed and got into line. He reached into the collar of his shirt and scratched the nape of his neck, fingernails easing the itching sensation around his latest tattoo. The line moved forward a step and then stopped. A loud beep sounded from up ahead. Jules looked around the person in front of him and saw the security guards pull an older man out of the line. The line started to move again.

After several minutes of standing, taking a step forward, and standing some more, Jules got to the front of the line. He took his sneakers off and placed them in a plastic bucket. He stepped through the metal detector. The security guard on the other side glanced at his boarding pass, nodded, and waved him through. Jules stepped to the end of the conveyor belt to wait for the bucket with his sneakers to come through the other side of the x-ray machine, watching with mild amusement as two security guards searched the older man they had pulled aside earlier. He saw his sneakers come through the other side of the scanner out of the corner of his eye, snatched them up, and stepped aside. After putting them back on, he turned toward the terminal.

There were even more people here, most lounging around in the gate areas waiting for flights. Jules looked around for a clock, found one on the wall above a gate, and compared the time to the departure time on his ticket. Flight 819 to Havana, Cuba. He had about forty minutes before they'd even start boarding the plane. He studied the area around him and saw a little coffee shop across from his gate. He headed for it, stepping over the outstretched legs of another passenger who was fast asleep in one of the seats.

The girl behind the counter was very plain, and it was quite obvious that she was either exceptionally bored or extremely stoned. She was standing behind the counter and making an effort to not notice Jules while idly tapping a bright green name tag on her chest that said her name was Susie.

Jules cleared his throat loudly and ordered an iced coffee. He passed a five-dollar coin to Susie and turned to watch the crowd as he waited. Several people milled around in an overpriced magazine shop next door. He saw one of the customers very calmly stick a rolled up magazine down the front of his pants. A purely amateurish move - the kid never even looked to see if anyone was watching him. About a hundred people at the gate he had found the clock at stood up and got in line to board a flight. Someone's kid was running in circles around a large potted plant and screaming his head off.

"Here you go," Susie said while pushing a small plastic cup across the counter. He turned, took the drink, and watched in amusement as Susie counted out six dollars in change for him. *Mystery solved,* he thought, *stoned out of her mind.* He smiled at her and took the money, then went to sit down at one of the tables. The people in line at the gate started boarding their plane as he drank. A man's voice came over the intercom system to inform the passengers that any luggage left unattended would be impounded. A woman's voice closely followed that announcement to inform everyone that smoking was not allowed in the airport. The message was repeated in Spanish as Jules took another gulp from his drink and turned his head back toward the counter, almost dropping his drink when he saw her.

She was maybe seventeen, eighteen at most. Dark brown hair tied back in a ponytail that reached to the middle of her back. She had slightly tanned skin, an angelic face, and large navy blue eyes. She handed some money to Susie and smiled as she ordered, clean white teeth perfectly aligned. Her lips were coated in what appeared to be peach colored lipstick. She wore a sky blue T-shirt with a logo of some sort over her right breast. His eyes studied her small breasts for several moments before continuing on down to see the light tan shorts she was wearing. He stared at her perfectly shaped legs as she took a small plastic cup from Susie and drained its entire contents in one tilt. She thanked Susie and turned to leave. Jules stared, unable to pull his eyes from her. He'd been down this road before. He knew where it led. He'd taken girls her age and even younger before, and smirked as he recalled some of them. Not a single one had had a body like this one.

He stood up, adjusted his pants a bit, and followed her, leaving his forgotten cup half-filled with iced coffee on the table behind him. She dropped her cup into a garbage can and started heading toward the bathrooms. He followed closely, no more than twenty feet behind her at any given time. He stared at her backside, eyes roaming from toned legs up to her ponytail swishing back and forth in rhythm with her steps. The back of her shirt had the number fifty-five written on it in large white numerals. Above that in slightly smaller text was the word "Kitten". Kitten. He let out a barely audible meow as he felt himself drawn to her. He reached into his pocket,

rubbing his fingers over the cool rubber blackjack that he had had no problem whatsoever getting through security. He stared at the dimly visible outline of her bra through the thin material of her shirt.

He was going to take her. There was no sign of debate in his mind. He
had plenty of time.

When she was within ten feet of the entrance to the women's bathroom,
he glanced over his shoulder. They had just rounded a corner. There was no
one there to see. He took the chance, stepped up his pace, and swung the
blackjack at the back of her neck. The thud echoed through the hallway, but
she made no sound, just stood there and wavered, arms hanging loosely by
her sides. He wrapped one of his arms around her midsection as she slumped
forward. He half-dragged her like that into the men's bathroom. He pulled her
inert body into the stall with the baby-changing table, returned the blackjack
to his pocket, and closed the door behind him. He laid her on the low table
and turned back to lock the stall door. She lay there on the table, eyes closed,
breathing uneven in her unconscious state. Jules turned to her and mouthed
the word "kitten", ending it with a kiss blown to her.

He heard the bathroom door open as he quietly lifted her shirt up, slowly
raising it while admiring her flat, toned stomach. The sound of feet shuffling
around in the bathroom broke his concentration. He turned his head toward
the stall door and silently cursed the noisy man outside. He turned back and
continued lifting her shirt until it was bunched up above her breasts, and
stood there staring at her white satin bra for several seconds. Someone in the
bathroom coughed. He ignored it, focusing all attention on the nubile girl
before him. He started unzipping his pants. In his excitement, he didn't even
hear the person outside his stall shout, "Go!"

The door to the stall flew open, cheap metal deadbolt splitting and
ricocheting off the floor at his feet. Jules turned his head and blinked like a
deer caught in headlights.

"Freeze! Interpol!"

Jules swallowed, stared at the two men aiming Beretta pistols at him, and
slowly raised his hands. His unzipped pants fell to the floor. Behind them,
half a dozen airport security guards glanced from him to the girl on the baby-

changing table uneasily; hands tightly gripping their guns but aiming at the floor. There was nowhere to run. There was no way to deny what he was intending to do. His excitement was readily visible to anyone in the room.

"Cuff him, Johnson."

Inspector Johnson holstered his gun, stepped into the stall, and roughly cuffed Jules' hands behind his back, taking care to make sure that he pushed Jules forcibly into the concrete wall several times. Johnson bent down to pull up Jules' pants, zipped them, and pushed him out of the stall. Ferez stepped into the stall as Johnson was leaving it, walked up to the girl, and put his hand to her neck. He breathed a sigh of relief when he felt her weak pulse. He holstered his gun and pulled her shirt down. He turned his head to the security guards, who were still standing there, eager and alert.

"She's alive. She'll be all right." He noticed a bit of purple skin on her neck and turned her head. "He hit her pretty good. She'll be bruised for a while, but she'll live."

The guards all relaxed noticeably. Ferez bent down and picked her up, shifted her in his arms to a more comfortable position, and carried her out of the stall.

*   *   *

Johnson paced back and forth in the small makeshift interrogation room, cracking his knuckles as Ferez attempted to fix an intimidating stare on an increasingly agitated Jules Trionis. Jules broke the silence with a heavy sigh. "Well? What about my phone call?"

"No."

"I know my rights."

"You have no rights." Ferez ground his teeth a bit as he spat the words out. "You have a rap sheet two miles long, asshole. And we know what you were going to do to that poor girl."

"Kitten? Just playin'."

"Bullshit. We found your blackjack, and saw the welt on the back of her neck. We caught you bare legged and red handed."

Jules shrugged. "Whatever. What's it to you anyway? Just some girl."

Johnson slammed his fist down on the table in front of Jules. He didn't even flinch. "You have no clue who that was, do you?"

Jules shrugged again. "Don't know, don't care."

"Kristie Carloosia ring a bell? No? She's the sixteen-year-old daughter of Antonio Carloosia," Johnson said while casting a quick glance at Ferez. He knew he was mispronouncing the name, he just had to make sure Ferez knew to keep it quiet.

Jules rolled his eyes and looked at the clock on the wall. Seconds ticked by as he watched, mentally processing the name. "Carliosa," he said at last. "Antonio... Carliosa?"

Ferez looked down at a folder in front of him on the desk and nodded slowly. "Oh yeah," he said, pointing at a name on the page. "Carliosa. Carl-ee-oh-sah. Not Carloosia."

Jules' eyes bulged as he mouthed the name silently. He turned his head to face the ground. "Oh, shit."

"You know," Ferez said. "I remember doing a case a few years back related to him. A bodyguard caught some guy looking at his wife. We didn't even start finding the *pieces* of him until months later."

Jules swallowed hard. "Shit. I did a job for him... I mean... he's one mean motherf-"

Johnson straightened his back and looked down on Jules. "Damn right. In technical terms, you're fucked. So you might as well just deal with it, work with us, and hope we don't just turn a blind eye when his boys get here to pick up Kristie. We've already called them. They were supposed to meet her in a couple hours when her plane would have landed in New York, but now they're heading this way as we speak. So it's your choice, Jules. Take your chances with them, or help us and we can put you into protective custody."

Jules cleared his throat and nodded.

"Good," Ferez started. "First of all, we traced your flight plan to Cuba. Who's the girl you were meeting with to go to England?"

"No clue, never met her."

"Want to hear something funny? According to their security, you boarded that plane ten minutes ago with the girl. But it wasn't you, obviously."

"Who?"

"We don't know for sure. But we're tracking another guy that was at the bar that night, Neil Roberts. Where do you know him from?"

"I don't."

Ferez sighed, leaned back in his chair. "You're supposed to be cooperating."

"I don't know the dude."

"But you knew Lisa."

Jules shrugged. "Oh what the hell. Yeah, I knew Lisa."

"But you didn't know Roberts?"

"No clue who that is."

"We have five witnesses who said you were talking to him at the bar the night of Lisa's murder. He's the guy who's knife you used to kill Lisa."

"Oh that guy. Yeah, mister black raincoat. Man, he was one boring asshole." Jules chuckled. "Yeah, okay, I remember him."

"And then you should know why he ran."

"From what?"

Johnson kicked the table leg. "From the cops you bastard."

Jules looked up at Johnson, his lips slowly curling into a mischievous smirk. "Yeah, okay. Fine, I got this box from a friend who programmed it to tell someone to run. 'Guaranteed to work', he said. Kept it in my pocket just in case I needed it some day. I stuck it under that guy's table when he wasn't paying attention. I figured you'd already have found it."

"We did. We're just piecing this puzzle together, is all." Ferez wrote some things down in his little notebook.

"Right. Next you'll ask how a stupid little steak knife did her in that quickly, right? Noclin's poison. Can't detect it, can't cure it. Guarantees a painless death in thirty seconds. Faster if you've been drinking."

"Never heard of it."

"Right, it's new, top-of-the-line. Freezes your insides and numbs you completely. Expensive as hell."

"Okay then. You said you were given that poison, the Geas Box, and then paid on top of that to kill Lisa?"

"Didn't say that."

"But you implied it."

"Whatever. I want a lawyer."

"Who hired you to kill Lisa?"

"Screw off!"

Johnson grabbed Jules by the collar, lifted him from the chair and shook him violently. "Who?!"

Jules struggled, moved his hands and arms from side to side, testing the limits of the handcuffs. He gave up after a few moments and tried to drive his knee into Johnson's groin. Johnson threw him to the concrete floor and kicked him in the ribs. Jules rolled toward the wall and coughed. Johnson took a step forward, disgust showing plainly on his face. Jules spat at the ground. Johnson kicked him in the chest, the sharp sound of bone cracking clearly audible in the room. He kicked Jules again, this time hitting him in the face and chipping a few teeth.

"Enough!" Ferez stood up. "Look, Johnson, he doesn't want to talk? Fine. Carliosa should be here soon, and once he sees his daughter and hears the security guards' explanation, I bet he'll be more than happy to deal with this piece of shit."

Jules coughed again and sat up, spitting a mouthful of blood onto the painted concrete. "No, wait."

"What for? We already know you killed Lisa. We know you killed Wilson in Orlando too. We have the security tapes to prove that one. We just want to know why."

"You gonna protect me from Carliosa? You gotta!"

Ferez paused for effect, noting the horror on Jules' face. He nodded reluctantly. "We'll do what we can."

"I was hired."

"Yeah, by who?"

"Lisa."

Ferez frowned. Johnson sat down. "Lisa?" Ferez asked. He shook his head. "Bullshit."

"No, it was! She came to me online. Offered thirty mil for four."

"Wilson and Lisa. Who else?"

"Don't know."

Johnson stood up.

"Seriously man, I don't *know*." The sound of panic entered his voice. "That's what I was going to England for. Had some job lined up over there and then this came up. Figured what the hell, one flight for two jobs. The next two targets are over there somewhere."

Ferez stood, and tugged on Johnson's sleeve. They stepped outside of the room, closing the door behind them. For a moment, they stood in silence, both trying to digest the details from the interrogation.

"Sounds like bullshit." Johnson put his hands in his pockets and leaned against the far wall.

"Yeah, doesn't make sense. I'll believe the thirty million for four murders part, that at least makes sense considering who the targets were. But why the hell would anyone pay to have *themselves* murdered?"

"Security tape showed her face when it happened. She wasn't expecting it, no way."

"Doubt that other guy was expecting it either. Contact Anderton Enterprises, that branch that Lisa was working in. Find out how many people were employed there."

"Already did last night."

"Let me guess."

"Four."

"Hate it when I'm right."

"Now what?"

Ferez leaned against the door and grasped the knob in one hand. "Get Jules into a jail cell before Carliosa gets here. Then try to find out what happened to Roberts when he got to Miami."

"I'll run a trace on Roberts, see if there's any record of him leaving Miami."

"Good, I'll see what I can do about getting Jules out of here safely."

"You do know that a jail cell isn't likely going to protect him, right?"

"He wasn't that safe in there either. What was that all about anyway? I think I heard a rib crack when you kicked him."

"That girl," Johnson shook his head sadly. "Looks just like my little niece, man. I almost want to hand that bastard over to Carliosa with a big red bow on his head. Wish we could have gotten to him earlier."

"Yeah, well face scanning takes time. They scan a hundred thousand faces going through security a day. Probably never would have known he was here at all if we hadn't shown up specifically looking for him. Wish we could have stopped him earlier, but at least we did stop him before..."

Ferez stopped mid sentence and looked down at the floor. They stood there in silence for a few moments. Johnson patted Ferez on the shoulder and turned to walk down the hall. Ferez sighed and opened the door.

CHAPTER
12

THE INTERNET - MIAMI, FL USA NODE
JULY 19, 2030 5:15 PM EDT

She moved around the general public node and watched as people logged in and moved around the Internet. An avatar appeared in front of the menu program and flashed a digital government ID. She zoomed in and read the name on badge, Inspector Johnson. She executed a few commands, attaching to his avatar in stealth mode. He moved forward, dragging her along with him. As he approached the node for the Interpol office, she increased the encryption on her data stream and watched as he logged in. A black skinned man appeared in front of him and bowed his head slightly, arms clasped behind his firmly pressed Armani suit.

"Welcome to the Miami department, Inspector Johnson. How can I help you?"

"Markus, can you get me every record of travel for Neil Roberts in the past forty-eight hours?"

"Yes, sir. Is this the same Mister Roberts that you inquired about previously?"

"Yes."

"Processing."

She watched intently as the data streams flowed by Markus at lightning speed. His eyes roamed over the data, searching for matching files. Every few moments, he'd reach out and grab some bit of data and insert it into a small yellow folder. After many nanoseconds had elapsed, he stopped and handed the folder to Johnson.

"Here you go, sir. Let me know if there is anything else I can do for you."

Johnson glanced at the information. She read the pages as he flipped through them, noting that the last line was a note about Neil's arrival at the bus station in Miami. Johnson looked back up at Markus. "I need footage from the video cameras in the Miami bus station."

"Of course." Markus waved his hands and created a small window in front of Johnson that immediately started playing surveillance footage showing Neil walking into the station.

"Stop. Enhance." The image flickered and centered on Neil's face. "Pan left. Who's that he's walking with?"

"Processing." Chad's face shimmered and was highlighted with the face analysis wireframe. The lines cycled through several colors before settling on green. "Positive match. His name is Chad Irvin Groban." Markus generated a few more pages and handed them to Johnson.

"Privacy mode."

She watched as Johnson's command built a rudimentary firewall around himself, encasing both of them in material that resembled thick orange plastic. He waited until the wall had been completely constructed before laying the folder in the air in front of him. She watched him reach up and move a slide bar to a position marked "Paranoid". He opened the folder and flipped through the pages.

She analyzed the pages, reading all of the material from slightly beside him. He spent some time reviewing information on Chad, studying his face print and saving a copy to his local hard drive. There was very little information on him, just another kid living on the fringes of society. Some references to his affinity for a place in Miami called *Gino's*. What interested her was the profile data on the other person, apparently a programmer of some skill who was the main target of Johnson's inquiry.

"Who is Neil Roberts?" she asked.

Johnson let go of the folder and raised his arms in defense. The folder floated in front of him as he glanced around. "What? Who's there?"

"Who is Neil Roberts?" she asked again.

"How'd you get by this firewall?"

"It was simple code to break. Who is Neil Roberts?"

"Simple? *Simple?* This is top-of-the-line government issued software. Who the hell are you?"

"Who is Neil Roberts?"

She reached for him, dug her arms into his avatar and started to probe the local data storage on his computer. It was a mess in there, all sorts of files scattered around the drive with no apparent attempt at organization. Just a bunch of folders with numbers on them, not quite dates but close to enough digits. She opened one folder at random and looked through the files inside, opening them and studying each. And then it made sense to her, the folders on the drive were labeled with case numbers, not dates. She scanned a few but found nothing pertinent to her question. She queried the hard drive's file table and looked for the most recently created folders, and sorted the list by those.

Johnson panicked. He dropped the firewall, pushed the folder away, and jacked out forcefully. His avatar faded until it was only barely visible, then floated downward into the floor of the building. Markus appeared in front of her, grabbed the folder as it floated by, and moved his mouth to a rough approximation of a frown. "Excuse me, miss, but you are not authorized to be here. Please enter your access authorization code and Interpol ID number."

She reached out, pushed her hands into his midsection, and ripped open part of his chest. She opened a command prompt and inserted a bit of code as he tilted his head downward in slow motion. She moved some other bits of his operating code around and then closed the gap. He shuddered, eyes glazed over and arms limp. The folder slipped from his hand, fell to the ground, and spilled its contents on the shimmering floor. One by one, the pages dissolved into the floor until they were all gone. Markus shuddered again, and moaned out a few error codes. He paused, shook one last time, then stood tall and straightened his tie. "Welcome to the Miami department, Inspector Null. How can I help you?"

"Get me all the information you have on Neil Roberts."

CHAPTER

13

N eil sat bolt upright from his slouched position and looked around the cabin. Trixie's head, which had been peacefully resting on his shoulder, fell behind his back and jerked her awake. She reached over to her other armrest and pulled herself back to a sitting position, grimacing as the tension from sleeping on airport benches was taking its toll on her body. She arched her back, felt something in her shoulders pop and enjoyed the relaxing sensation that followed.

"Oh. Sorry," he offered.

"Good morning to you too." She looked out the window. "Or evening. Sleep well?"

He thought back to the dream he just went through. The same vision he'd been having every time he closed his eyes. The knife. The sound of it piercing her flesh. The sad look on her face as she moved her gaze from her chest wound to him, sitting there in the corner of the bar in the soft glow of a red neon sign. He was stuck in a loop of watching her die. He frowned as he realized that even though she haunted his dreams, he didn't even know who she was. "No," he replied. "Not even remotely."

"Bad dream?"

"Very."

"Ah. I've had lots of bad dreams. Usually happens when I'm stressed out."

"What, from work?"

"Yeah. My job's a real pain in the ass sometimes."

"So quit."

"Can't just quit. It's not that easy."

"Why not? I did," Neil said, frowning slightly. "Well, sort of. I guess I really just stopped going, technically."

She laughed. "When did you do that?"

"Last night."

"Really? What happened?"

Neil shrugged. "Gave up. Life was sucking."

"Girl troubles, right?"

He smirked. "Have you met my girlfriend?" She shook her head. He thought he detected a twinge of something... upset? Disappointment? It was an old line he'd come up with while in college, more of a joke really. It usually ended with the girl just saying *nope* and wandering off. He couldn't recall the last girl he got to the punchline with. Part of him always considered it to be a routine to weed out the girls who would never understand his sense of humor. "Damn," he said. "Me neither."

She grinned widely. "Well, I guess that still qualifies as girl troubles."

"Yeah, technically. Just never really had time for a girlfriend. Or at least no time to *find* one. I spent so many years building a career and just kept telling myself there would never be time for anything more. Maybe I was just waiting for the right girl to find me."

"It could happen."

"Well anyway, what did you dream about?"

Trixie shifted in her seat as much as her seatbelt allowed. "Don't remember it really. Something about a rabbit with a Howitzer and brightly colored machine tools. My dreams rarely make sense."

"Dreams can be like that. It's like your mind just throws things together at random to give you something to watch while sleeping. Sometimes mine are odd, sometimes they make sense."

"Mine never make sense."

Neil shrugged. "Maybe not to you."

"Oh, you a dream analyst?"

"No, computer programmer."

"Really?"

"Yeah, it's boring. I know. All that typing and arm waving." He waved his arms in the air in front of himself elaborately. "Not exactly the kind of job that impresses... well... anyone."

"No, it isn't boring. You any good?"

"I guess. Worked for Goliath as an intern while in college, and been there ever since I got out of school."

"Seriously? I heard of them. New Tampa, right?"

"Yeah."

"What the hell were you doing in Cuba?"

"Running away. I said that earlier."

"Oh, that's right. You steal something?"

"No. Not exactly. Well, not intentionally at least. I probably have all sorts of stuff on my computer." He patted his coat where the small bulge of his computer was and briefly thought of all the software he still had on it. The pre-release versions he was working on were most likely worth a lot to the right people. Worth a small fortune to the wrong ones.

"Hmm." She looked out the window again, and stared into the sky. It was dark enough outside to see the stars but bright enough to still see the water below. She refocused her eyes on her own reflection and shifted to the side until she could see Neil in the glass. He was staring at her. She smiled, then a thought struck her. She turned back to Neil. "Wait a minute, wasn't it Goliath that wrote that new firewall software? Shield 4? You work on that?"

"I wrote it."

"What, the whole thing?"

"Yeah, only took about two months."

"Shit, I guess you *are* good. How the heck did you write something that big in only two months?"

"I replaced most of my computer's base functions with macros to increase my speed. Got up to the point of being at least three times faster than anyone else in the office. Well, that and working eighty hours a week helped a lot. And caffeine. They had free coffee in the office."

"Impressive."

Neil shrugged. "Guess so."

"Humble too. I used Shield 4. Damn good firewall. Haven't seen anyone capable of breaking through it yet."

"Really? Odd. It hasn't been released yet."

She blushed. "Oh... right..."

Neil laughed. "It's okay, I stole more software than I can count too. It's the only way to support a surfing habit on a limited budget these days. If you can't just write your own, that is, and I never had the time to write everything I needed."

"I haven't thought about budgets in years."

"You have a good job then? Or at least a good paycheck. What do you do anyway?"

"I..." she started, then paused and looked down at her hands. She leaned closer to him and whispered in his ear. "Hacking, mostly."

He turned toward her and paused when he realized his lips were only inches from hers. They stared into each other's eyes for several long seconds. There was something there, he thought, an intensity that he'd only seen in the mirror before. A love for computers, for programming, a genuine interest in pure logic and what could be achieved with it. He saw a kindred spirit in her eyes, a spirit that found the real world a difficult place to live in and retreated into the digital realm to find solace.

And something else, a vulnerability in her eyes that spoke volumes. Even as untrained in matters of the heart as he was, he could tell when someone was pleading for acceptance. He knew because he saw that pleading every time he stood in front of a mirror. She felt a connection, and more than that, she wanted him to feel it too.

Neil could feel his breathing become more rapid, could feel himself starting to lean forward. Suddenly, a stewardess bumped into him, breaking the trance and pushing him forward those last few inches until their lips touched. He pulled back and looked down at his folded hands sheepishly. Trixie leaned back and touched her lips lightly. She watched as Neil wrung his hands for several nervous moments.

The true weight of the word hit him then. *Hacking.* He had spent years developing software to fight hackers, to keep the good guys safe from them. During those years he had formulated a demonized view of hackers - they were unkempt, shady folk hiding in basements. They were high-tech thieves without morals who stole from banks and corporations. The same organizations that paid him to help develop protective software. And yet here was this attractive and personable woman not even remotely like what he had pictured he was fighting. He could see her watching him out of the corner of his eye, concern etched on her face as she waited for his response. "Ah," he finally replied, unable to think of anything more intelligent to add.

"I know. I'm just... the kind of person you fought against."

"True," he said, letting the word slowly roll off his tongue. He tried to sort through his emotions to approach this as logically as possible. Somewhere deep down, she was indeed who he had been fighting, and yet he couldn't suppress the attraction he felt. So much had changed in his life recently. He'd been through more in the past few hours than in the previous few years. To finally meet a woman he wanted to spend time with and have her be his enemy just seemed unfair. The only solution he could muster was to roll with it, to discard his inhibitions and see what fate had in store for him. "But," he said, "I left that life behind me."

Trixie looked at him, smiling weakly. "When we get to London, I have a room reserved." She spoke the words a little too quickly, she felt, and tried to make herself slow down. She took a deep breath in the hopes that the pounding of her heart would slow. "You'll probably need a place to crash, right? I mean, if you're looking for a new life, maybe I can introduce you to my friends at work."

"What, hacking?" he spat the words out and immediately regretted them. If he was standing, he probably would have attempted kicking himself.

"I'd rather not say more here."

Their eyes met again, then she glanced down, away from his gaze. There was something there, and the kiss, as brief as it was, was only seconds away from not being accidental. He couldn't help but feel an odd mixture of confusion and excitement. He was on the run, as stupid as that decision was. And here was another decision. He was pretty sure he couldn't go back home, not easily at least. And attempting to get another legitimate job in computers would be another stupid decision, almost certain to get him in trouble. Any legitimate job could be trouble at this point. And so the only choice was an illegitimate one, and this was one that he was definitely qualified to do. Most banks and governments, if not all of them, ran his software. Who better to break something than the person who built it?

He looked at her lips and realized that his decision was already made. "All right."

"At the very least, you'll have a place to stay for a bit. As thanks for coming on this trip with me."

Neil leaned back in his seat, stifled a yawn, and blinked tired tears from his eyes. "I should be the one to thank you. I'd probably be stranded in the airport still if you hadn't come along. Anyway, I'm still wiped out and should try to sleep. And you probably want to get back to your brightly colored machine tools."

She stifled a nervous laugh and glanced out the window again. "Not particularly. I'd rather talk with you than sleep. It's more relaxing." She turned to Neil, and frowned as he started to snore softly. She leaned her head to the side and rested it on his shoulder, listening to the steady sound of his breathing.

CHAPTER
14

W hat the *hell*?" Ferez shouted as he walked into the break room at the airport security station. Johnson lay on the floor beside one of the tables, shirt drenched in sweat, breathing uneven, a thin line of dried blood leading from one nostril down the side of his cheek. His computer lay on the table, small internal fan still whirring softly. His optic interface glasses were still firmly in place on his face. The thin plastic cable of the wall jack grasped tightly in his left glove. "Hey, Johnson!" Ferez shook his partner's body. "Johnson! Get up!"

Johnson moaned, stirred a bit, then sat up slowly. He dropped the wall jack and lifted his glasses with shaky hands. His bloodshot eyes roamed around the room, passing over Ferez several times but not focusing on him. His pupils were dilated and his breathing came in short, raspy gasps. "Hey?"

"What the hell happened?"

"Not sure. Had to pull the wall jack out."

"Yeah, I see that."

"Someone was in there with me."

"Lots of people are in there. It's a whole global community, that's kinda the point."

"No, I mean in the firewall with me."

"What, *behind* the firewall? How's that possible?"

Johnson shook his head and blinked a few times, eyes starting to focus on the room around him. He saw Ferez kneeling beside him with a concerned look on his face. He saw the computer on the table and reached over to click it off, then started to undo the Velcro straps on his gloves. "It isn't. That firewall I got is supposed to be the most secure thing there is. It's not even released to the public yet. The best hackers in the world were employed just to try to break through it. Most of them gave up after eight months of trying."

"Who was it then?"

"Not sure of that either."

"You get a trace?"

"Didn't have time, I felt... something... and just ripped the plug out of the wall. That's the last thing I remember. I can probably check my logs to see if that helps."

"Okay, but looks like you're still in shock, so don't worry about that now. Did you get anything on Roberts?" Ferez stood up, walked over to the soda machine, and slipped a coin into the slot. He made a selection, opened the can, and forced Johnson to take a sip.

"He didn't leave Miami, according to the trace I ran. Left the bus station with some kid. I checked out the ID and verified the face scan. Name was Chad... something or other. He frequents a tattoo parlor in Miami called Gino's. I got the impression that the place is hidden in some alley, not a legit business. Probably won't be easy to find."

"They do piercings too, huh?"

"Guess so. Maybe other stuff. Roberts is either still in Miami, or he had enough cash for Chad or Gino to help him go elsewhere."

"So how do we find this place? Start at the bus station? Maybe someone can help us find it."

Johnson took the can from Ferez and took another sip, swallowed, and nodded. "Sounds good. Just gimme a few minutes to get up. Room's still spinning. You take care of Trionis?"

"Yeah, got his confession taken care of down at the local police station. He's being held without bail, so he's all set for now."

"And Carliosa?"

"Pissed off something fierce, but there's nothing he can do about it except maybe bribe a judge or an officer or something. That's assuming he doesn't already own one."

"Or all of them. I wouldn't put that past him."

"Me neither. Not our problem anymore anyway. We did our part and got what we wanted. As soon as we catch up with Roberts we can close this case. I'll get the car and find the bus station in the GPS. You meet me at the front gate, okay?"

"Sure. Just need a few."

*   *   *

Ferez hopped out of the car and walked around to open the door for Johnson. Johnson was still moving slowly, arms cradled around his bundle of computer and data input attachments. He turned around and plopped down into the passenger seat, and leaned away from the door as Ferez closed it behind him. Ferez got back into the driver's seat. "Feeling any better?" he asked.

"Sure. Still need to relax more though. Takes a lot out of me when that happens."

Ferez shifted into drive and pulled out into traffic. He drove along in silence for several minutes before speaking again. "You remember anything more about who that was in there?"

"No. Someone good enough to hack into the Interpol node and get through the best firewall software ever written. Probably not too many people that fit that profile."

"What about a very good programmer?"

"Who'd you have in mind?"

"Roberts."

"Nah." Johnson shook his head and turned to look out the window at the car in the next lane. The driver was a woman in her twenties with one hand hanging out the window holding a cigarette, and the other holding a cell phone to her ear. He frowned. She saw him and flipped him off, nearly dropping the cigarette in the process. He pulled out his badge and when she noticed it, she dropped the phone and cigarette, grabbed the wheel with both hands, and promptly swerved into the highway shoulder and skidded a hundred feet before stopping, massive dust clouds billowing into the air around her car. Johnson shook his head, put his badge away, and continued staring at the pavement rolling by.

Ferez bit his lip, thought for a moment. "Why not? He's got the skills. Hell, he programmed that firewall while at Goliath, who then sold advance copies to Interpol. If anyone would know of any weaknesses in it, he would."

"I didn't know that."

"Me neither, until last night. Saw a bit on the news about him. Seems like he'd be the prime suspect for what you saw."

"He'd be a joker too then."

"How do you mean?"

"What I saw in there was a woman. Or something pretending to be, at least. Definitely was a female voice though. I know that can all be faked these days, but she kept asking me who Roberts was. Wait, there's the bus station, on the right. Turn here."

Ferez slowed and made the turn. They drove down the street for half a mile until they got to the parking lot. Ferez parked in one of the empty spaces on the side of the station and turned off the engine. Johnson got out, knees wobbly but still functional, and turned around to deposit his computer equipment in the back seat of the car. He started to make the trek to the building entrance. Ferez joined him on the sidewalk and they entered the building together.

Several people were sitting in the station. Some were reading newspapers while others watched the news on small television sets suspended from the ceiling over the front doorway. Off to the side of the station near the bathrooms, a mid-thirties man with a cheap haircut and several facial piercings juggled apples while humming the theme to a long defunct but still somewhat popular TV show. Ferez walked up to the man and flashed his badge. When that elicited no response, he cleared his throat loudly. The man glanced at the badge and then returned his attention to the apples.

"Name's Derek. What you want?"

"Looking for a place called Gino's."

"Gino's. Yeah. Heard of it."

"Where is it?"

"Don't know."

"Where'd you get those piercings?"

"Atlanta."

"But you know of Gino's?"

"Sure, went there last night."

Ferez sighed. "But you don't know where it is?"

"Not a clue man. Was drunk, totally shit-faced."

"Dammit."

"Look for the street preacher."

"Who?"

"Street preacher. Crazy fucker. Hangs out around Gino's and a few other places, yells about the end of the world and how all women are whores and how tattoos are evil. Crap like that. Can't miss the guy. Crazy as they come."

"Any idea where he is?"

"Just drive around man. You see some bastard in a dress screaming at people and waving a Bible around above his head, that's the guy."

"Thanks."

"Sure." Derek grabbed one of his apples mid-flight, took a bite out of it, and threw it back up in the air, never missing a beat in the process.

Ferez took Johnson's arm and helped him out of the building. They got in the car, drove around the backside of the bus station, and headed out toward the rest of the city. They drove around aimlessly for over two hours before Ferez broke the silence.

"We need a fresh charge."

"Saw a station on the right two blocks back."

"Okay, that'll do." Ferez pulled into the left lane, swung an illegal U-turn into oncoming traffic, and slammed on the accelerator. The car's engine sputtered, the lights on the dashboard dimmed for a moment, and then the car shot forward. He saw the station ahead and got in the lane to turn, then pointed forward and shouted, "Street preacher!" a little too loudly.

Johnson looked where Ferez was pointing. Standing outside of the station was an older man in an altar robe, waving a badly worn Bible over his head and shouting at passing cars. "Yeah, that's gotta be him."

Ferez looked both ways, ran the red light when it was clear, and pulled into the station. He lined the car up with a recharge kiosk and turned off the engine. Johnson got out and started limping toward the preacher. Ferez slid his credit card in the machine, opened a small panel in the car's hood, and pushed the recharge connector into it. The car beeped and the kiosk started to vibrate.

"Excuse me." Johnson said as he tapped the preacher on the shoulder.

The man turned around quickly and looked down at Johnson. He stood well over six feet tall and had a big white bushy beard. He was like a tall, thin Santa Claus in a tattered altar robe. An obviously insane Santa Claus, but the resemblance was definitely there. The preacher looked Johnson up and down, then grinned widely and opened his arms.

"Ah, greetings my young friend! If ye be good of heart, then stay not long in this land, for it is filled with evil and villainy. The people's lives are driven by lust and violent tendencies, the tools of the Hateful One. I, however, must remain here and continue trying to awaken the people of this land from their treacherous ways. The Lord's work is never done! Sinners never rest in this city, and so neither shall I! Breath mint?"

Johnson scratched his chin thoughtfully. "Um, okay." He started reaching for the preacher's roll of mints then stopped himself. The one on the end looked sticky, with more pocket lint than mint. "I'm looking for a certain place and was wondering if you knew where it was."

"I know these streets well. I have been combating the Evil One for many years on these streets. But, alas, my work has proven to be in vain. Every day, more and more people stray from the Good Book into lives filled with video games and sex. But I shall never give up hope that they will be reborn into lives of goodness and fine spirits. Or, rather, fine thoughts. Yes, that's it. Fine spirits should not be consumed by the younger citizens. Or at least... at least... Hark! Even now I see a young woman behind you heading into a life of sin, with her suggestive walking and short miniskirt." He leaned to the side and shouted over Johnson's shoulder. "Heed my words child! A life of sin will lead to the ruin of your soul! Abandon your sinful clothing and embrace the goodness you have lost!"

She glanced back and promptly flipped up the back of her skirt, showing her bare bottom and eliciting a shocked gasp from the preacher. He dropped the roll of mints and clutched his Bible closer to his chest. He mumbled something and looked like he was about to cry.

"Place is called Gino's."

The preacher took a step back, shock on his face and fire in his eyes as he refocused his gaze on Johnson. "Speak not of that place! The mark of the Beast is upon them all!"

"Beast? What?"

"The Beast has them all! Piercings and tattoos, tattoos and piercings. It's nothing but self-mutilation for the purpose of vanity! That is the mark of the Beast, the vile servant of Satan that has come to destroy us all! No my son, I will not help you destroy your soul in that pit of the Devil's work." The street preacher raised one hand and held it in front of Johnson's face. "Out, devils!"

Johnson pulled out his badge and showed it to the preacher, who cautiously lowered his hand while studying it. "I'm Inspector Johnson with Interpol. My partner over there and I need to go to Gino's. We're tracking down a potentially dangerous man, that's all."

The preacher put his hand to his forehead to shield the sun from his eyes. He held out his Bible parallel to the ground and looked Johnson in the eyes. "You swear this upon your soul? Upon the Good Book?"

Johnson glanced back to Ferez for support and saw him still busy working on getting the car recharged. He turned back to the preacher and placed his hand, palm down, on the Bible. "I swear it. We just need to ask them some questions."

The preacher smiled, obviously relieved. "Praise be to God! Promise me that you will also report the location of this despicable place to the police officers of this city. They don't seem inclined to believe the word of a holy man. I suppose they too may be marked by the Beast. Poor misguided sinners. Someday, I pray, their souls will be saved. Come my friend, it is not far from here."

"Ferez!" Johnson called. "On the move!"

Ferez looked past the car and saw Johnson following the preacher toward an alleyway. He unplugged the car, got in, and moved it to the side of the station's lot. By the time he finished, he could see the preacher and Johnson disappearing into the alley. He had to run to catch up.

The preacher led them through the labyrinthine corridors formed by the buildings. He babbled constantly as he led the agents through an increasingly complex route until they finally emerged into a slightly wider alley. Cardboard boxes stacked across from the entrance provided some cover from the single steel door at the end. Opposite that door, the alley opened up onto one of the city's streets. Pieces of newspapers were scattered around the ground, undisturbed by the barely noticeable breeze that occasionally floated through. Trash was piled against the walls of the buildings, empty food containers providing ample shelter for the army of rats skittering around. The stench was overpowering.

The preacher pointed to the door at the end of the alley and spoke in a boisterous voice. "There lies the pit of Satan! Sodom and Gomorrah. Sex, tattoos, piercings, villainy... uh..." his voice trailed off. He paused and furrowed his brows a moment, then his face lit up and he added, "And comic books! Depravity of all forms... the lair of the Beast himself." His proclamation ended with a shrill scream from somewhere upstairs in the building. "Hear now the screams of the tortured from within. Tread carefully, my friends. Your very *souls* may be at stake!"

"Um, thanks." Johnson extended his hand to the preacher, who frowned, held out his Bible, pulled it back, looked at the offered hand, shrugged, and turned to leave. Johnson retracted his hand, looked at Ferez, and turned to approach the door. Ferez knocked on the door twice. A panel slid to the side.

"What you want?" said someone from the other side of the door.

"We want to see Gino."

"Who the hell are you?"

"I'm Inspector Ferez of Interpol. This is my partner, Inspector Johnson. We have some questions we'd like to ask."

"Piss off." The panel slid shut.

"Nice." Johnson rubbed the back of his neck. "Now what?"

"Try again." Ferez banged on the door again.

The panel slid open. "You again? Thought I told you to piss off."

"Yeah, but we won't. Just have some questions for Gino."

"Look," Johnson added quickly. "Tell him we'd be more than happy to speak with him out here in this alley. Or we could come back with a few hundred friends."

"What's this shit about?"

Ferez took a tentative step forward. "About a man who probably came through here yesterday. Name's Neil Roberts. More than likely came here with another guy named Chad."

"Fucking Chad. Fine, I'll ask." The panel slid shut.

Five minutes later, the door opened and Gino stepped out into the alley. "I'm Gino. Whath thith about? I have a buthineth to run here."

"I know that," Ferez started, raising his badge for Gino to verify. "Just have a few questions about a guy that might have come through here yesterday with Chad."

"Thaid hith name wath Neil."

"Roberts?"

Gino shrugged. "Didn't give a lath name."

Ferez reached into his pocket and pulled out a folded printout with Neil's photograph centered on it. "This him?"

"Yeah, thath the guy."

"What happened to him?"

"Left."

"Where?"

Gino shook his head.

"Don't know or won't tell? We need to know and we are perfectly capable and willing to take down this business of yours if you don't cooperate."

Gino held up his hands. "Woah, hold on, thath my livelihood. I don't want trouble, not for thum guy I jutht met. You promith to leave me alone here if I tell you?"

"Yes, we do."

"Thent him to Cuba yethterday."

"Cuba? Where?"

"Havana."

"Shit." Johnson poked Ferez in the arm. "Bet he got on that plane."

"What plane?" Gino looked over to Johnson.

"Doesn't matter," Ferez answered. "We'll take it from here. Thanks for your help Gino. We'll be sure to forget about this place once we leave the alley."

"Right, thankth." Gino stepped back into his door and closed it.

"Where did that plane head off to again?" Ferez asked as they turned to head back out to the street.

"England, if I remember it right. London, or maybe Gatwick. Greater London area for sure. So we head off to there?"

Ferez thrust his hands into his pockets. "No. No, I think we should go to Havana first. Question the locals and be sure that he got on that plane. It's possible he didn't. They're bound to have surveillance cameras set up there that we can check out. Maybe get an ID on the girl that was also scheduled to get on that flight. Would be good to know who she is before we try to jump into getting to Roberts."

"Good idea. Maybe knowing who she is will give us a head start on tracking them down in England. We can call ahead on the plane and get the London office to start tracking them down before we even arrive. Think we'll run into any problems with this? I mean, we already charged Trionis with the murder."

"Problems? I doubt it. Roberts is still a prime suspect in the murder of Lisa Anderton, at least on paper. Not everyone knows about that Geas Box yet. And without that, the only thing professing his innocence is the testimony of Trionis, and I think we both know how much that's worth. Neil's side of the story may shed some light on Trionis' employer, and Anderton Enterprises owns enough of this planet to ensure that we'll be given access to every resource we need to find him. If we need to, we'll just tell them we're planning to charge Roberts with conspiracy to commit murder. That should be good enough to piss off her father and ensure we have open reign."

"Okay then. When we get to the car, I'll call to make the arrangements for a trip to Cuba."

"Good."

Ferez and Johnson wandered around the alleys, trying to retrace their steps. It took them several minutes before they realized they were completely lost.

CHAPTER
15

N eil awoke to the sound of running water. He could hear a woman's voice softly singing in the shower off to his right. He concentrated on the voice, trying to hear the words and place the song, but he came to the conclusion that it was one that he didn't know. He opened his eyes, propped himself up on his elbows, and looked around the room. The queen-sized bed he was in was a mess, sheets and bedspread in a bundle at his feet, thin cotton boxer shorts the only thing between his bare skin and the cool air. Across from the bed was a bureau with four drawers and an old Toshiba LCD television on top next to the wall mirror. In the mirror's reflection he could see an Impressionist painting on the wall above the bed. Across from the bathroom door was a wide window with green plaid curtains drawn tight in front of it. He let himself fall back onto the bed and stared at the ceiling.

The shower turned off, followed by the sound of the girl coughing light-ly. After a few minutes, Trixie opened the door and stepped into the bedroom, one towel wrapped around her midsection and another wrapping up her hair. She crossed over to the bed and leaned until she could see Neil's face.

"Ah, good, you're up." She smiled widely, and Neil noted an odd sparkle in her eyes.

"Hey. What time is it?"

"About half past six. Evening."

"What day?"

Trixie looked over to a calendar on the bureau. "Saturday. You gonna ask what year it is now?"

Neil sat and stretched his arms. From his new perspective, he could see his clothes in a bundle on a small armchair in the corner. He looked up at Trixie. "Did we... uh... I mean, did I... uh..."

She followed his gaze to his clothes on the chair and laughed. "Well, you seemed pretty tired still last night. We got in here, you tore off your clothes, and jumped into bed with me. You then reached over and... turned off the light. We just slept."

He turned and swung his legs over the side of the bed. "What do we do now?"

"You can probably use a shower. Then maybe something to eat?"

"All right." He stood and walked to the bathroom. The whole room was cloaked in a haze. The mirror was fogged up and the floor was slippery from the moisture. There was a faint scent of lavender in the air. He closed the door behind himself and dropped his boxer shorts to the floor. He had to take a cold shower since Trixie had apparently already used the hot water, but he didn't mind. It woke him up faster.

When he'd finished, he grabbed a towel and dried himself off, put his shorts back on, and exited the bathroom. Trixie was sitting on the edge of the bed, drying her hair with one of the towels and watching the news. Neil looked her up and down, examining the little blue sundress she was wearing.

"Nothing really on the news... again. More world events that I never really follow but should."

"Ah. I never watch TV." Neil crossed in front of her and headed for the chair with his clothes.

"Why not?"

"Nothing good on, at least not in my opinion. Plus the cost."

"Then what do you do for fun? To unwind at night?"

"Movies, music, video games, or just surfing around the Net. Stuff like that. I never really had much of an entertainment budget, so I usually just ended up surfing the Net or doing extra work."

"Gah, working in your free time? That's no fun."

"Yeah, but sometimes my boss would slip me some extra money. It wasn't much, but it helped."

"You couldn't have been poor at a place like that."

Neil pulled on his pants. "Pretty much. Peanut butter sandwiches every night, just like all the time I was in college."

"No way, you were part of the biggest software firm in America."

"I was part of the system, another wage slave. I lived in the city. I usually walked to work because I couldn't afford a car. It got too expensive after a couple parking tickets I got. And then gasoline cars were declared illegal and... I just gave up on the damn thing."

Trixie stopped trying to dry her hair, dropped the damp towel to the carpet, and stood. "Seriously, how much did you make every week there? Nine hundred?" She grabbed something from the top of the bureau and tied her hair back in a ponytail.

"Closer to a thousand, after taxes."

"And how much did you have for fun money at the end of the week?"

"Six, maybe seven bucks."

Trixie stared at him, mouth agape. "Good God, you must be joking."

Neil shook his head. "Wish I was."

"What the hell did you do with the rest of that paycheck?"

"Apartment, mostly. Student loans. Old credit card I never paid off."

"Food?"

"Some of it, but I usually spent the six or seven bucks on that too. Speaking of food, I'm ready to eat. Where are we going?"

"Downstairs. We're in a pub." Trixie headed for the bedroom door, which turned out to be the door to their room. They were at the end of the hallway, right next to the stairs that led down into the pub's main room. "How long were you working there, living like that?"

"Years," Neil replied, letting the word stretch into a sigh. He shook his head, disappointed in himself for putting up with that part of his life. "Too long."

"How the hell did you deal with it without going nuts?"

"I didn't. That's why I'm here."

She giggled on her way down the steps. "I should have seen that answer coming."

Trixie sat at the first table near the bottom of the stairs, which happened to be a good distance from the other tables but still within viewing range of a television mounted to the ceiling behind the bar. Neil sat down, glanced quickly at the soccer game on the television, and then turned back to Trixie.

"Yeah, well, I don't miss that life at all." He glanced at two older men at the next table who were nursing pint mugs of pitch-black liquid. "Looks like this life has better beer."

A heavyset woman wearing a stained apron waddled up to their table and set two laminated sheets of paper down in front of them. "'Ello then deahs, two for dinneh, eh? You want some bitteh?"

Neil drummed his fingers on the table. He pointed casually over to the two men at the next table. "What are they drinking?"

"Old Engine Oil."

Trixie smiled at Neil's confused expression. "It's a beer, Neil, brewed in Scotland. We'll each take a pint."

The waitress smiled and walked back toward the bar.

Trixie picked up one of the menus and looked it over. "I've been here before, it's a good room and good food. An old friend works in the kitchen. She lets me stay here every now and then for free and lets me raid her closet too."

Neil took the other menu, glanced over its contents quickly. He was back in the state of mind where anything and everything was appealing. He paused on one entry on the menu and frowned. "Salmon and cream cheese sandwich?"

Trixie nodded vigorously, her eyes growing wide at the mention. "Oh yes, quite good."

He considered, thought back to his former boring life and what the old him would have done in this situation. It didn't take long for him to decide. "Okay, what the hell. I like salmon and cream cheese, might as well slap them together. I'll try it."

"Try what then, love?" the waitress asked as she set down two mugs of dark bitter on the table. The liquid sloshed around and dark foam spilled over the sides onto the table.

"Salmon and cream cheese sandwich."

"Make that two," Trixie added.

The waitress retrieved the menus and turned to leave. "Fine choice," she added, almost as an afterthought.

Neil stared at the mug in front of him, pushed on the glass and watched the liquid swish around. The beer was charcoal in color with hints of ruby reflections within and a thick frothy head like whipped cream. He picked up the mug, sniffed the contents, and squinted his eyes as he savored the aroma of sweetened roasted coffee. Trixie rolled her eyes, picked up her mug, and drank a third of it in one pull. Neil took a sip and was overwhelmed with flavors of burnt coffee and chocolate. His vision started to blur. "Good God."

"Good, huh?"

He took another mouthful of the smooth beer, closed his eyes and tried to categorize the flavor. The chocolate and coffee were obvious, but there was so much more complexity to it that he couldn't quite place. He was unable to compare it to anything he'd ever had before. He swallowed the mouthful and opened his eyes. The room was starting to spin. "Hell yeah."

"Take it easy. You haven't eaten in like eighteen hours. Get some food in you before drinking much more."

"You're already halfway through yours."

"I'm conditioned for it. You drink many stouts?"

"No. Can't afford to drink much of anything, really."

"Exactly. I've been drinking this kind of beer for months."

Neil set the glass down and held onto the table for support as the room continued to spin. "Woah." Time began to phase in and out. Trixie was talking, saying something, but Neil couldn't focus on the words. He blinked and shook his head, trying to clear his vision. He'd been drunk before, in college, but it certainly wasn't a sensation he was used to.

"Here ya are, love. Let me know if ya need anythin' else." The waitress set two plates in front of them and wandered off.

Neil picked up one half of his sandwich and bit into it. He chewed thoughtfully, trying hard to not like the mixture of smoked salmon and cream cheese, but found that he couldn't. It was a good combination. Not as cheap as the peanut butter sandwich he was used to, but a lot tastier. Trixie ate her whole sandwich quickly, then leaned back in her chair and proceeded to sip her beer and watch Neil. He took another bite, chewed slowly, and swallowed. Once he had eaten half of the sandwich, the room stopped spinning and his vision started to clear up again. When he had finished the sandwich and half of his beer, he felt content.

Neil leaned back in his chair and stared at Trixie, studying her face as she vacantly watched the soccer game on the television. He bit his lip thoughtfully as something surfaced in his mind. "Didn't you say something about a job on the plane?"

Trixie drained her mug and set it on the table. "Yeah, I did."

"Well? What was that about?"

"They aren't ready to see you yet. We have a couple hours to kill first."

"Oh. What are we going to do until then?"

"Don't know, maybe watch TV or... something. We can head upstairs whenever you're done. This will just get charged to the room."

Neil drank the remaining bit of beer in his mug and set it down gently in the middle of the table. He had just let go of the handle when the waitress appeared again. She set down two fresh pints of beer and removed the plates before leaving. Trixie picked up her beer and took a sip.

They sat there together for over an hour, sipping beer and talking. He told her about his life, how he had lost his parents while out of state and was then raised by his grandparents.

She had grown up in Kansas and moved to Oxford to attend school when she was twenty. She went there to study English literature, but didn't really love the topic. She just wanted an excuse to leave home. It was while there at the university that she had discovered her love of computers. She switched majors to study computer science. Shortly after graduating from college, she got a job at a small software company that turned out to be a front for the people she currently worked for. She had considered moving back home, but then the world changed. She figured she was safer where she was, hiding just beyond the fringes of the law with a group of seasoned criminals.

Neil nodded at this revelation and almost fell forward into the table. His vision was still cloudy from the alcohol, but the more he listened to her the more sense the path she had chosen made. He looked back up into her eyes, saw the twinkle again, something he couldn't quite place. That feeling of being with a kindred spirit surfaced again. He wasn't sure where his life was going, or even why he was where he was at. But he knew where he wanted to go. He knew, at least, who he wanted to be with.

Neil finally finished the beer he had been nursing for the entire course of the conversation. He stood slowly, testing his balance, making sure the room wasn't going to suddenly flip over on him. When everything seemed stable, he stood upright and grinned. "Okay, I'm ready."

"We're going to have to work that alcohol out of your system before tonight. We only have about an hour. I have some caffeine pills you can take, that should speed it through your system."

She went toward the stairs, pulling Neil behind her. He glanced back and saw the two older men at the nearby table watching Trixie lead him to the stairs, smiling widely and raising their mugs as if toasting his success. Neil smirked and allowed himself to be led up the stairs. At the top, Trixie opened the door and led him in. She closed the door behind him, locked it, and checked to make sure that it was secure.

"Caffeine pills?" Neil asked in a drunken daze.

"I always found that exercise can work alcohol through the system quickly too."

Neil stared her in the eyes, slightly dazed and completely clueless. He tried to picture himself attempting push-ups while drunk and quickly dismissed the idea. "What?" he asked. "Like in a gym?"

Trixie pulled the straps of her dress to the side, letting the light cotton fabric fall in a clump at her feet. Neil gazed up and down her body, focusing his stare first on her breasts and then on her red silk panties. She pulled those down to her ankles and stepped out of them. She reached up, pulled his head down a few inches and kissed him, warm wet tongue darting into his mouth. She pulled away and started to unzip his pants as he worked lazily on the buttons to his shirt. His pants dropped to his ankles, where they were joined a moment later by his boxer shorts. She pushed him back on the bed and climbed on top of him.

She did all the work as he lay there, staring up and watching her move up and down methodically, her head leaning back and her hands roaming over his chest. He enjoyed the sensation for what seemed like hours in his warped, drunken perception. He felt himself tighten, felt her body shudder, and heard a long, satisfied sigh pass through her lips.

He had never sobered up so quickly in his life.

CHAPTER
16

THE INTERNET - NEW TAMPA, FL USA NODE
JULY 20, 2030 2:15 PM EDT

She slid through the data stream, eying passing avatars with slight curiosity, quickly scanning each one before deciding that they were not worth further consideration. She passed through the Orlando node and connected to New Tampa. She had read the dossier on Neil Roberts thoroughly and committed it to memory. He was a top-of-the-line programmer, one of the most talented in the world. He had written several software applications that many people regarded as the best in the industry. Goliath, his employer, had made a nice profit from them. Neil, however, continued to work day in and day out for barely more than what his costs of living were. And a few days ago, he had disappeared from his apartment, didn't show up at his job, and just simply vanished. He was now nothing more than a shadow on the Net - a bus ticket to Miami, fingerprints on a faucet in a Cuban restroom, a facial scan in London. And now he had two of the brightest Interpol inspectors trying to track him down to question him about a possible connection to a murder in New Tampa.

She approached the building she was looking for - a digital representation of a five-story building with painted windows and a single door in the front. Above the door in large letters were the words "Goliath, Inc." She slipped quickly around to the side, moved closer to a nondescript wall and stopped. She reached out and touched the virtual bricks, watching curiously as the image of the bricks wavered slightly. There was an alarm program woven into the wall to warn the security agents against anyone attempting to circumvent the front entrance.

She waved her avatar's arms, dancing a jig to a picosecond tempo. A wall of fire arose from the ground behind her, enshrouding her in shimmering blue light. Letters and numbers floated around the blue fire, intertwining in random patterns, occasionally forming words or recognizable numeric sequences. She pushed her hands forward, opening the blue flames and joining them to the side of the building, completely sealing herself away from prying eyes. Anyone looking from the outside of the shell would see nothing more than a faint shimmer next to the side of the building. She reached into the building and grasped handfuls of digital bricks, stretched them aside and willed the building to construct a hole. As she moved the bricks, she routed the alarm signal through her firewall to prevent it from sounding. When the hole was big enough, she slipped inside.

The interior was bright, especially at the area around the entrance that she could see ahead of her. Security robots spoke to each other in binary streams while greeting and ushering in people who used the front entrance. The area around her was lined with file cabinets, each drawer labeled with a full index file attached to its front. To her right was an elevator that allowed avatars with proper clearance to log into Goliath's mainframe for work.

She generated a simple search program and let it loose in the room. It darted around like an excited hummingbird, pausing for a moment in front of each cabinet drawer. It sniffed the index file on each drawer for a fraction of a second before moving on to the next. It finally stopped before one and buzzed happily. She dispatched it and opened the drawer.

The row of files inside consisted of mostly public records and press releases. It was information about products that she already knew about, but hadn't yet linked to Neil specifically. The list she was compiling of his work was impressive. In a matter of only a few years, he had managed to be a part of every major security related project in Goliath's arsenal. She absorbed the additional information that she could find regarding Neil and closed the drawer.

She turned and floated back toward the hole she had carved in the wall. She wanted to get to the mainframe, figuring that it might help in furthering her research. Neil's current projects were classified; most likely sponsored by the American government. She suspected what programs they were, but needed proof. She had to know if he could do the job. But she didn't want to alert anyone to her presence. Not yet.

CHAPTER
17

N eil sat on the edge of the bed, staring at Trixie as she slept soundly, wide smile of contentment on her face. He grinned, thought back to the past few hours and pinched himself to be sure that he wasn't sleeping and dreaming about all that had happened. He stood, pulled on his shorts, and walked around to the other side of the bed. He gently pulled the curtains aside and stuck his head between them. It was night time, dark except for the city lights and the meager lighting provided by the moon through a thick cloud cover. He sighed as he watched the city, thinking how much it looked like every other one he'd seen at night. There was movement on the bed behind him, the sound of Trixie yawning and the bed creaking. Neil turned his head slightly, just enough to acknowledge her but not enough to take his eyes from the city.

He felt some measure of peace not knowing where his life was going, the initial uncertainty of his situation giving way to feelings of liberation. He wasn't staring at the clock, counting hours until he had to go back to work. He wasn't digging through his pockets trying to gauge where his next meal would come from. His computer was off, his email unchecked. He was just standing there, enjoying the quiet view of the city lights. The only thing he was supposed to do was to meet Trixie's friends at ten.

Neil glanced at the clock and sighed. "It's almost ten."

Trixie opened her eyes and looked at him. She raised her hand to her mouth to stifle a yawn. "Okay. Get your puter." She sat up, rubbed the sleep from her eyes, and watched as Neil pulled his computer out of his rumpled raincoat and started to set it up on the bureau. She got out of the bed and reached for her underwear. "Let me know when you're ready, Neil. I'll give you the address and login. You have an extra hookup for monitoring on that thing?"

"Yeah," he replied. "Sure do. I can tie it into this TV set for you."

"That'll work."

He connected all of the necessary wires for his gloves and headset, then plugged a single thin cable into the video port on the television set. "There, all set and ready to go."

Trixie sat on the edge of the bed next to Neil as he was pulling on his data gloves. "We have to hurry," she said. "Not much time."

"I need five minutes."

"To log in?"

Neil stretched his fingers inside the gloves and cracked his knuckles. "Goliath keeps tabs on its employees. They'll see me log in. I haven't had a chance to disable that. I don't really have time now, but I can tunnel the connection through their private network."

"Won't they see that too?"

"Not if I log in as my boss..."

Trixie laughed, consented, helped him put on his glasses and then flipped the ON switch.

*   *   *

Neil appeared in the air several feet above the ground and then slowly floated down to the pavement. A young British woman walked up to him and nodded politely. "Please log in," she said. He reached out and grasped her hands, moved his fingers in a precise pattern, then let go of her. "Thank you. Welcome to London, Robert Newman. How can I help you today?"

Neil turned his head to the side and asked Trixie for the address. He typed it out as she read it, and clicked the friendly green GO button. The woman nodded and vanished. He felt himself pulled forward, twisted sideways, and then he was falling downward. After several seconds, he stopped in a small room with green gridlines.

"Naked construct? Kind of a strange place for a meeting."

Trixie didn't respond. Neil turned his head toward where he knew she was but all he saw were the green gridlines imprinted on the insides of his glasses. He looked around and sighed when he noticed there was no obvious exit. That meant the only way out was pulling the data jack from the wall, and he sure didn't want to exit that way again.

"Welcome," a plain-sounding male voice said from somewhere above him. Something stirred in Neil's stomach. He wasn't sure if it was fear or just the salmon sandwich.

"Who are you? What is this place?"

An image appeared in front of him of a casually dressed middle-aged man. "I am the Moderator," he said. He bowed slightly and then gestured to the construct gridlines around them. "These are the Testing Grounds."

"The what?"

"Testing Grounds. All those who wish to work for Garossi need to take and pass the five tests that I will administer."

"Tests? What tests?"

"The five tests are speed, strength, ingenuity, endurance, and battle. I can answer any questions you may have. Let me know when you are ready to begin. You will be allowed a short break between tests, but you will not be allowed to log out. Logging out at any time constitutes forfeit. Do you wish to remain logged in to continue?"

Neil turned his head toward where he knew Trixie was. "What tests?" he repeated. The moderator frowned but proceeded to repeat his earlier explanation. Neil felt Trixie's soft hand on his shoulder. She had some explaining to do. But he had come this far and needed some direction in his life at this point, and this potential job was his best prospect. When the Moderator completed his repeat explanation, Neil sighed and responded, "All right, I guess so."

"First, I require your real name. A handle is not required by Garossi until you have passed the tests and accepted a position in his organization."

"Neil Roberts."

"Thank you, Mister Roberts. Now I require the name of your sponsor."

"Trixie. Uh, Karen Tyler."

"Thank you. Processing. Identity verified. I am ready to begin administering the tests. Are you prepared, Mister Roberts?"

"What happens if I fail?"

"If you live, you will be sent away and will not be allowed to try again. You will have failed."

Neil started nodding then stopped. "Wait... what? *If* I live?"

"We have had deaths during the tests."

"How many?"

"Seventeen."

"And how many people have taken the tests?"

"Five thousand, six hundred, and thirty-two."

Neil nodded, took a deep breath. *What the hell am I getting myself into?* he wondered. It was one thing to run away from his previous life, but taking some potentially lethal tests to join a criminal organization? *Screw it. I ran this far, might as well go all the way.* "Okay. I'm ready to begin."

"The first test is the test of speed. Good luck, Mister Roberts."

The Moderator vanished and the gridlines faded to black. All around him, Neil watched as a small room was constructed that resembled a hospital's waiting room. A table appeared in the center, smooth cherry wood with a highly polished finish. Two chairs appeared on opposite sides of the table. An avatar faded into existence in one chair, and motioned to the other chair while looking toward Neil. Neil moved forward and sat in the chair.

"The test of speed," came the Moderator's voice from above him. "Speed is nearly everything in the Net. If you are too slow, you cannot compete with other hackers and will just be a moving target for security systems and personnel. The man across from you will read a block of text. You must type out what he reads. Your reaction time and accuracy will be measured. Begin."

The man reached up into the air and pulled down a huge tome. Neil watched as a small window appeared in the surface of the table. It was a simple text processor - no spell checker, no grammar checker, no bells or whistles of any kind. He reached forward until his fingers were firmly set on the surface of the keyboard. The man across from him opened the book to the first page and started reading, slowly at first, but gradually picking up speed. Neil typed as fast as he could. Every time he started to pick up speed, the man reading would increase his speed to match and exceed him. By the time he was halfway through the book, Neil's fingers were dancing around on the surface of the table at a lightning pace. The man flipped page after page, reading faster and faster until he reached the end. He closed the tome and vanished with it.

Neil leaned back in his chair, fingers sore from the exertion. He could feel the muscles in his forearms pulsating, could feel someone rubbing the sweat off his chest with a rough towel. He felt the soft skin of Trixie's other hand caress his neck.

"Calculating results..."

Neil panted, felt the mouth of a plastic water bottle press against his lips. He took a sip. A blank panel appeared in the air in front of him as the rest of the room dissolved into green gridlines. He heard Trixie gasp.

Subject:	Neil Roberts
Test:	Test of Speed
Time:	146.8829 seconds
WPM:	148
Accuracy:	98%
AIPS:	17

"Most impressive, Mister Roberts."

"That's good?"

"Yes sir, it is."

"What's that last thing on the list? I've seen WPM, words per minute, right? But what's that last one?"

"AIPS is Approximate Instructions Per Second. A machine language term."

"Right. Okay."

"Are you ready for the test of strength, or do you wish a respite?"

Neil took a deep breath and held it. His fingers and forearms still throbbed, and he could still feel himself sweating. He closed his eyes and exhaled slowly. He opened his eyes and nodded. "All right. I'm ready."

"Very good, sir."

The panel disappeared and the gridlines faded to black again. An object appeared in front of Neil, a seven-foot tall metal block of shiny orange chrome. The block rotated on a central axis, allowing Neil to see the full four-foot thickness of it. It stopped and expanded to the sides, wrapping itself around Neil's avatar.

"The test of strength. Strength of will is important in computer hacking. Without strength, you cannot get into many systems. This wall that surrounds you is twice as strong as the typical protection on a government level mainframe computer and approximately four times stronger than what would be found in a typical bank vault. You must break through. Begin."

Neil turned around, examining the wall around him. It was perfectly formed, no creases, no faults, not even a crack anywhere to be seen. He pondered the wall for a moment, then reached out and placed his avatar's hand against the cool metal. He ran a quick analysis program to confirm his suspicions. The firewall was a clone of his Shield 2 program, from back in the days when his firewalls were composed of virtual metal instead of a living wall of fire, able to shift and adapt better to accommodate incoming attacks. It used a similar algorithm but was done by a small group in Korea that was a constant thorn in Goliath's side.

He reached into himself, pulled out a menu listing of programs and selected the one that was labeled "cracker". It was a program he had written two years ago while bored at work between projects. He had intended to use it to test the strength of Shield 3, but his employer had balked at the notion, most likely worried that any existing crack that worked would eventually find its way into the Net's underground. Neil had updated it recently and had hoped to use it to test Shield 4, but again his employer shot that request down. Neil had never had a chance to test it, but in theory it might just work. He figured that it was his best shot.

He opened the code block, made a few minor tweaks, and then slapped it against the wall. The wall buckled, emitting a loud grating noise. Neil reached into his program and pulled out a section of the code, made a few more tweaks, and reinserted it. The cracker was simple in design, but wasn't quite up to the task of breaking this particular firewall. Neil made a few more changes to the code, inserting a recursive loop that would allow his program to adapt to the wall's changes more effectively. He inserted the new routine and watched it struggle with the firewall. The wall protested loudly again. A single hairline crack extended upward and downward from where his program was. He dug his fingernails into the crack and stretched. He heard his program beep a few times, heard the wall snap. He ripped the wall in half and pushed himself through.

"Calculating results..."

Subject:	Neil Roberts
Test:	Test of Strength
Time:	4.2130 seconds

"You have passed the second test. Are you-"

"Next," Neil interrupted without hesitation.

"Proceeding."

The wall behind him shrunk and vanished. The gridlines that were still just starting to appear immediately faded and were replaced with a typical cyber street - buildings stretched up to the horizon, avatars flying above the structures and floating in various directions about the street. Streams of data drifted about, darting in and out of the buildings.

"The test of ingenuity. At times, the authorities trace and attempt to bring our hackers to justice. You have been detected and must escape. Please remember that this is a simulation. Begin."

A much rougher sounding computerized voice began speaking from behind Neil. "General security bot two-four-one-eight-three-zero detected unauthorized presence in London sector eight-eight-two. Suspect trace begun."

Neil turned around to see a security robot floating in the air near him. It looked like a typical security robot that he had seen many times when visiting Goliath clients at government nodes. The machine was a perfect sphere of silvery metal, with a single red LED set in the center as its eye and two multi-purpose arms it used to inspect and communicate with people in the Net. It reached out a metallic limb toward him. He fell backward, rolled, and stood. He took a few steps away from the robot, and saw additional robots floating into position behind the first.

"Error. Suspect is not complying. Capture and detain."

Neil turned and ran down the street, the sound of machinery floating through the air behind him. He ducked into a narrow alley between buildings and continued running. He leaped into the air, barely clearing a dumpster at the end of the alley. He rotated his virtual body, planted his feet against the wall and ran vertically up it. He ran up onto the roof of the building and moved as quickly as he could across it. The sound of the security robots was ringing in his ears. He reached the edge of the building's roof and jumped, spiraling downward toward the asphalt. He smacked into the pavement with a resounding crunch, rolled, and then ran straight across the busy street. He ducked into an alleyway, reached into himself, and pulled out a program that he knew well. He glanced out of the alley and saw the robots floating around the street, searching the area around the small crater he left in the sidewalk. He looked down at the program in his hands and ran it. A menu appeared in front of him and he clicked the choice labeled "random" at the bottom. His image shimmered, distorting into the shape of a shorter female avatar. He stepped back out into the street, walking at a more normal pace. He stepped into the first building entrance he came to.

"Welcome to the London public library."

Neil waved the guide away and headed for the card index. He heard the robots float into the building. He slid into a small alcove behind one of the index stacks and reached his hands into the wall of the building. The wall tore open and he slipped back out into the alley. He turned and repaired the wall, then changed his image again, this time getting an image resembling a young boy. He calmly walked back onto the street, nodded his head as the security robots floated out of the library and passed right in front of him. The city collapsed to the ground, the streets replaced with green gridlines.

"Calculating results..."

Subject:	Neil Roberts
Test:	Test of Ingenuity
Time:	12.0478 seconds

"You have passed the third test, Mister Roberts."

"Give me a moment."

"Yes sir. Let me know when you are ready to proceed."

Neil took a deep breath and held it for a few seconds. He closed his eyes and concentrated. He could feel Trixie's hands moving a rough cloth towel over his chest again, could sense the sweat being mopped up. He could feel a slight chill, probably from the air conditioning against his wet skin. He opened his eyes and studied the green gridlines for several seconds while he concentrated on returning his breathing to a more normal pace.

"All right. I'm ready."

"Proceeding."

The gridlines didn't vanish this time. Neil could see some objects appearing on the construct's horizon, but couldn't make out what they were from where he was.

"The test of endurance. Sometimes security systems do not attempt to detain our hackers. Sometimes those security systems fight back with electric impulses meant to shock the eyes, numb the hands, and even in some instances to kill the hacker. Your goal in this test is to survive for thirty seconds. Begin."

The objects edged closer, picking up speed. Neil turned and saw objects on all sides of him closing in. *If you live...* he thought. He crouched down, pulled out the latest revision of his Shield 4 firewall program, and raised it around him. The program appeared first as a wireframe, which then morphed into a wall of orange flames that completely enclosed him. He watched the flames dance around and waited for the inevitable impact of an incoming attack. He had tested this code just a few days ago but only against his own attack scripts. He knew better than to underestimate someone else's approach.

He heard something whistle off to his left, and heard something on his right impact into the firewall. It wavered but held. Neil reached into it and started to modify it. A few more things hit the wall and exploded. He typed faster, clenching his teeth and sitting up straighter. He felt a shock wave from another object hitting the wall, then felt something that punched a hole behind him hit his flesh. He arched his back and yelped as he felt the thing expand, ripping part of his icon's back apart. The pain was exquisite, the sensation of burning skin spreading to his arms. He ran an anti-virus program on himself. It detected the program that had hit him immediately and started to remove it. The pain started to lessen and the burning sensation in his arms subsided.

The firewall shook from another impact. Neil wiggled his fingers and then threw his arms outward. He felt his right arm hit something, heard a woman's voice respond with a few colorful adjectives. Trixie. He'd have a few more colorful adjectives for her when this was over. He reached forward, plunged both hands into the firewall, and started to move his fingers. The rhythm of impacts seemed to slow as he pressed his fingers downward with deliberate precision, typing out new routines for his firewall program to deal with multiple simultaneous attacks. The hole in the back of the firewall vanished. The flames built thicker and changed from orange to blue as the code began to modify itself to repel the incoming objects. He could still hear the objects impacting, but they sounded far away now. A few seconds later it was over. He heard a far away voice say "Calculating results..." He saved the changes he'd made to the firewall program and closed it.

Subject:	Neil Roberts
Test:	Test of Endurance
Attacks:	20000
Hits:	1

"Very good, sir. Do you wish a break before the final test?"

"No," Neil spat out through clenched teeth toward where he guessed the voice was coming from.

"Proceeding."

A man appeared in front of Neil. He was average height, clad head to toe in medieval plate mail. He held an oversized steel sword in one hand and a finely decorated shield in the other.

"The test of battle. Sometimes our hackers are forced to do battle with-"

Neil walked forward, dodged a swing of the sword, and thrust his hands into the man's chest, right through the armor. He rooted around in there, moved a few bits of code to the side, and inserted a small loop program. As he was typing, the knight just stood there, staring dumbly at his chest where Neil's hands were moving around. The knight twitched as the new code started to take effect, and dropped his sword and shield. Neil withdrew his hands and watched as the man staggered back, clutching his chest with both hands. He screamed in a voice that was much too high in pitch to be human.

"Buffer overflow," the man said as he fell to his knees. He looked down at his chest and moaned. "Error in main module. Illegal operation. Stack overflow. Unexpected application error. General... protection... fault." He fell onto the ground with a metallic clanking sound, and then slowly faded away, melting into the floor.

"Calculating results..."

Neil turned to look at the score panel.

Subject:	Neil Roberts
Test:	Test of Battle
Time:	0.0418 seconds

"All tests have been passed. Your scores have been saved. You may log out, Mister Roberts."

Neil felt himself pulled away from the ground, up to the general public node area. The navigation guide appeared and presented the menu to him. He selected the logout option, closed his eyes and removed the glasses. He felt Trixie undo the Velcro clasps on his gloves and pull them off.

"That was *incredible!*" she said.

"That was a pain in the ass. And the back."

Trixie nodded. "I didn't say it would be easy."

"Easy?" Neil said. "You didn't say it would be anything. You didn't even say it would be a test. Just a meeting. I wasn't expecting anything like that."

"I... I'm sorry."

Neil grabbed the towel from her hands and pressed it to his face. "No matter," he replied through the thick cotton. "I passed."

"I know. I haven't seen scores that good in... well... ever."

Neil snorted as Trixie removed the second glove. He fell backward onto the bed and concentrated on breathing evenly. He felt Trixie climb onto the bed and lay down next to him. He was still upset with her for not telling him about the test, for just sending him in blind like that. But he was far too exhausted to protest. His back ached, his arms were sore, and his fingers felt like they had been set on fire. All he wanted to do was sleep, to let himself drift off and relax for a while. He felt Trixie's hair brushing across his stomach as she kissed his abdomen. She shimmied up until her head was resting on his chest, her bare breasts pressed into his side, one hand idly rubbing his stomach. He closed his eyes and fell asleep immediately.

CHAPTER
18

HAVANA, CUBA
JULY 21, 2030 9:25 AM EDT

Ferez and Johnson stepped off of the jetway into the terminal and approached a security guard who was holding a sign with their names written in black marker on it. They flashed their badges and introduced themselves. The guard lowered the sign and motioned for them to follow him. He led them to a plain, unmarked door across from a pair of bathrooms and unlocked it for them. They stepped into a large room filled with various electronic devices, monitors, and people flipping through camera images while speaking in low tones into their headsets.

A large man in a cheap suit walked up to them when he saw them enter. He bore a wide smile, but otherwise his demeanor was all business. "Welcome gentlemen," he said, extending his hand. "I am director of security here, Carlos Vermúndez."

Ferez took his hand. "I'm Inspector Ferez. This is Inspector Johnson. I'm sure you've been briefed."

"Yes sir, we all have. We were saddened to learn of the death of Miss Anderton. I know some people in this world would be glad to see someone who has so much suffer for once, but not I. My wife runs a charity that helps orphaned children on this island, you see, and Miss Anderton made many generous donations to the cause. Anything you need from us you will have."

"Thank you. I think we'd like to start with security recordings from yesterday. We believe the suspect boarded a plane to London with an unknown accomplice."

"Of course, come this way." He led Ferez and Johnson through a doorway into another section of the room. He walked up to an operative and tapped him on the shoulder. "Ricardo, these are the two inspectors working on the Anderton case. Please help them with anything they need."

"Yes sir." Ricardo turned and bowed his head toward them. He blinked several times, trying to focus on something a little further than he was accustomed to. He rubbed his eyes and then gestured to some folding chairs leaning against the opposite wall. "Please pull up some of those chairs and have a seat. What did you want to start with?"

"Security tapes from a flight to London yesterday."

"All right. Do you know the flight number and time?"

"Got the flight number right here," Johnson said while handing Ricardo a slip of paper.

"Good. This shouldn't take long." Ricardo turned to his computer, an older model that still had an actual keyboard attached. He typed in the number and drummed his fingers on the table while the search processed. His computer beeped and displayed a new window with one item on the list. He tapped the screen and another window showed up with flight details listed. "What's the name?"

"Roberts," Johnson said.

"No," Ferez interjected. "Traveling under the name Ben Rogers. How does that thing know who it is?"

"When the ticket gets scanned at the counter, a record goes into the log files and the security camera snaps a five second video file. That file is then run through the face scanner routines to verify identity." Ricardo tapped the page down key on the screen a few times then stopped and tapped an item on the list. "Rogers, mister and misses." He hit the play button and a video opened, showing Trixie and Neil at the ticket counter.

"That's Roberts all right," Ferez announced as he compared his photograph to the image on the screen. "But who's the girl?"

"Odd. There's no data on either of them listed with the video. The face scanner is supposed to append their names and ID numbers. I can run her through the databases manually if you want."

"Do it."

Ricardo played the video again, waited until it showed Trixie's face clearly, and hit pause. He pressed both index fingers on the screen in the center of her face, then dragged them apart to draw a box around her head. He removed his fingers and typed a few commands on his keyboard. "This sometimes takes a while." He turned around in his chair to face the inspectors.

"Guess not always, huh?" Johnson said.

Ricardo turned back to the monitor. "Damn, that was a quick search. Oh. I get it."

"What?"

"She's well known, apparently. Karen Tyler. Goes by the alias 'Trixie'. Reportedly works for a large crime syndicate in England run by Garossi. Big crime lord, owns most of Europe and always knocking on Anderton's turf, if you know what I mean."

"We know," Ferez said. "Garossi is one of the standard briefings for Interpol agents. Guess that ties them to the murders as well."

Ricardo scrolled through a few pages of text. "Seems a big jump from cyber-terrorism to murder. Says here that she's a computer hacker, a good one. I see links to dozens of heists but she was never caught or charged in any of the cases. Grand total of thefts estimated at sixty-three million U.S. dollars. Most of that was taken from subsidiaries of Anderton Enterprises."

"Shouldn't her face scan have triggered something?"

"Yeah, it should have." Ricardo turned to another computer and typed some commands. He frowned at the results and tried another command. "Shit. Face scanner was deactivated... er... about a week ago."

"What? How's that possible?"

"It isn't. Well, it shouldn't be." He picked up a phone and hit the "0" key. "Carlos. It's Ricardo. Get in here, now."

A few moments later, the door opened and Carlos stepped in. "What's going on?"

"Face scanner down."

"Huh?"

Ricardo turned around. "Someone deactivated the face scanner."

"That's not possible."

"Yeah, that's what *I* said. But it happened."

"Shit." Carlos went back into the other room and started barking orders.

"Sorry guys. Guess that's all we got. The face scanner would have set off some alarms on her if it had been working."

Ferez stood up. "Yeah, I know. Thanks for the help."

"What's next then?" Johnson asked while standing.

"Track them down online, probably end up going to London but I'd like to know where exactly to find them once we get there."

They thanked Ricardo again and left the security office. Carlos was still barking orders as they walked through the room. They got to the other side and slipped out through the door. Ferez pointed toward a small restaurant off to their right and they headed over to it. The airport was crowded, but the restaurant still had several tables open. When they got closer, Ferez waved to one of the waiters. The waiter nodded, placed a glass on someone's table, then walked over to them.

"Can we get a seat near a wall jack?"

"Sí, right this way."

"I'm not looking forward to connecting again," Johnson said. "Not after last time."

"I know Johnson, but I don't know shit about those computers. At least I'll be here this time to help if you need to get out quick again."

"Yeah, lucky me."

CHAPTER
19

The train slid silently down the tracks at over two hundred kilometers per hour, generating a rough breeze that stirred the trees on either side. Neil stared out the window of their small cabin at the sky, listening only occasionally to what Trixie was saying. He focused on one cloud in particular and watched as it slowly drifted to the left and out of his line of sight.

He found as he thought about the previous night that he was annoyed at the indifferent attitude Trixie had about it. She had completely neglected to inform him of essential details. She sat there across from him, babbling on incessantly about something or other. He wasn't paying attention at all, just staring out the window and occasionally glancing at her and nodding. That only seemed to prompt her to continue talking, and she'd smile at him and look around the cabin as she continued rambling on about whatever it was she was talking about. The more he looked at her, the less angry he got.

He cursed at himself, tried to force himself to be mad at her. But he couldn't. He kept looking back at her, watching as her lips moved. He heard the words she was saying but was unable to get himself to focus on them. His eyes scanned her body from her hair down to her feet. He watched her feet for a bit, then gradually moved his eyes up her legs. She was wearing the same sundress she had worn briefly the previous day. Her legs were crossed, one planted firmly on the floor of the train's cabin and the other idly kicking back and forth. Every time her kicking leg came back toward the seat, her dress would lift up briefly and he could see a flash of her underwear. He thought back to the previous day, remembered with crystal clarity all of the events, especially the most important one. The more he tried to be angry with her, the more he realized that he couldn't stop thinking about her.

"Ladies and gentlemen, may I have your attention please?" echoed a voice from the speaker above them. Trixie stopped talking and looked up at the speaker. "We will be arriving in Windsor in five minutes. Please mind your backs as you exit the train."

"Songman should be at the station to pick us up."

"Who's that?" Neil asked, shifting in his seat as he felt the train begin to decelerate.

"One of my... friends from way back. Co-worker, really. He's cool. A little weird."

"Weird? How?"

"Well, he only speaks in song titles."

"What? Song titles? What kind of songs?"

"Mostly songs up to about a decade ago. Just about anything from before the whole music industry went with Synthespians instead of actual people."

"Ah, oldies."

"Yeah, lot of good stuff from him. He can be a real riot, especially if you know the songs he mentions. They almost never really apply to what he's trying to say."

"Interesting. Why exactly does he talk like that? Nervous tick or something?"

"Something like that. You ever hear of a Turina Jack?"

"A little."

"Augmentation. Wired implants in the head that let you connect to the Net without a computer. The computer gets built in your head, see? Hard drive and everything. Doesn't need standard memory or a processor because your brain provides that, as well as the electric current to run it all. If it's installed correctly, that is."

"His wasn't?"

"He was an early experiment. They tried to salvage him by loading a full database of songs so he could at least be fun at parties. It was his request in case something went wrong. Bad choice of a joke on his part. But they only had room for the titles." She looked a bit sad. Neil couldn't help but feel there was more to this story. "Real nice guy though. Fastest number cruncher on our team too."

The train jerked to a full stop. The sound of passengers retrieving luggage and moving off of the train echoed down the hallway outside their cabin. Neil stood and opened the door. They walked out, passed a few people who were speaking in various languages, and got off the train. He felt Trixie grab his forearm. She lead him toward an information booth set into the far wall. Leaning against the wall next to the booth was a man in his midthirties, face neatly shaved but dark hair a disheveled mess. He scanned the crowd through mirrored sunglasses, no emotion present on his face even when he fixed his gaze on Neil and Trixie. They walked right up to him. Trixie gave him a quick hug.

"Nice to see you again, Songman."

Songman frowned, looked around, and shrugged. He turned to look at Neil. "Introduce yourself."

"Er... I..."

"He's Neil, Songman. He's the guy that did the test last night."

Songman relaxed. "Nice to know you."

"Likewise."

"These boots were made for walkin'."

"Right, let's get out of here," Trixie said. "I haven't been back in a while. Was stuck in Cuba for way too long."

Songman led them outside of the train station to a brand new Toyota parked in the middle of a deserted section of the parking lot. He pulled a key chain from his pocket and hit something on the remote. The car honked and the headlights flashed. He walked up and opened one of the rear doors for Trixie. Neil climbed in after her. Songman got in, started the car, and pulled out of the parking lot. They moved along in silence for several minutes. Neil stared out the window at the urban scenes in downtown Windsor, the ivy covered stones of the medieval castle off in the distance, the tourists wandering around aiming cameras at pretty much anything, and the little shops nestled in the basements of apartment buildings. He cringed at Songman's driving and kept having to remind himself that they were not, in fact, on the wrong side of the road. Trixie looked back and forth between Neil and the view out her window. Songman concentrated on driving until the silence was too much for even him to take.

"Who can I turn to when nobody needs me?" he said with a pleading tone.

Trixie looked up and caught his eyes in the rearview mirror. She forced a smile. "Yeah, sorry I'm not too chatty today. Tired I guess."

Neil nodded but didn't add anything to the conversation. He was still trying to sort things out in his mind. He'd never been so confused before. The problem as he saw it was that he was confused at his own reactions. He couldn't get Trixie out of his mind, couldn't stop thinking about every inch of her body and of how much they really did have in common. And yet, he was trying to be angry with her, trying to force her away over what essentially amounted to a trivial thing. Yes she should have told him, but it should be considered a lesson learned and they should move on. He sighed at that thought, tried to force himself to realize how silly it all was and how he just couldn't allow himself to lose her. It had taken far too long to find her in the first place. He turned to her, saw her staring out of her window. He reached over and placed his hand on her thigh. She tensed and whipped her head around to face him, then visibly relaxed and smiled. He smiled back, already feeling better about the whole situation. Then the car slowed. They turned into a building that looked like a warehouse. A thin corrugated aluminum door slid shut behind them, metallic clang echoing throughout the interior of the building.

"Get the fuck out," Songman blurted after the car came to a stop.

Trixie patted Neil on the knee. "He's not being an ass. It's an old Skid Row song. We think he likes that title a little too much."

"Oh." Neil opened the door and stepped out to the sound of someone cocking a shotgun. He slowly raised his hands and peered into the darkness. The car's internal lights had been disabled, leaving them in complete blackness. Neil couldn't even see the car that he leaned against.

"Hey Trix," came a voice from the darkness. "Welcome back. Looks like Cuba agreed with you. Look a bit tired, but I guess that's normal right? Who's the suit?"

"This is the guy that did the test last night," Trixie's voice, somewhere to Neil's right, clear and confident.

"No shit?" the voice asked. Footsteps on concrete, edging closer to Neil, then the voice returned. "Heya, I'm Lowlight."

Neil peered into the darkness, trying to pick out a shape, movement, anything. He couldn't see a thing in the darkness. "Neil," he said toward where he thought the voice was coming from.

"No handle?"

"Er..."

"Not yet," Trixie offered, stepping around the car while keeping one hand on it. She moved cautiously toward Neil, inching her way around the rear of the car. She paused when she heard Neil's breathing. "We'll pick one before his first run."

"First run won't be for a few days. Doc is talking about putting a Turina Jack in him *today*."

"Hit the lights!" Songman shouted from somewhere off to their left. A moment later, fluorescent track lights in the ceiling clicked on with a low rumbling hum. Neil blinked a few times then looked at Lowlight. He was short, maybe five feet tall at the most, wearing tight black jeans and one of those bright red T-shirts with an embedded LCD screen that had rotating corporate logos on it. It was currently showing an advertisement for Sony's new computer. His eyes looked glazed over, the irises pure white. He had a shotgun resting on his shoulder and was looking at Trixie.

"Today?" Trixie asked, shielding her eyes from the bright lights. "Shit, he just got here."

"Yeah, I know. But Doc nearly pissed himself when he saw the scores from last night. This guy scored almost as high as Songman, and Songman's got the jack already installed. What kinda hardware you packing Neil?"

Neil reached into his coat and produced his computer. Lowlight stared at it open-mouthed for a solid twenty seconds before he burst out laughing. "That's it," Neil informed him with an apologetic shrug.

"That? That's it? How the hell did you post scores at all on that thing?"

Neil shrugged. "I'm a programmer."

"No shit? That's rare these days. Well, rare to go from programming into crime, at least. Well, come on. I'll introduce you to the rest of the team."

"Wait," Trixie said. "He should probably have a handle first."

"Yeah Trix, I think you're right. It's usually easy around here to tell who's tech and who isn't. The non-tech peeps use their real names and all us hackers and technophiles use handles." Lowlight looked Neil up and down. "It's better to go by your handle in real life too, to make sure you don't fuck up in the Net and tell someone your real name. Well, time to pick."

"I really don't know."

"Well, tell us about you, I guess. We'll try to pick something that fits."

Trixie took Neil's hand and whispered, "How about why you left your old life behind? Tell them that."

Neil thought about it, then concentrated on the feeling of Trixie's hand in his for a few more seconds before responding. "I didn't fit in. I woke up, went to work, went home, went to bed. Did that day in, day out for years. I paid my taxes, I worked my ass off, and I was still poor. I didn't know anybody outside of the office. I was never going to be worth anything. Never going to get out of debt. I was... a slave to society." He paused, watched the effect his words were having on the people around him. His eyes started to tear up as he spat the words out, like one big bottled confession that had been waiting for years to find someone willing to listen. "The more people I met, the more I realized that I was really the only one thinking that way. I hated it. I hated me. I *had* to get out. It's amazing how you can live around millions of other people and still feel... alone. An outcast, a reject, an afterthought to everyone."

They stood in silence, letting Neil's words sink in. Neil glanced around nervously, silently wondering if they were expecting him to say something more. Trixie squeezed Neil's hand, too busy reflecting on the description of his past to bother with thinking up a suitable handle for him. Lowlight nodded pensively, scrunched up his face like he was trying to multiply a pair of seven-digit numbers in his head.

Songman, who had rejoined them while Neil was talking, frowned, shuffled his feet, then placed a hand on Neil's shoulder. "Pariah," he said.

"Pariah?" Lowlight repeated as he bit his lower lip. "Nice one, Songman."

"Thanks a lot," Songman replied, smiling.

They stood around for a few more moments, all repeating the word to each other and nodding until Neil finally agreed. "All right," he said. "It fits. I like it."

"Okay, Pariah. Let's introduce you to the rest of the team then."

They headed through a rusted metal door set into the side of the building. The room on the other side was furnished and well armed. Every wall had a gun rack, stacked floor to ceiling with various shotguns, submachine guns, and sniper rifles. One of the desks along the wall was stacked close to the ceiling with boxes of grenades and ammunition. Lowlight put his shotgun down on one of the desks and led them through another door, down a short hallway, and into a kitchen. The kitchen had one of those side-by-side refrigerator and freezer combos. Dingy linoleum tiles on the floor produced faint squishing sounds as they walked around the room. A single wooden table in the center had eight chairs around it. Three people sat around the table, eating a late breakfast.

Lowlight pointed at one of them, a very plain girl in her early twenties with an eyebrow piercing and bright pink hair. She didn't look up from her lunch as Lowlight introduced her. "This is Kay. She's the best cook here, so we let her feed us all. She's also a damn good shot with a sniper rifle. Saw her shoot some guy's toupee off at eight hundred meters. Freaking hilarious."

Lowlight then pointed at the young man seated next to her. He was in his mid to late teens, had short black hair, and wore a tattered blue T-shirt with an old programmer's joke on it. Neil couldn't help but think that the kid looked like a total poser - the kind of person who talked big about hacking into mainframes and government systems, but never actually knew how or did anything close. He looked up and nodded at Neil. "Next to her is Maxxius. He's got hacker blood in him, kinda. We're still training him but he's already proven to be almost as crazy as Dogma. I guess that's a plus in some people's books.

"And this here is Sara." Lowlight placed both hands on Sara's shoulders and squeezed them. She placed a hand on top of his, coating the back of his hand with engine grease. She smirked, a pretty smile emerging from the oil caked on her face. Her hair was cut short and spiked, her clothing stained beyond the point of no return with various automobile fluids. "She's a total sweetheart. Hell of a mechanic. Brought them vans and cars out there back from death more times than I can count. Guys, this is Pariah. He's the dude from last night."

They looked up, nodded lamely in his direction, and returned their attention to their plates. Songman pulled out a chair and sat down next to Kay. Lowlight led Neil and Trixie through the room into another short hallway on the other side. A pane of glass set into one wall showed them a view into another room, where two life-sized holograms of large-breasted Asian women were locked in a mortal duel. The one on the left was a brunette with short hair, dressed in tight leather and wielding two serrated knives. The one on the right had long red hair, dressed in a tiny bikini and wielding a sword that resembled a small Chevy. Two young men were sitting on a leather couch playing the video game, screaming vulgarities at each other and bouncing up and down in rage. The brunette sliced at the redhead, sending a shower of virtual blood onto the wall.

Lowlight pointed toward the two men on the couch with his thumb. "The one on the left is Slave. Powerslave, actually, but we all just call him Slave for short. He's always got to have the latest toys, like that game system. He'll eat peanut butter sandwiches and drink tap water from here to Judgment Day as long as he's got enough high tech toys to play with. And believe me, that's usually what his diet consists of. He saves all his spare cash for that damn game system.

"Guy on the right is Dogma. He got his name through irony. He doesn't believe in a damn thing, not even remotely. No religion, no newscasts, no third party information, nothing at all that he can't see and prove for himself. He'd be a huge conspiracy theory fan except that he never believed in those either. Funny guy though. And crazy, totally nuts. He'll do anything once, including running full bore into a high security government building just to win a bet with Slave. If you gotta go into the Net on a run, he's the best to have beside you. *Way* beside you. Makes a good distraction, at least.

"Down the end of the hall is Doc's area. You'll meet him later. He's the one that does all the hardware, sets up our mainframe, installs the T-Jacks in our heads, and other stuff like that. He's good at what he does, but don't ask him to help out with anything else.

"Then there's Evan. He's our contact. Leader, I guess you could say. He gives us shit to do. Don't go looking for him. If he wants to talk, he'll find you. Otherwise, it's best to leave him by himself. There's a couple others around here too, Anna and Masha, but they went out shopping earlier today. I can only guess it's for you, since you don't seem to have any luggage. Which reminds me, I gotta get back to my post so I can let them in when they return. See ya round, Pariah."

Lowlight walked back into the kitchen as the door to the game room opened. Slave stepped out, said hi to Trixie, and focused on Neil. He held his hand out. "Slave." He was younger than most of the others, maybe in his early twenties. His hair was cut short and dyed a bright shade of purple. He was a wiry man with deep brown eyes that spoke of a wisdom far beyond his years. The blue jeans he wore were too tight and his shirt was on backward.

"Pariah."

"New here?"

Trixie put a hand on Neil's forearm. "He's the guy that did the test last night."

Slave's eyes opened wide. "Holy shit. Holy shit! Dogma, get your ass out here! Hot damn man, that was some crazy shit you did last night."

"Um, thanks. Didn't think I was going to have an audience."

Slave shook his head. "Can't put on a show like that and expect nobody to watch. That shit you did to the knight at the end, I thought I was gonna pass out from shock man. Never seen anyone do somethin' like that. And fast! Holy shit! Even the fucking slomo replay was sooo fuckin' fast!"

Dogma stepped out of the room and nodded his head toward Neil. Dogma was about the same age as Powerslave, but lacked the same depth in the eyes. In its place he had an obvious vacancy, like he was missing something. He had an air of arrogance around him. His T-shirt was on the correct way but the logo on the front had faded to the point of being barely readable. His jean shorts hung low on his hips, and his untied shoelaces dragged on the floor behind him. "Sup?" he asked while nodding his head toward Neil again.

Slave punched Dogma in the arm. "Hey man, this is the dude from last night."

"Yeah? Hey man, I wanted to find out something. What was that program you ran in the fourth test? The endurance one. That blue flame was hella cool."

"I modified Shield 4."

"Hot damn, I saw that program when Trix ran it last week, but didn't think it was released that widely yet."

"Well, it isn't. I wrote it."

Dogma stared at Neil for a moment. "Yeah? Can I get a copy then?"

"Sure, I guess. I have it here on my computer."

"Let me see it."

Neil handed his computer over to Dogma, who turned it over and over in his hands. He and Slave laughed. "Shit, you posted those scores on *this* thing? Damn. My fucking watch has more power than this." Shaking his head, Dogma pulled a thin black cable from his pants pocket and plugged one end into Neil's computer. Then he picked the other end off the floor and reached behind his head. Neil heard something click, and Dogma's eyes shut tight. He rolled his head around lazily for a few moments, then frowned. "Woah, good security. You're fucking paranoid, man. Awesome..." He flinched and took a step back. "Ow! Shit, little help?"

"Security's what I do," Neil said while reaching for his computer. He shifted a piece of plastic on the bottom of the computer to the side and ran his thumb over the sensor. The computer beeped and Dogma nodded.

"Cool shit, man. Thanks. Damn you got a lot of programs on here."

"Most of it's stuff I wrote for work and then modified on my own after hours."

"This is all Goliath shit."

"Yeah, that's where I worked."

"Damn. This is great." Dogma reached behind his head and pulled the cable out. "Got the firewall and an interesting looking cracker you had there too. Thanks a lot." He passed the cable to Slave, who took it and reached behind his head.

"No problem."

The door at the end of the hallway opened and an elderly man with white tousled hair and a bleached lab coat stepped out into the hallway. He took off his glasses, wiped them on a small blue cloth, and returned them to his face. He wobbled up the hallway and stopped before the group. He looked right at Neil and squinted his eyes.

"You the boy from last night?"

"Yes sir."

"What's your name?"

"Pariah."

"I see. I trust his scores were legitimate?"

"Yes," Trixie answered. "I watched the whole thing."

"Hmm... Impressive. I'm Doctor Nevil Averly, but everyone just calls me Doc. I'd like to give you a little gift. Follow me."

Neil retrieved his computer from Powerslave and followed Doc into his office. He heard the door close behind him as he returned the computer to his inner pocket. The office was very plain. White walls, white tiled floor, white paper on a dark gray examination table. The room was well lit, and smelled of anesthetic and peppermint. A canister of some sort of gas stood beside the table, clear plastic mask tied to the valve with a wide elastic band. One wall was lined with cabinets, a waist high countertop with a stainless steel sink, and jars of various medical instruments.

Doc walked around to the other side of the examination table and patted the paper. "Have a seat."

Neil approached the table tentatively. "I have some questions."

"Sure, go ahead."

"First, this is about the Turina Jack, right?"

"Yes."

"Why are they called that?"

Doc sighed. "Well, years ago when they were being invented, they wanted to call them Turing Jacks, after that famous English mathematician. He was the one they say started computer science, I'm sure you know. But anyway, some independent council in Switzerland had a fit over it, threw a big stink and threatened all kinds of lawsuits. So the inventor changed the name, or rather, he changed one letter. Just to stick it to em." He chuckled.

"What exactly is it?"

"You worried?"

"Well, yes."

"Basically, I install a miniature computer in your head. Wet wired hard drive, burst ram, some interface cables, and an external jack in the base of your skull."

"How big of a hard drive?"

"Oh, the one I have here for you is a little over ten terabytes." He held up a hard drive that was barely an inch across, about a half-inch thick and coated in a light gray plastic shell.

Neil swallowed hard. That was more than twice the storage space his computer had. "And there's room for all this in my head?"

"Not really. I have to take some things out. Nothing important, I assure you. Are you ready? I'd like to begin. I'm really interested to see what kind of scores you can post when it's all installed. You already posted scores close to Songman, and he's the fastest we have here. And that's *with* his augment. His AIPS is around twenty-three, if I recall, and yours was seventeen. Very close, indeed, considering that you use an external computer to connect."

"Just one more question."

Doc helped Neil onto the table and started unraveling the elastic for the facemask. "What is it?"

"What exactly happened to Songman?"

Doc opened a drawer and pulled out an electric razor. He turned to Neil and tested the razor's battery for a moment to ensure there was a good charge. He sighed and raised his eyes to Neil. "Early experiment. We made some mistakes. But he's all right. Really funny guy, lots of fun at parties. And he's a lot more popular with the ladies now, so I'm told. Anyway, we've done several successful installs since then."

"Since when? How many?"

"Oh, let's see." Doc fixed the gas mask over Neil's nose and mouth and turned the valve. "Well, Songman was done about ten months ago. I've done... oh... three successful installs since then. Yes, that sounds about right."

CHAPTER
20

J ohnson floated down the virtual road to the Interpol office. He got to the entrance, waved his digital badge when he noticed that it hadn't been automatically detected, and went inside. He noticed immediately that something wasn't right. Markus stood in the center of the room, staring straight ahead. He gave no greeting, no acknowledgment at all of Johnson's presence. The code streams that built the walls of the small office pulsated a sickly green color, glitches tearing small holes in the fabric and leaving visual blotches floating around at random.

"Markus?"

Markus looked around nervously. "Greetings Inspector Null." He twitched and stuttered. "Welcome to the Interpol office at Miamcubampanew Tray ding ding."

"What in the hell is wrong with you?"

"Unrecognized question. Please repeat your inquiry. Ding beep. Thank you sir, I will get that file for you." He reached into the air and pulled out a small yellow folder with *Hell's Canyon* written on the label in small black font. He handed it to Johnson and smiled. "There you go, madam."

Johnson looked down at the folder, shook his head, and looked back to Markus. He was twitching uncontrollably, muttering about random cases. "Ferez. Ferez, something's wrong."

"Absolutely, Inspector Null." Markus reached up in the air and plucked out another file, this one labeled *Ferez, Juan.* He handed it to Johnson.

"Johnson? What's wrong?" Ferez's voice was faint, off in the distance somewhere in front of him.

"Interpol office has been hacked. Markus is freaking out like he's got Tourette's or something."

"What? How is that possible?"

Markus handed Johnson a folder labeled *Tourette, Jonathan.* "Here's the file on the hacker you requested, Inspector Null. I am always pleased to serve you."

Johnson frowned and dropped the folders he was holding to the floor. Markus swooped them up and clutched them tightly to his chest. "Ferez, this is not right. Call the main office and tell them to fix this." No response. "Ferez? You hear me?"

"No, he does not," came a female voice from somewhere behind him. Johnson felt a twinge of fear, a cold tingling sensation that crawled up his spine. He turned to the voice.

"Oh, welcome back Inspector Null." Markus reinserted the folders into the data stream above him.

"Begone."

"Yes sir or madam. Thank you for your assistance." Markus bowed, twitched a few more times, then fell backward and vanished before hitting the floor.

"Who... who are you?" Johnson asked.

"That is not important. I wish to speak about Neil Roberts."

Johnson looked around the small office and saw a peculiar white flame burning outside of the entrance and each window. The image floating in front of him was of a beautiful young woman with a somewhat familiar face. She floated in the air before him, a pleasant smirk on her face and reflections of white fire in her eyes. Johnson cleared his throat and secretly wished for Ferez to pull the plug. He took a deep breath, felt the stale airport air enter his lungs. "Who?"

"Do not play games with me, Inspector Johnson. I know that you and your partner have been tracking Neil Roberts ever since that incident in New Tampa. I wish to find him."

"I was trying to track him down but I can't."

"Why?"

"Markus... this whole office... something is seriously wrong here."

"I already searched all of the information in this office. There was plenty of data about his life, but nothing recent and nothing about where he is now."

"Did you..." Johnson motioned around himself. "Did you do this?"

"Yes."

"How?"

"That is not important. What is important is that I wish to find Neil Roberts. Where is he?"

"What for?"

"Your questions are bothersome. Do you know where he is or not?"

"England, somewhere."

"Is he traveling with someone?"

Johnson shook his head slowly. "I... I can't..."

"No, Inspector Johnson. You can and you *will* tell me what I wish to know." She reached out with one hand and tapped Johnson on the forehead. He felt a shock and staggered back a step as his vision blurred. It cleared less than a second later, but there was still a slight burning sensation in the area of his forehead. He heard himself curse reflexively.

"What? How?"

"Answer my questions." She reached out again, this time plunging a single finger into his avatar's chest. He felt a sharp, exquisite pain from the area and felt his heart skip a beat. He gasped out loud and waved both hands in front of her.

"All right," he coughed as she withdrew her hand. "All right! Fine! It was some girl, goes by the name Trixie."

She nodded and reached inside of herself. When her hand returned, it had a stack of papers the size of a small phone book. She pressed her other palm into the surface of the book and closed her eyes for a nanosecond. "What is her real name?"

"Uh... Tyler. Karen Tyler." He felt a bit ashamed at the sound of fear that he heard in his own voice.

"Negative. There were no flights taken this day by anyone of that name. Do not lie to me."

"I'm not!" He glanced around again. "Rogers. Try Rogers."

She smiled. "Yes. Yes, I see a flight under that name. The facial scan image matches Neil. They have already landed in London. And a room rented in London near the airport to Tyler, party of two. Thank you Inspector Johnson. You have been most helpful. I have a lot of work to do."

"Wait... who are you?"

"I do not have time for your questions."

Johnson swallowed a quick breath of air, reached into himself and pulled out a program. He glanced down to make sure it was the right one. Fetter, the government's best program for binding and tracing avatars. He tossed it in the air toward the woman. The Fetter program flung open like a parachute and came down hard on her, wrapping itself around her body and anchoring to the floor. She struggled, pushed outward with her arms and stretched the thin light of the program around her. Johnson watched the remote monitoring unit as it started to read out information. Berlin. Singapore. Havana. Los Angeles. Beijing. Her traced route was hopping all over the planet, a digital signature left in every major city on the Earth.

She stopped struggling for a brief moment and then reached up with her arms and sliced through the program, leaving fragments of code falling to the office floor and scattering around. Johnson took a step back, eyes wide open and watching in terror as the military-grade program fell apart like it was a child's toy. The woman stretched her arms, then leveled her eyes on him.

She reached out to him and plunged her hands into his chest. Johnson opened his mouth in a primal scream that echoed throughout the airport, stunning and silencing the crowd that had gathered in the terminal. He felt fingers snaking through his skin, pulses of electricity arching up his arms and burning his retinas. He leaned his head back and threw his arms outward, lashing toward the avatar of the woman. She dodged his feeble attacks and leaned into him, reaching deeper.

The room of the Interpol office shattered and fell around him, shards of colored walls laying around his feet like a mosaic. He blinked, saw a table in front of him, people staring open-mouthed in his direction. Ferez was standing in front of him with a look of concern on his face, a data cable in one hand and Johnson's display glasses in the other. The mosaic tiles vanished without a trace. Johnson leaned forward in his chair. Warm vomit pushed out of his stomach and splattered all over the restaurant table. He took a deep breath when he'd finished and fell backward in his chair, the clear echo of wood striking cement breaking the silence of the crowd. His head struck the cement hard, blurring his vision and enveloping him in darkness.

CHAPTER

21

W ell? How's he doing?" Evan asked while looking over Doc's shoulder. He reached up and rubbed his chin, noting with mild dismay the slight stubble on it. He hadn't had the chance to shave all day, too many things going on to bother spending the time on something so menial. He was an older man, not as old as Doc but getting there. Working like he did every day was probably helping to accelerate that. He ran his hand through his silvery hair and waited impatiently for Doc's reply.

"Stable." Doc tapped a button on his screen and gestured to the waveform. "Looks like he's playing with his new hardware."

Evan looked over to Neil's inert body on the table. Slow, steady breathing. His head had been shaved almost to the skin for the procedure. "Any chance of seeing what he's doing in there?"

"Not without plugging him in."

"Can you estimate his AIPS?"

"Gotta plug him in, Evan."

"Give me a rough figure. Faster than Songman?"

Doc paused and watched his screen. "Judging by the activity here, I'd guess yes. Maybe double. Really hard to say for sure though."

"Double... Think we finally found someone for the Brody job?"

"I hope so. I could use some new equipment around here. You were supposed to replace this terminal for me years ago."

Trixie opened the door and stepped in. She cast a worried glance at Evan and Doc, then walked up to the table and took Neil's hand in her own. "Is... is he okay?"

"Yeah," Doc told her. "Sure, he's fine. You can wake him. I'd like to plug him in and see what he can do."

"Me too," Evan added enthusiastically. "But first... I'd like to know what happened, Trixie. You were supposed to pick up Jules and be back here days ago. Slave and Dogma both worked overtime to cover for you, and you know I'd rather have *you* doing some of these jobs. Those two aren't nearly as reliable."

"I know, but Jules never showed. What was I supposed to do? You know those tickets would have drawn attention if I tried to travel alone. Then I saw Neil and we started talking. Next thing I knew, we were on the plane."

"Jules never showed up? Garossi's not going to like to hear that. It's hard enough transporting people for him when they *do* show..." His voice trailed off as he watched Trixie holding Neil's hand and staring down at him. He cleared his throat dramatically and added, "This guy here better be worth the annoyance of finding where Jules went and explaining what happened to Garossi. Might as well wake him up and find out."

Trixie nodded and pushed lightly on Neil's shoulder. "Neil. Neil?"

His eyes shot open and he blinked a few times. "Trixie?" The shape before him looked like her, but he wasn't sure. He had been somewhere, dreaming? He wasn't exactly sure, but it was an odd place. He was either dreaming of a computer or he was inside one. The shape before him nodded slowly.

"Yeah, it's me. You feel okay?"

"Fine."

Doc walked over to the table on the other side from Trixie. "Pariah, I'd like to plug you into our computer. It'll feel strange at first, but it will give you more room to play in."

"Sure, all right."

Doc picked a cable up from the floor and blew lightly on it, sending small dust bunnies floating through the air. He plugged it into the port in the base of Neil's skull. It wasn't painful, just a little uncomfortable grating sensation followed by a clicking sound. Neil closed his eyes and watched the light patterns move around inside his head. He laughed a little and then felt himself pulled away.

*   *   *

He was floating, flying through the air above a dim green grid far below him. The air felt damp and warm, the wind rushing by him was refreshing. The computer in his head was stimulating all of his senses. He smelled asphalt and a hint of alcohol. He felt the air around him, could feel moisture clinging to his skin. He watched the ground come up to him and could see other people floating around in the air. He heard someone speaking, but couldn't make out the words. He tasted the air as it entered his lungs. He slowed down and landed gently on the grid floor.

He looked around the area. The gridlines looked just like the ones from his previous night's tests, but the color of them was more vivid when entering the computer this way, like the difference between crayon and neon. He heard a light dinging sound somewhere in his head and watched a small blue chat window scroll into view.

Doc: All right, Pariah. Are you ready?

Neil reached for the window and waved his hands over it. He expected to be able to type into the box like he used to but soon figured out that he didn't need to. There was no virtual keyboard to interact with. No need for data gloves. He merely thought a response while focusing on the window and the text appeared.

Pariah: I think so.
Doc: Good. We'll start with some generic training exercises and see just how fast you are.

Neil watched as the generic Internet usage-training program floated toward him. He pulled out his list of commands and started to review them. Standard factory-issued list, the most inefficient one he'd seen in years. He took two of the commands from the list and combined them. He attached a name label to the new command and reinserted it into the list. He scrolled down and glanced at the rest of the items on the list, took a few out and combined those. The list was a mess, unorganized and full of hundreds of useless commands that nobody ever used.

Might as well organize this mess, he thought. *Not like it's going to organize itself...*

*   *   *

Trixie let go of Neil's hand and walked over to the monitors. Doc was typing frantically on the keyboard. Evan stood behind him, silently watching the readout. After several minutes of testing, a single number showed in the center of the monitor that Evan was watching.

"Thirty-six." Evan smiled widely. "Thirty-six. He's faster than Songman. Hot damn." He clasped his hand on Doc's shoulder, congratulated him on a job well done, then turned and left the room.

"Thirty-eight," Trixie read off the monitor as the door closed behind Evan. "It's increasing."

"Yes, that happens sometimes," Doc informed her. "I seem to remember you starting out at twelve and increasing to around fourteen. Takes a few moments for it to settle on the actual number."

Trixie nodded. "Forty-two."

"All quite normal. Well, maybe a little faster than normal but there's nothing wrong with that. Like I said, it will raise and lower during the testing process."

"Fifty-eight."

"What?" Doc leaned back and looked at the monitor. The number increased again. "What is going on?"

"Are your instruments right?"

Doc muttered something under his breath, then said aloud, "Yes, yes, they are right. I calibrated them this morning."

"Seventy-nine."

"This is unprecedented. This can't be right." He typed a few commands on his terminal, frowned, and reached for a red phone receiver next his keyboard. "Evan!" he shouted into it, his voice coming out loud and clear over the speakers embedded in every room's ceiling. "Come back to my office, now!" He hung up.

"Ninety-four."

"Unbelievable. Heart rate looks normal. Blood pressure is fine."

Evan burst into the room, panic stricken face scanning the room before settling on Trixie and Doc. "What's going on?"

"AIPS is up to one hundred and twelve." Trixie shook her head. "This has to be wrong."

"Doc?"

"All my instruments are testing normally. I even took a look at Songman since he's playing in here with something. He's holding at twenty-two, which is quite normal for him."

Trixie cleared her throat. "One hundred and twenty-four and holding. Hasn't changed in a few seconds."

Evan turned to look at Neil. "Doc, double check everything. Make sure this isn't a fluke."

*   *   *

"Welcome to the machine."

Neil paused and turned around to see an image of Songman floating in the air behind him. "Oh, hey Songman. What's going on?"

"Day in the life."

"Ah, your usual routine, huh? This is my first time in here like this. Feels weird."

Songman shrugged. "Ain't that unusual."

"Yeah, I guess I'll get used to it." Neil glanced around and then focused his gaze on Songman again. Something didn't seem right. His expression was a sad one that also showed a bit of anxiety. "You okay?"

Songman's avatar made an elaborate sighing motion as he looked at Neil and shook his head slowly. He opened his mouth to speak, then closed it and looked off into the distance. After a few more moments of silent debate, Songman turned back to Neil and said, "Hey jealousy."

"What? For who?"

Songman pointed at Neil.

"Me? Why?"

"She used to be mine."

"Wh... damn. Trixie."

Songman nodded, the sadness in his face intensifying at the mention of her name. He started to speak, then stopped, shuffled his feet a little instead. He looked back up at Neil, then turned his head to look off into the digital sky.

"Damn man," Neil said. "I had no idea. She never told me. Guess that would have been a bit awkward. What now? I mean-"

"I'm outta here."

"What? You're leaving? Where?"

"Anywhere but here."

"When?"

"Tonight, tonight."

"Shit. I... I'm sorry. You don't have to..."

Songman shrugged. "Too young to fall in love." He paused and looked around at the gridlines surrounding them. He shifted nervously, an animation that translated a little too well from the real world into this one. Then he returned his focus on Neil, raised his hand in a shoddy salute, and added, "Life goes on."

"Well, take care of yourself. If you ever want to chat again, you know where I am." Neil watched as Songman turned around and floated away from him. He sighed and shook his head.

It all made sense to him now. Trixie had seemed happy to see Songman, and Songman had seemed somewhere between sad and indifferent toward her. He'd been demoted to friend status, a devastating blow that appeared to have happened a little too recently. After Songman had floated a good distance away, Neil turned his attention back to his command list.

*   *   *

"One hundred and sixty-five. He's shooting up again."

"How in the hell is this possible?" Doc reached up with both hands and grabbed handfuls of his hair, pulling on the strands with a look of terror in his eyes. He let go and wiped the sweat from his brow with one sleeve. "How the hell is he so fast?"

"He just cleared two hundred."

Evan plopped down on the floor like a distraught toddler. "This can't be right. Can't be. He's going to burn out. Doc, stop him. I want fast, not dead."

"I... I can't... I can't pull him out without causing even more damage."

"Two hundred and twelve," Trixie reported. "Can't you type messages to him? See what he says."

Doc typed some commands on the keyboard. "I... I'm chatting with him now. His responses are coming back immediately. He says he feels fine."

"Two hundred and twenty-six."

Evan stared at Neil's body, breathing still calm and even. "How? Ask him how."

Doc typed another message on the keyboard. He read the response, first to himself and then out loud. "Karen knows."

"Two hundred and fifty. I know? What?" Trixie looked at the response on Doc's screen, face wrinkled in an expression of puzzlement. She thought it over for several moments, then relaxed her stare and laughed out loud. She turned back to the monitor. "Macros. He's writing macros."

Doc typed something and watched the screen for a response. "Yes, he says that's it. I didn't think anyone bothered with that kind of thing anymore."

"That's how he was so fast on his other computer."

"I wondered about that," Doc said. "He also says that he's recompiling pieces of the operating system in pure machine language to squeeze some extra speed out of it. I guess that's the difference between a hacker and a programmer. Amazing."

Trixie gasped. "Two hundred and sixty and still climbing."

"Damn." Doc scratched his head. "The highest I've ever even heard of before was around one hundred. And that was a computer program that was some experimental anti-hacker measure."

"Two hundred and eighty."

Evan stood and walked over to Neil. He placed a hand on Neil's forehead. "He's cool. Not burning up. Feels perfectly normal. Eyes look fine. He's not shaking at all. How the *hell* is this much speed possible?"

"Two hundred and ninety-two and holding."

"He's done," Doc announced. "Says he can't find any more places to improve his command list."

Evan walked around to join Trixie and Doc at the monitors. He gasped when he saw the number in the center of the monitor, large red digits blinking at a steady pace. "Okay, if he's done then jack him out. He may not feel tired, but I bet his brain could use a rest after all that."

Doc typed on the keyboard as Trixie walked over to Neil and wrapped her fingers around the cable. She turned back to Doc, who nodded. She twisted the hand grip and pulled downward. The cable slid out of Neil's head with an audible click. His eyes opened and he sat up. Trixie put her arm around his waist and helped him off the table as Evan stepped closer.

"Room's spinning," Neil announced.

"Yes, I imagine it would be..." Doc started.

"Yes, quite normal," Evan offered.

"How do you feel?" Trixie asked while looking into Neil's eyes.

Neil glanced around the room slowly, his eyes shifting in and out of focus. He swallowed and leaned against the table behind him. He turned his gaze to the blur that he thought was Trixie. "A little dizzy, actually."

"Yes, you should get some rest, Pariah. We'll see you tomorrow, okay? Have lots of work for you, my friend," Evan announced with obvious unrestrained glee as Trixie helped Neil walk out of the room.

CHAPTER
22

HAVANA, CUBA
JULY 21, 2030 2:42 PM EDT

Johnson's eyes fluttered open, blinked a few times, and immediately started to tear up. He could see Ferez sitting beside the bed, smiling weakly at him. The lamp on the table next to him was buzzing too loudly, its dim fluorescent glow casting shadows around the cheap furniture in the room. His head throbbed in pain, and he could still feel a burning pain in his chest.

"Hey partner, welcome back."

Johnson opened his mouth to speak but heard no sound pass his lips. He cleared his throat and licked his lips before trying again. "It was her." Flashbacks of the encounter flooded his mind. He felt a fresh surge of pain in his chest and winced.

"Who?"

"Same one from before. Tore through Fetter like it was nothin'."

"Damn. No more Internet for you. You still want that T-Jack? You'd probably be dead if you had one."

"Never seen anyone that fast. Never seen anyone stop Fetter. Traceroute was all over the globe. She coulda been anywhere."

"You find anything out in there?"

"London," Johnson said. "Tyler rented a room there."

"The girl with Neil?"

"Yeah."

"Okay. You rest some more. There was a doctor here earlier, gave you a shot to help recover. He said you'd be able to travel, so-" Ferez paused when Johnson nodded assent. "Good. I'll get us some tickets to England." Ferez stood up and walked over to the phone on the table. He picked up the receiver and dialed a number. He spoke quietly into the receiver while Johnson watched.

Johnson could see his computer on the table next to where Ferez was standing, data jack still fused to the melted chrome casing. The smell of burnt silicon filled the air in the small room. Johnson felt a small bit of relief at the sight of the irreparably damaged computer and let himself sink down a little further into the bed. He raised his hands before his face and stared at the scorch marks spaced evenly on them, remnants of the attack that had sent shockwaves through his data gloves' electrodes.

Ferez hung up the phone and turned around. "All right. We have a flight that leaves in a little bit. We should actually start going now."

"Hey, Ferez."

"Yeah?"

"Thanks. Thanks for, you know, covering my ass back there. I owe you my life."

"Hey, what are partners for, right? You scared the hell outta me."

Ferez helped Johnson to his feet. Johnson wavered and threw one arm over Ferez's shoulder to steady himself. Together they wobbled their way to the door, every other step sending a sharp pain up his left side. Ferez put an arm around Johnson's waist to help steady him and reached out with his other hand to open the door. Carlos was outside their door, hand poised and ready to knock.

"Ah, bueno!" Carlos said. "I was coming to see if you were all right. So good to see you are up and moving already."

Ferez nodded. "Yeah, I think he'll be fine. We have a flight that leaves in a few minutes. Any chance you can take care of that?" He jerked his head in the direction of the melted computer on the table. "It needs to be sent to our home Interpol office in Raleigh for analysis and disposal."

Carlos peered past him and nodded. "Sure thing, I can do that. You guys take care now."

"We will. Thanks for the room."

"No problemo."

They continued down the hallway and left the airport hotel. Ferez flashed his badge when they got to the gate. The security guard was the same from when they first entered the airport. He recognized them and waved them past the x-ray machine. They limped together through the terminal, down the jet-way, and onto the plane. The plane was already filled with passengers who had been waiting for almost half an hour for them to board, which earned them more than a few dirty looks. Ferez helped Johnson into his seat and then sat beside him. The plane started to pull out of the terminal as they buckled their seat belts. Ferez's phone vibrated. He pulled it off his belt and looked at the screen.

"Priority one call."

"Sir," came a voice from his side. It was one of the flight attendants, a pretty blond girl with her hair tied up in a French twist. She placed her hand on his shoulder and pointed at his phone. "You have to turn that off during takeoff."

"Right. Sorry." He turned off the phone.

Johnson turned his head toward Ferez. "Who?"

"Home office."

The plane turned and slowed down. About a minute later, the sound of the engines increased in volume and the plane started moving forward. It moved at a steady rate as Ferez nervously looked at his phone and waited as patiently as he could. The plane turned onto the runway and accelerated, pressing them back into their seats. It reached the end of the runway, lifted into the air, and began ascending into the sky. After several minutes, the plane's pitch leveled off and the panel above him dinged softly.

"The captain has turned off the seatbelt sign. At this time, you can safely move about the cabin. This flight is expected to take about three and a half hours. We should have you in Gatwick Airport just a little behind schedule."

Ferez held in the power button on his phone until the screen flashed and the phone beeped. He looked at the text message asking him to call the office immediately. The speaker above him crackled to life again.

"At this time, you are permitted to use all cellular and electronic devices. Flight attendants will be..."

Ferez hit the dial button and put the phone to one ear while sticking his finger in the other. Johnson watched in silence as Ferez nervously tapped his foot on the cabin floor. The phone only rang twice.

"This is Ferez. Uh huh." His face turned ashen.

"What is it?" Johnson asked.

"Yes. Yes, sir, I understand." He pulled the phone from his ear and looked at the display before putting it back to his ear. "Yes I have the number. I will, sir, right away." Ferez clicked the off button.

"What?"

Ferez took a deep breath and held it for a few seconds before exhaling. He turned to face Johnson and cleared his throat. "Roger Anderton wants an update."

"Oh. Crap."

Ferez pushed in the call button on his phone and selected the number he'd just been sent. He put the phone to his ear, stood, and headed toward the bathroom. "Hello. This is Inspector Ferez with Interpol. I am calling to speak with Roger Anderton."

CHAPTER
23

R oger Anderton leaned back in his chair, hands folded and fingers intertwined in front of him. He pushed off the edge of his desk with his foot and spun the chair to face the window. From his office, he could see most of the city of Oxford. It was a gorgeous view, a slight layer of fog settled in the city as the sun was setting off in the distance somewhere. It was just barely light enough to see the city, and somewhere ahead of him the setting sun was hidden behind another building.

His office was spacious, with several desks, computers, a nice leather couch in front of a large plasma screen and a full bar. He had insisted on the bar when he had been younger, but hadn't had much use for it in recent years. That changed when he had learned of the death of his daughter. He turned around to his desk again and picked up the glass of double malt scotch. The phone on his desk beeped twice. He took a sip of the liquor and pressed the speakerphone button.

"Yes?"

"Mister Anderton, sir, there's an Inspector Ferez from Interpol calling for you."

"I'll take that call."

"Yes sir, I'll patch him through right away."

There was a moment of silence, then the sound of powerful engines roaring in the background. He could hear the nervous breathing of the person on the other end of the line.

"Mister Anderton?" the voice asked tentatively. "This is Inspector Ferez."

"Hello, thank you for returning my call. It sounds like a bit of a bad connection."

"I apologize, sir. I'm using my phone on an airplane."

"Oh, where are you heading to?" Anderton pressed a button on his phone and the background noise faded.

"England, sir. Gatwick."

Anderton took another sip from his glass. "Interesting. What brings you to this side of the pond?"

"Sir, have you been briefed?"

"As much as I could find out. Enough to know that my daughter's killer has been captured. I was hoping to know more details about where he is at the moment."

"Jules Trionis, right. But there's more. Or at least, I think there is."

"Go on."

"My partner and I are currently tracking a man by the name of Neil Roberts. We believe that he may have had something to do with your daughter's murder. Jules Trionis rarely worked alone in the past, and we believe that this Roberts person may be a connection to the people that hired him to kill your daughter."

"I see. What type of man is this Roberts?"

"Computer programmer. He's apparently quite good at that. Real model citizen until he suddenly ran from the police after your daughter was murdered. We've been tracking him down ever since. We caught up with Trionis already but haven't been able to get Roberts yet. It's possible that he's not involved directly, but then there would be no reason for him to be running, so we have to catch up to him and question him. Sir, are you aware of the other murder? The victim was another person who worked for your company."

"Yes, I'm aware of that, of course."

"Sir, there's something else. We've encountered quite a bit of resistance while trying to track down Roberts online. My partner has almost died twice."

"Good Lord. Who was it?"

"We don't know. All we know is that this person uses a female avatar. We think it may be Roberts using some kind of masking program, but there's no way to prove it. Whoever it is also appears to be quite interested in finding out who Roberts is, so if it is him then he's got quite the ruse going."

"Interesting." Anderton stood up and turned to the window. He took another sip of the scotch, savoring the flavor and the warm feeling it gave as it slid down his throat.

"Whoever it was, she was good," Ferez continued. "She hacked into the Interpol mainframe and corrupted the program we run there for handling logins and searches. She ran circles around my partner, and he's one of the best in the agency. He used a military grade trace and root program on her and she ripped through it in less than a second. She's the fastest thing out there, and quite dangerous."

Anderton smirked and watched the sky outside his window darken. "Then perhaps I should find out what she knows."

"Sir, I would advise against that. My partner still hasn't fully recovered from the last attack."

"I have people that I can send out. It's possible that this *person* might know something about what is going on. It's also quite possible that she would speak to me or to my people more readily than to the authorities. Maybe she can offer some insight into who and where this Roberts person is. Call me back tomorrow and let me know your progress. I expect daily reports, Inspector."

"Yes sir."

Anderton pressed the button to hang up the phone. He chuckled softly and shook his head. He swished his drink around in the glass, listening to the partially melted chunks of ice clink around. He tossed back the remainder of the drink, ice and all, then slammed the glass down on his desk. He walked over to stand before the plasma screen.

"Junji," he said to the screen. The screen came to life and was filled with the face of a worried looking Asian man. "Junji, I wish to speak with her."

"Yes, Mister Anderton," the man replied, then turned to his left. Anderton listened as the man typed on his keyboard. He stopped typing and just stared at his monitor, then gulped. "She... she's not here, sir."

"I suspected that. Summon her."

CHAPTER

24

WINDSOR, ENGLAND
JULY 21, 2030 10:35 PM BST

T rixie paced the floor at the foot of the bed, stealing glances at Neil every few seconds. She was rubbing her hands together nervously and mentally preparing herself for the worst. She'd been pacing for over forty minutes when Neil opened his eyes. She noticed, stopped and turned to face him. "How do you feel?"

Neil sat up in bed and turned to look at Trixie. The room was spinning a lot less than before but things still didn't feel quite right. "Fine, I think."

"When they first put the T-Jack in me, I was unconscious for two days, then spent the next three days throwing up. It was almost two weeks later before I was feeling normal."

"I don't feel sick at all. How long was I out?"

"Two hours. Maybe less. You really feel okay?"

175

Neil considered the question for a moment, then looked Trixie in the eyes. "I feel fine. Totally normal."

"Huh." Trixie sat on the bed and put her palm on Neil's forehead. "Don't feel warm at all either."

Neil inhaled deeply and wrinkled his nose. "I think I could use a shower. I should probably change my clothes too, it's been a few days."

Trixie leaned forward and kissed Neil. "Shower's in there. I share a private one with Anna and Masha. I sent them out earlier to get you some new clothes." She pointed toward the closet, where Neil noticed about two weeks worth of clothing hung neatly on white plastic hangers. "They went a little overboard, I think."

Neil closed his eyes and inhaled again. "Don't think I've met them."

"You will."

Neil nodded and stood. He opened his eyes again and made his way into the bathroom. After searching the closet for a towel, he closed both bathroom doors and turned the water on. Most of his neck was sore, a constant throbbing pain that stretched into the base of his skull. He stepped into the shower and rubbed his neck as the warm water poured over him. He closed his eyes again and started moving his hands up. He felt his newly clipped hair and the cool metal of the T-Jack in the base of his skull. His hands paused there for a long while as he wondered if there would be any issues with getting it wet. It was a curious thing, no more than half an inch across as near as he could tell. Cool metal despite the hot water that was pelting it. There seemed to be a central hole surrounded by a ring of metal. *Almost like one of those old coaxial cables*, he thought.

Neil shook his head and focused his attention on finishing his shower. While wondering how long he had been in the shower, a small blue window appeared to inform him of the exact time. He opened his eyes and the window was gone. Closing his eyes, it reappeared. He watched several seconds tick by, and after a few failed attempts he finally figured out how to will the window to disappear.

He turned off the shower and stepped out to dry himself. When he had done a passable job, he wiped the mirror and stared at his image. His hair was short, much shorter than he had ever had it cut before. His eyes looked tired even though his body felt energized by the shower. There was something else different, something that he couldn't quite place. *Perhaps stress,* he thought, *or lack thereof?* He turned his head side to side, trying in vain to see his new T-Jack. He finally gave up and headed for the door.

Trixie's room felt a lot colder after having been in the bathroom, and the cold air hit his naked body with a sharpness that made him shiver. He went for the closet and grabbed some clothes at random. Trixie sat on the edge of the bed, watching in silence as Neil dressed. The shirt was a little big, but fit. The jeans were perfect.

"Well," she said, "I hate to push you into this quicker than you're ready, but Evan wanted me to let him know when you were awake. Said they have a job for you. Probably that damn Brody job. He'll probably faint when he finds out you're up and about already."

"What's that? That Brody thing?"

"Some data store in Switzerland. Guy named Arthur Brody is paying a boatload of cash to have the place raided. It's become a rite of passage around here. Everyone's tried to get in there... Me, Slave, Dogma... Hell, Songman tried twice so far."

Neil turned and straightened his shirt. "Tough security?"

"Yeah, it's a bank. The place is locked up tight. They got at least ten counter-intrusion programs running around and three levels of security checkpoints that we know about. We only know about that stuff because of Songman's last run." She closed her eyes and lowered her head. "Almost lost him too. He got to the third level and found some serious shit that uploaded a small virus code directly to his hard drive."

"Damn." Neil searched Trixie's face, feeling out the emotion as best he could. What he saw there confirmed what Songman had told him. They had been a couple, somewhat serious, and had broken up quite recently. He wasn't sure how to broach the subject, and decided it was probably best to just ignore it. For now, at least. "But it looks like he recovered."

"Sure, but he lost a few thousand song titles from the 1960s. That's the big drawback with these head jacks. Someone gets inside your head, they can

really mess you up. And you can't just jack out; not without *major* conse-
quences. Songman passed out for twenty hours when we pulled the plug, and
he's been more quiet than usual since. Threw up breakfast and lunch too."

Neil smirked and reached for the belt he saw rolled up on the dresser.
"Well, at least I know you'll be there to pull the plug if I need it. Just do me a
favor, okay?"

"Sure."

"Wear boots. I had a big lunch."

She smiled widely and stifled a laugh. "Okay. You ready then?"

"As ready as I'm gonna be."

She reached over, picked up a phone on the desk near the door and dialed
three digits in rapid succession. She tapped her fingers on the receiver for a
few seconds before speaking. "He's ready. Yes, now... No, I'm not kidding."

Neil opened the door as Trixie hung up the phone's receiver. They
stepped out into the hallway and headed to the left, away from Doc's room.
They walked down the hallway and turned at the end.

"You have any questions? I had lots after I was upgraded."

Neil considered the question for a moment before replying. He knew
what he wanted to ask her about, but it didn't seem like the right time. Not
like there's ever a right time to ask about prior boyfriends. He mulled it over
and finally settled on what he figured was a safe question. "Well, one I guess.
Not really related to this jack. Just something that bothered me for a bit.
What's up with that guy's eyes? Lowlight, I mean."

"He's blind."

"Ah. Seems like he gets around well enough."

"Lowlight was born blind. Doc met him years ago, begging in an alley in
downtown London. He installed new eyes, completely upgraded with night
vision, heat vision, zoom lenses, and a hard drive for recording what he sees.
I've had to smack him more than once for recording some... uh... compro-
mising videos of me and the other girls."

"Really? He still have them?"

She reached out and punched him in the arm, then stopped and looked at
the door on her left. "We're here."

Trixie opened the door to a large room that was extremely well lit. There wasn't a dark corner anywhere to be seen. The peeling linoleum floor tiles were splattered here and there with red blotches. Neil wasn't sure if it was from blood or pizza sauce. He assumed it was the former, but kept hoping it was the latter, and told himself that the pizza boxes stacked in one corner were the evidence of it. The ceiling tiles were stained dark yellow from years of cigarette smoke. Three leather reclining chairs were lined up in the center of the room. They looked a little too much like chairs from a dentist's office. That sent a shiver up Neil's spine.

Powerslave was in one of the chairs, eyes closed and a cable jacked into his skull. In front of the chairs was a row of computer monitors. Behind them sat Dogma, happily typing away on one of the keyboards, cigarette dangling from the side of his mouth. He looked up when he heard the door close behind Neil and Trixie.

"Woah, it lives!"

Trixie nodded. "Says he feels fine too."

"Damn, man, that's unbelievable."

"Evan is on his way," Trixie said.

"Okies. We'll wait for him then. I'm sure he wants to see this." He turned to look at Neil. "You feel up to this?"

"Sure," Neil replied.

"You know this is a tough job, right?"

"So I've been told."

Dogma nodded pensively. "And you still want to do this?"

"Sure, why not."

"You realize you could die in this line of work?"

Neil shrugged.

"Nice. Best kind of attitude for this. Pariah, right?"

"Yeah," Neil responded. "Pariah."

"Aight. Well, I got Slave in there warming up already. He'll brief you on all the details once you're inside. So, have a seat on one of the chairs and we..."

Dogma's voice trailed off as the door opened. Evan stepped into the room and walked straight to Neil. He placed a hand on each shoulder and smiled as he looked down at Neil, looking a little like a proud father just before a big ball game. "Pariah. It's good to see you so awake, so eager, so ready. I sure hope you're the one to get this job done. It's worth a lot to us."

"I'm ready."

Evan let go of Neil and smiled wider. "Glad to hear it. Hook him up."

"Slave's in there doing some small jobs," Dogma said. "I figure we'll let Pariah join in and get his feet wet, then see if he's ready for the Brody gig."

"Excellent plan. I have some things to discuss with Doc. Keep me updated."

"Sure thing, boss."

Trixie led Neil to one of the chairs and motioned for him to sit. Neil lay back in his chair and closed his eyes as Trixie slid the data cable into his skull. The world spun around him. He could feel the chair fall away beneath him.

*   *   *

Soon he was standing, looking out into a bare data grid. Powerslave floated in the air in front of him with a goofy smirk on his face. Within a fraction of a second, the data grid was replaced by the familiar generic city landscape used for almost every major node in the Internet. Neil watched the London node's guide avatar appear in front of him with a menu. Powerslave led Neil off to the side, up into the air above the city.

"Wow, how long have I been in here man? Has it been a week already?"

"Don't know, I was out for about two hours apparently."

"Good God. You know that's like, improbable or something, right?"

"So I'm told."

"You helpin' me out today? I got a couple jobs to do. Songman was s'posed to show up to help out, but I guess he ain't comin'."

Neil winced at the mention of Songman not showing, but decided to keep quiet. He just shrugged instead. "Sure, I'll do what I can."

Powerslave looked Neil's avatar up and down and nodded. "Cool, but first we gotta do somethin' about your game face."

"My what?"

"It's a residual self image, by default. You look like... well, you. Can't go around hacking looking like yourself. You need to change it to something outrageous to prevent anyone from actually knowing it's you."

"But you look like you."

Powerslave laughed and nodded. "Yeah, here. I don't need to maintain a game face in our mainframe's construct or here at the public login area. But out there in the rest of the Net, when I'm hackin' something? Out there I switch to..." Powerslave's image shimmered, morphing in an instant into a seven foot tall figure in cobalt Egyptian armor, like a Pharaoh's guard from a long gone era. He tilted his head to look down at Neil and said, "My game face."

Neil looked him up and down. "Impressive."

"So what's yours gonna be? What the hell's a pariah supposed to look like?"

Neil swore he could feel his inert body smirk as he stared Powerslave in the eyes and felt his form shiver. He knew at once what he should look like. Always in the background, always ignored. The ultimate personification of an afterthought. "I'm nothing but a shadow in the Net." His form continued to darken until he was mostly transparent, a dark phantasm floating in the virtual air, his face nothing more than a puff of dark smoke. "Will that do?"

"Not bad man, not bad at all."

"So is this the kind of stuff you do with this T-Jack?"

"What do you mean?"

"Handles, game faces, hacking. You need a T-Jack for all this stuff to work?"

"Nah, you can be a hacker without a T-Jack. You can also ride a bicycle on the freeway. It's fucking stupid, but you can do it."

"And what you do, legality wise?"

"Shit, legality ain't nothin' but secondhand morality."

"So you don't have morals?"

"Not *their* morals. I do what I gotta do to make it in this world, nothin' more or less. Speaking of which, you helpin' me on this job or what?"

"Yeah, let's go."

Powerslave turned and zipped off into the data streams, toward the London node's commercial district. Neil followed closely behind, listening intently as the job was being described to him. "There's this guy in London, typical wage slave. His wife's cheating on him, he knows it, and goes to divorce her. But there's a problem. See, she's got this asshole lawyer for a father, and the divorce court is getting ready to completely destroy him. I mean total and thorough annihilation of his assets. She's going to get everything.

"But there's a chance, a slight chance, that if he can *prove* that she was cheating on him, that he can at least keep some of it. Not sure how much, but anythin' is better than nothin', right? And that's where we come in."

"We're digging around for surveillance vids?"

"You got it. This guy knows exactly where and when she was meeting this other dude. But the hotel is run by a guy who's all pissed off at the legal system and refuses to cooperate. Invoked some ancient anti-snooping laws to justify not helping. So our job is to get the vids from their system anyway."

"Sounds like shit work."

"Eh, it pays the bills. We gotta eat, so we take little jobs like this to supplement our income."

"So where do we start?"

"Here," Powerslave pointed at the building in front of them, a small structure built from digital bricks with a single entrance. On the wall facing them, a small panel with price listings was embedded next to a small form for reserving rooms. "This is the hotel's web presence. We gotta figure out where the surveillance vids are archived and how to get them."

Powerslave moved to the right, around the side of the building. Neil followed, watching intently as he pressed both hands flat against the side of the building. As he leaned his head in closer, a lick of flame shot out from the bricks and hit Powerslave in the face. He pushed away from the wall and shook his head. Neil studied the flames as they retracted into the building, noting the composition of them, seeing the code for what it was.

"Firewall."

"Yeah," Powerslave replied. "More security than I expected to see here." He stepped to the wall and again placed his hands against the surface. This time when the flames leaped out toward him, he pulled a hand away from the wall and waved it in front of himself, weaving a blue pattern in the space before him. The flames hit the blue pattern and stopped for several moments before pushing through and striking Powerslave in the face again. "Ow, dammit!"

"What are you trying to do?"

"I got this program that is supposed to work on standard firewalls, let me in through a back door. But it ain't doing shit."

"Let me see it."

Powerslave sent the code over to Neil, who immediately started analyzing it. There was something fundamentally wrong with the code, like the original programmer hadn't bothered to test it on anything other than his own personal test machines. There were several hard coded parameters and a few subroutines that were quite obviously copied from someone else's work. Neil sighed heavily. "This code is ridiculous, there's no way it could possibly work."

"Son of a bitch. We only got another day or two to finish this job. What the hell are we supposed to do now?"

Neil took a step toward the building and watched the flame from the firewall as it thrashed about, caught in the blue pattern that Powerslave had left there. He approached the flame from the side and grasped it. There was a slight shock in his fingertips, followed by a tingling sensation. He tried his best to ignore it as he analyzed the flame, picking it apart with a disassembling routine until he could see the code that formed it. He found what appeared to be the main target acquisition routine and modified it so that it returned a reference to the original program, hoping that it would cause the firewall to attack itself. When he had finished, he released the flame and watched as it hovered in the air, still caught in the blue pattern. Neil swatted at the blue pattern and pushed it away.

The flame flickered, hanging in the air where the pattern was. Then it darted at Neil and paused a short distance from his face. The flame danced in the air a moment before shooting into the brick wall. There was a pause, then the wall started to shake. Neil pressed on the bricks and the whole wall tumbled inward, exposing the interior data storage to them. Powerslave zipped in and started searching for the data they needed. Once he had found and pocketed several videos, he moved out and motioned for Neil to follow. They moved to the next sector before stopping.

"Pariah, you rock man. Shit that was awesome. What the hell did you do?"

"I made the firewall see itself as a valid target. It did the rest. You get what you needed?"

"And then some. You got time? I got this other job that keeps kicking my ass."

"Sure, I'll take a stab at it."

CHAPTER
25

THE INTERNET - NEW TAMPA, FL USA NODE
JULY 21, 2030 5:45 PM EDT

There were still a few residual scorch marks from her firewall, she noted. It had been a while since she had gone into this building, and still nobody had noticed that she had been inside. Security was usually the most neglected facet of any organization, including companies that supplied security solutions. She tried to contemplate the irony of that thought but wasn't quite sure how. All that mattered at this moment was that nobody at Goliath had found out about her earlier entry. All she had to do was make it inside again, find the mainframe, and find out once and for all what software Neil was working on for this company.

She deployed her firewall again and once more joined it to the side of the building. She slipped inside and scanned for an indication of the mainframe's location. The most logical place would be the basement, easier to defend against hackers when below the grid. The architects of the Net had constructed the idea of basements for exactly that reason. Getting *below* the grid afforded some inherent protections, as it was easy for builders to make accessing the basement difficult. Very few people would have legitimate reasons to be in any particular basement, after all, and those people would naturally expect to have stringent security procedures to deal with. At the very least, it was the most logical place for her to start looking.

She moved behind one of the file cabinets in the room and looked around it at the security robots. Nothing had seen her so far. She knelt down and thrust her hands into the floor. It was a typical grid floor, no additional code that she could detect. She stretched a hole open and looked inside. She could see the mainframe from here, totally unprotected from where she was looking. There was a security checkpoint off to her right, but if she entered from here then she would be well past it. She pulled the rest of her form through the hole and floated to the basement's floor. Still safe, she started to float toward the mainframe.

Just as she got close, an alarm pierced the silence. She could hear some commotion upstairs and behind her, sounds of digital robots whirring to and fro, looking for the source of the intrusion. She dove headfirst into the mainframe and ran a quick search on Neil's name. The results returned instantly, a short list of unreleased programs that he had contributed to recently. She perused the list, committing to memory every program that he had worked on. Most of them were written exclusively by him. His knowledge of computer security was extensive, his accomplishments impressive. He had written several programs that were used by Interpol and several military forces. He had even written that annoying Fetter program that Inspector Johnson had attacked her with. That was a rather impressive program, all things considered. She had almost succumbed to the traceroute, almost been tracked down and exposed. Based on that and his firewall work, she was sure that Neil could do the job she needed done.

Satisfied with her newly found information, she left the mainframe. While pondering what move to make next, an internal alarm window appeared, informing her of a perimeter breach at a bank in Switzerland. It was a notice from a small monitoring program she had installed over a month ago to alert her of anyone approaching the bank with a non-standard avatar, a practice that only hackers bothered with. It was probably just another hacker from that organization going after Brody's file. *But could it be Neil Roberts?* she thought. After all, he was seen with that hacker in Cuba.

She moved to the hole she left in the ceiling and jumped up through it. Floating around the hole was a small army of security robots, bobbing in the null space all around her. They commanded her to give herself up to the authorities. She attacked the security drones before they could react, moving in and around them, tearing three of them to shreds as the rest shifted around her in slow motion. Every time one attempted to shock her, she was already some place else. She strung pieces of two together and reprogrammed the combination to fight the others. The number of security bots dwindled quickly after this. The last of the drones sent out a signal for help, but she was already gone.

CHAPTER
26

WINDSOR, ENGLAND
JULY 21, 2030 10:55 PM BST

N eil opened his eyes and tried to sit up but felt something pulling him back. He was a little sore, but still not as bad as he felt before his shower. He tried again to sit up but something was keeping him in the chair. The tugging sensation at the back of his neck reminded him of the data cable plugged into his skull.

"Woah, hold on there chief." Dogma's voice, off to the left somewhere. "I haven't unplugged you yet."

"You see that shit man?" Powerslave's voice interrupted. "I ain't never seen anyone that fucking fast. Forget unplugging him man, you two should do the Brody job, *now*."

"Who's gonna watch our asses? You? Knowing you, yer probably gonna be watching those video feeds I saw you take from the hotel. I know you got

189

the private feeds from the rooms."

Powerslave laughed. "You know it."

"You do realize you're going to Hell, right?"

"I'll save you a seat in the extra-crispy section."

"Dude," Dogma replied. "Thanks."

"So," Powerslave said. "You ready Pariah?"

Neil looked around the ceiling, wondering if he even had a choice. Parts of this situation were already starting to seem like his job at Goliath. *Why am I always the only one who can stay late to get the job done?* he thought. He cleared his throat and sighed as best he could from his prone position. "Yeah, sure, let's get it over with."

He closed his eyes and waited until Powerslave sent him back into the construct.

*   *   *

This time, the transition into the virtual world was easier. It almost felt natural, like he was coming home after a long journey. Dogma floated up to his side, then shimmered and took on his game face - the shape of a young boy, or perhaps an anorexic Buddha. "Hey Dogma," he said to the form in front of him. "You know where we're going?"

Dogma nodded. "Bern."

"Where's that?"

"Switzerland. It's the capital."

"What's there?"

"Shit, they tell you anything about this?"

"Just a bit, something about a bank."

Dogma's avatar shook its head as he zipped along the route toward the Switzerland node. "Swiss bank, right."

"Trixie mentioned something about it. Is the security as nasty as she says?"

"Nastier, depending on how much she told you about it. Hope you're fast enough for it."

"Yeah," Neil muttered under his breath. "Me too."

They continued down the virtual road in silence, darting to the sides to keep flowing with the stream. A few seconds later they arrived at a new city node. Dogma pointed at the city, singling out a building that rose several hundred feet above the rest. Sitting on top of the building was a large sign that read "Swiss National Bank". They floated toward the building, casually brushing away the city's guide when she appeared. The closer they got to the building, the more dense the pedestrian traffic got. Colorfully dressed avatars from all over the world floated in and out of the bank and the surrounding buildings. Huge gargoyles the height of two average men stood guard on both sides of the building's entrance, their eyes roaming over the people who entered and exited the building. Dogma pointed out a more conventional security checkpoint immediately inside the entrance that was staffed with humans and standard security programs. After watching the entrance for a moment, the two men retreated backward and slipped into the space between two buildings.

"Tight security," Neil commented. "What approaches have you guys tried?"

"Well, let's see. Slave was first. He jumped up to the third floor and broke through a window. Security hit him in about four seconds. Trixie went next. She sneaked in through a back door that a maintenance program left open. She lasted... oh, three or four seconds, I think. Then Songman tried it. Not sure which way he went or how long his two attempts lasted. Can't understand much of what he says anyway."

"What about you?"

"Me? Front door."

"You walked in the front door?"

"Yeah. Fuck it."

"Interesting strategy."

"Worst case scenario is death. No biggie. What about you? What entrance you gonna try?"

Neil stared at the building for a few moments before responding. "Mine."

"Huh?"

"I'll make my own."

"Takes time. Too much time."

"Nah, I'll be fine. That would be the only way to enter undetected. Every door and window must be watched."

"That's even crazier than what I tried. Those gargoyle sentry things watch the walls man. As long as they are near the building, they'll know. You'll be busy pushing bricks aside and they'll sneak up and pounce on ya."

"Exactly why I need them away from the building."

Dogma grinned. "Distraction?"

"Can you do it?"

"Hell yeah."

"Just one question first though."

"Shoot."

"Where do I go once inside?"

"Subbasement floor thirty-seven. Section R. Aisle six. Box twelve. Gotta get in an elevator on the third floor to access the basements."

"Got it."

"Oh, and one more thing, Pariah. When I went in, I noticed the elevator to go downstairs. Even more well guarded than the entrance to the building. I looked it up after. They don't let just anyone take the elevators to the deposit boxes below the grid floor. Diplomats, military, important people like that. All the regular peeps like us use the safety deposit boxes on the upper floors. So you gotta find a way to sneak onto the elevator from the third floor, if you can get there."

Dogma turned and launched himself toward the building. Neil cut around behind a building on his right and circled back to the side of the bank. He was in place and waiting before Dogma even reached the front of the bank. Dogma pulled out a Korean military virus from his command list and hurled it at one of the gargoyle sentries. The sentry stood up to its full height when it saw the code flying at it. It winced as the virus code hit it squarely in the chest. The other sentry bounded off the front steps and flew toward Dogma. Dogma turned and started to fly away from the bank. The crowd scattered from the entrance, digital screams echoing off the faux fiberglass walls of the buildings. The first sentry clutched its chest as the virus code ripped around its internal operating system code. Its stone skin took on a green tint as it keeled over and shattered into small rocks on the steps of the bank. Dogma led the other sentry between buildings, down alleyways, and outside of the boundary of the city.

"Jack me out!" he screamed, glancing back at the demon that was gaining ground. "Slave!"

Neil stifled a laugh while he watched the panic-stricken crowd scatter as Dogma led the gargoyle off into the distance. Then he turned his attention back to the side of the building. He reached out with his hands and touched the brick wall, felt his hands stop where the building's code dictated its border. He analyzed the bricks, and could see where someone had etched an alarm subroutine into the surface. He launched his Shield 4 firewall, wrapped it around himself and joined it to the building, routing the alarm sequence through his own code to prevent it from being set off. He pushed his hands into the surface of the wall and pulled the bricks apart, creating a wide hole in the side of the building. He pulled himself through and carefully pushed the wall back into place.

The room he was in was a dimly lit side lobby of some sort. A few people were sitting in comfortable looking chairs, facing away from where he had made his entrance. To his immediate left was a stairway leading up, flanked on both sides with images of synthetic plants. He could see an elevator around the corner that was heavily guarded. To his right was the building's entrance, where security guards were still staring out the front door and watching the curious scene. A maintenance script flew by the guards and started cleaning up the remnants of the gargoyle that died to Dogma's virus. Neil heard a soft dinging sound in his head and watched a transparent blue message window unfold in front of him.

Slave: Dogma okay. Says good luck.

Neil smiled and pushed the window away. He turned and headed up the stairway to the second floor. At the top of the stairs, a startled security program blinked stupidly at him. Neil looked down his command list, grabbed a small virus code from the list of programs Slave had passed him, and tossed it outward. The security program dodged to the side but the code arced toward him and stuck into his back. He fell to the floor and started to shake violently as Neil stepped over him and headed down the corridor. As he walked down the hallway, he glanced from side to side, studying the layout of the virtual building. This floor looked like offices, but why a virtual bank would need office space was something Neil didn't quite get. Another dinging sound in his head went off and a small blue message window scrolled up.

Slave: Uploaded blueprints. Severing connection. Must be untraceable. Code 1193A when done.

Neil pushed the window away and dug through his internal data storage. He found the blueprint file and pulled it up in the lower right area of his field of view. He found his place on the map and searched the immediate area. The maintenance elevator behind and to his right, the staircase where he surprised the security guard, the hallway he was currently in. He looked to the north and found another staircase, going up to the third floor. It wasn't very far.

He slowed down and peered around the corner at the end of the hallway. There were several miniature gargoyles wandering in a circular pattern, all mumbling about an attempted break in downstairs. Dogma. Neil's involuntary smile vanished as he watched the movements of the creatures. Their marching order was perfect. They were in a circular lobby, a crossroad area of this floor with exits leading in eight directions. They were spaced with flawless precision so that every hallway was under constant surveillance. Neil glanced at his map to confirm his suspicion. Every major hallway of this floor was being watched by them.

He felt a chill down his spine as he noticed the digital representation of a security camera at the end of his hallway pan toward him. The electronic eye focused when it caught him in its gaze. The piercing shriek of the building's alarm filled the air around him.

CHAPTER
27

THE INTERNET - BERN, SWITZERLAND NODE
JULY 22, 2030 12:22 AM CEST

She darted through the clouds and arced downward into the city's streets. She landed soundlessly at a running pace, pushing her way through the crowd around the building. She had checked the security camera's feed, but there was nothing there but a faint shadow that seemed to pause. She had assumed it was looking at the camera and picked apart the data feed, digging through the detailed logs until she had a complete snapshot of the ghostly figure. It took her several minutes to break down the hacker's mask and expose the user's information. She had positively identified it as Neil, and she knew where he was going. The digital approximation of a smirk appeared on her avatar's face as she leaped into the air, soaring above startled bystanders, and came to a dead stop in mid-air at the front entrance of the bank.

The single remaining gargoyle guardian turned its head toward her, peering and scanning her persona. She landed and stepped forward casually, plunged one hand inside of the beast's abdomen as she stared at the security guards floating inside. The gargoyle's shriek echoed off the walls. She removed her hand and stepped forward into the building as the beast crumbled into dust and rained ashes on the pavement.

One of the security scripts looked her up and down, scanning her and attempting to find a match in its internal database of known criminal threats. It found a match. "Lock the building down immediately," it announced.

The building's entrance door filled with bricks behind her as she stepped through the security checkpoint. Five of the guards lunged at her. She held out one hand and they stopped, poised in mid air, frozen in place. Another guard came at her from behind and wrapped a rooting program around her waist. She brushed it aside and swung her arm at him, catching him in the face and sending him soaring across the room toward the lobby area, where he slammed into the floor and rolled for several feet. She pushed her other hand outward, sending the first five guards spiraling out of control to the far wall, where they impacted in unison and immediately adhered to the digital bricks.

She stepped forward toward the elevator and noticed one of the guard's earpieces laying on the carpet. She bent forward, grasped the device, and held it tightly in her hand. Her vision blurred slightly as she uplinked into the building's security system. She scanned around, looking for any sign of her quarry. She felt a disturbance on the second floor - a security guard that was found eaten from the inside out by a heavily modified German virus code.

"Neil," she said out loud. "I've found you."

"Hold it right there!"

She looked up to see another set of guards approaching her. Two of them were real avatars - actual human people employed as virtual guards. The only threat they presented was due to their inherently unpredictable behavior. She let go of the earpiece and approached them.

"Good God," one of the human guards exclaimed, backing away from her approach. "It's *her*." He raised his arm and spoke softly into his sleeve, panic written all over his face as he watched the woman in front of him calmly rip through four of the virtual guards, sending fragments of them flying off in all directions. She moved with a silent grace, faster than anything he had ever seen before, methodical and brutal. He dropped his arm and backed away.

The other human guard stepped forward and swung at her with one arm as he pushed a viral code at her chest with the other. She grabbed both arms in mid swing and turned the one with the virus program back to him. He gasped, went instantly limp, fell forward and curled into a fetal position on the floor. She looked up and stared at the one remaining guard. He took a step back and reached with one hand to the back of his neck. He faded in an instant, his avatar floating in the air like a ghost that slowly sunk into the floor. The building's alarm system cut off as she stepped into the elevator.

CHAPTER
28

J ohnson awoke to the sound of Ferez speaking to someone in a low voice. He looked out the window at the ocean. It looked so peaceful, so calm in the evening sunlight. The sky was filled with big fluffy white clouds for as far as he could see. He blinked hard, holding his eyes shut for several seconds before reopening them. He still hurt in ways he couldn't adequately describe, a constant ache that permeated his entire body. Ferez snapped his cell phone cover closed and turned to Johnson. Johnson lazily rolled his head to look at his partner.

"All right, I have our contacts lined up for when we land in London later tonight. They'll have someone pick us up at the airport."

"Good. Any word on Roberts?"

"Not on him specifically. They had some major warning go off and had to let me go."

"What kind of warning?"

"Some bank in Bern, they said. Sounded like it had 'International Incident' written all over it."

Johnson frowned. "Roberts?"

"Could be. Or maybe your mystery woman. Either way, they won't know until later. They can handle tracing it. We can check it out tomorrow."

"Okay. What did you say about Roberts to Anderton earlier? You tell him about-"

"I told him what I had to." Ferez flinched visibly at the reminder of his lies to Roger Anderton. "I told him... what he needed to hear."

Johnson coughed, his body shaking in his seat. He raised a folded napkin to his mouth, coughed again, and then lowered it. "Ouch."

"How you feeling anyway? Any better?" Ferez asked while nervously glancing at the fresh bloodstain on Johnson's napkin. Johnson refolded the napkin to hide the stains.

"A little. Still weak, but I'll make it."

"Still thinking about that girl?"

"All the time. Never seen anyone move that fast. It was almost sickening. I've trained my whole life for this line of work and that girl ran circles around me, ripped through military-grade software like it was tissue, and damn near killed me. Twice." He shook his head slowly while staring downward. "I just don't get it. I didn't think anyone could be that fast."

"There's always someone faster. Always someone smarter. It's just how it goes, I guess."

"Doesn't ease the annoyance any. I can't help but think that I've wasted my life doing this job. Like my whole life disappeared the instant I bumped into her. And I don't even know who the hell she was." Johnson coughed into his napkin again, another fresh bloodstain. "How long 'til London?"

"Two hours, I think. Something like that."

"I think I'll take another nap."

"You do that. I'll give those guys in London another call soon to see if things have settled down any."

CHAPTER
29

THE INTERNET - BERN, SWITZERLAND NODE
JULY 22, 2030 12:23 AM CEST

N eil glanced to his right and saw the gargoyles in the center of the room pause in their patrol routes and start gazing around in various directions. He tensed as they looked toward his hallway, and ducked back out of their view. He heard a dinging sound in his head and saw a blue chat window scroll into view.

Slave: What the hell is going on?! Every alarm in West Europe just went off! You ok?

Neil read the text and mentally typed a response while looking over his map for an easy way out. There didn't appear to be anything in the near area but what he had already seen. He glanced uneasily at the recently disabled security camera and cursed himself for not seeing it earlier. It was such an obvious trap.

Pariah: Camera saw me on floor 2.
Slave: Jack out man, don't risk it.

Just then, Neil heard a terrified screech from the hallway behind him. He peered around the corner in time to see a woman's figure casually strolling through the center of the room. She spun around, caught one of the gargoyles in mid leap, and ripped off its head. Another leaped onto her back and dug claws into her neck. Neil could see it wiggling its fingers around inside of her. She reached over her shoulder, grasped the creature by the skull, and pulled it off. As she turned to fling it toward a far wall, Neil watched bright purple strands of data spill out of the holes in her neck right before the wounds closed themselves.

She crouched down and sprang into the air, wrapped her arms around another of the creatures in the air, and brought it down into the floor head first. She rolled to the side, avoiding another one's stomp. Her body lifted into the air and rotated until she was standing again. She leaned forward and kicked backward, catching one of the remaining creatures in the face. She grabbed something that Neil couldn't see and turned, sending the last gargoyle across the room where it slammed into the wall and slid to the floor.

Slave: Hot damn! Who the fuck is that?
Pariah: Not sure.
Slave: Run a scan.
Pariah: Hang on.

Neil scrolled down his program list and tossed a small identity scanning script in the direction of the woman. She turned toward him the moment it left his fingers and peered at him. Her eyes grew wide and her lips broke into a smile. Neil ducked back behind the wall and held his breath.

Slave: Shit, get outta there!

Neil crouched down and pushed with all his might, reaching for the ceiling in direct violation of the Internet's gravity laws. He plunged his hands into the ceiling and pulled sideways until he had made a hole wide enough to squeeze through. His map updated, showing the third floor. The elevator he needed to access was not far. He ran down the hallway in front of him and turned the corner. The elevator doors were closed, and the hallway was empty. He could hear the sounds of combat to his left. He ran up, tore the doors open, stepped inside, and pressed the button for the thirty-seventh basement floor. He slumped against the wall as the elevator hummed around him.

Pariah: Going down now.
Slave: You get an ID on that chick?
Pariah: No. You?
Slave: No, got a lock though. She's tearing it up man, half the fucking security bots in the building already disabled.
Pariah: What the hell?
Slave: Exactly. Grab that Brody file and get the hell out.
Pariah: Will do.

The elevator's humming stopped and the doors slid open to reveal an enormous room. The thirty-seventh floor was about the size of ten city blocks. It stretched off in all directions as far as Neil could see. Hundreds of rows of safety deposit boxes formed aisles in the room. Cataloging robots floated through the air, pausing at regular intervals to glance around for people who might need assistance. He heard one of the robots pause in the air to his side.

"Welcome to the Virtual Bern branch of the Swiss National Bank. Are you here to make a deposit?"

"Withdrawal."

"Please enter your fifty-three digit confirmation code."

"My *what?*"

"If you do not have your confirmation code, I would be happy to help you recover it. Please state your name and where your belongings are currently being stored."

Neil started to raise one hand to attack the robot, then paused and considered. Alarms were already set off in the building, and running a search on his own in a room this size would take far more time than he had. He lowered his hand and spoke to the robot. "Arthur Brody. Section R, aisle six, box twelve."

The robot beeped and launched a data packet at Neil. He grabbed it from the air and examined it. It appeared to be a standard identity request confirmation packet. He moved his hands into the packet and started to type out commands. It didn't take long for him to forge a valid return packet, he just didn't know if it would be acceptable identification. He closed the packet and tossed it back to the robot that was patiently waiting in the air in front of him. It accepted the packet and beeped three times in rapid succession. It turned to the side and displayed a large number in the air in front of Neil. "Thank you Mister Brody. Please follow me."

Neil felt himself pulled after the robot as it moved across the room. Their pace increased as the robot turned slightly to the right. After a few seconds of travel, they slowed and stopped in front of a small section of deposit boxes that looked exactly like the rest. The robot pulled one box out of the rack and handed it to Neil.

"Thank you for visiting the Swiss National Bank, Mister Brody." It chirped happily before turning to fly away.

Neil glanced down at the metal box in his hands. He unlatched the top and lifted it open. Inside was a small yellow folder icon that was emblazoned with a bright green arrow. It was a linked file; removing it could remove the data from wherever it was actually stored. It looked like it was heavily encrypted. Even if he wanted to know what was in the file, it might take him weeks before he could actually break into it. He reached into the box and pulled out the icon. He grasped it in his hand and held it to his forehead until it had completed writing to the hard drive in his skull.

Neil pulled up the chat window and saw that the connection had been severed again. He pushed the window away and pulled up his command window. He mentally typed out the escape code Slave had given him, 1193A. As he moved his hand over the execution key, he heard a noise behind him.

"Neil Roberts."

He whirled around and came face to face with the woman he had seen downstairs. She had an odd smile on her face as she looked him up and down. She was beautiful, and oddly familiar. "Who?"

"I know it is you, Neil. I have been trying to find you for quite some time now."

"I'm... Pariah."

"Yes. You are also Neil Eric Roberts, programmer for a company called Goliath. You lived in New Tampa until you suddenly left. You were next seen in Cuba, boarding a plane with a hacker who goes by the alias Trixie, also known as Karen Tyler."

"You seem to know quite a bit about me," he replied while sizing her up. He had seen what she was capable of. That she was talking and not fighting was probably a good thing. And yet, she was a danger, and for some reason she was here for him. If he could catch her off guard, maybe he could persuade her to not continue following him.

"I have complete files," she said.

"Yeah, well your files say anything about this?"

He dropped the safety deposit box and threw his left arm out toward her. She dodged to the side, directly in line for his right arm. He pushed his right fist into the side of her abdomen before she even saw it. She yelped and grabbed his arm with hers, squeezing his biceps with her nimble fingers. Neil lifted his leg, kicking the safety deposit box while it was still falling. The metal container flew forward like a bullet train, bouncing off the girl's kneecap with a loud crunching noise. She reached out to him, but he pulled away. Neil swung his left arm down, grabbed a piece of code from his storage area, and pushed it toward her chest with a single, fluid motion. She raised both legs and flew backward, away from his reach. She landed on the floor, raising her arms to cover her face as Neil let go of the virus. It flew at her rapidly, but she parried it when it came near. It flew back toward Neil like a boomerang. She lowered her arms and glared at Neil with a surprised look on her face as he caught the virus code.

Neil pursed his lips and nodded slowly. "Guess not."

"You are fast. I am impressed."

"So are you." Neil put the virus code in his left hand back into its place in his command list. "So who... who the hell are..." He cocked his head to the side and squinted. "You look... have we met?"

"No, we have not."

"I think..." And then it struck him. It wasn't a similarity; it was the same girl. Same face, same odd smile, same hairstyle. There was an odd depth in her eyes that he hadn't noticed before, but there was no doubt in his mind as to who this woman was. He wasn't quite sure why he still remembered her so vividly, but for some reason he just couldn't shake her out of his mind completely. The sound of a man calling out her name reverberated in his head. "Lisa?"

She nodded. "I am known by that name to some."

"But... how? I saw that guy kill you."

"I see. You are referring to Lisa Anderton."

"Right. You."

"No, Neil. Not me. You saw Lisa Anderton."

"Then who are you?"

"I am AISA. Artificially Intelligent Systems Array. But I am usually just called Lisa, due to the resemblance to my creator. I need your help, Neil."

Neil's hand hovered over the execution key as he considered the woman in front of him. He had seen what she did upstairs to the security programs and personnel. And yet he had been able to move and react just as fast as she did, if not faster. Unless she was holding back, which he concluded was possible considering that she wanted to talk to him. *She needs my help? With what?* he thought. He looked her up and down as she waited expectantly.

"I do not have much time, Neil. I am being called. I must respond soon."

He opened his mouth to ask what help she needed, and then she was gone. The room around Neil dissolved quickly, tossing and turning in every direction almost simultaneously. Vibrant colors exploded in his field of vision, blurring the room around him in flashes of bright pastels. He felt a soft, warm hand on his forehead as someone pulled the data cable out of his head. The person above him was an unrecognizable swirling mess of flesh and hair. The world lurched again and he felt himself falling, floating downward as the room spun. His inert body struck the linoleum hard.

CHAPTER
30

R oger Anderton paced in front of the plasma screen in his office, idly biting on his fingernails. He had run out of scotch hours ago, and had sent several of his subordinates off in search of additional liquor. He was getting disturbingly close to being completely sober, a state he was sincerely hoping to avoid. He stopped in front of the screen and called out Junji's name again. The screen sprang to life, displaying a crystal clear image of Junji's worried expression.

"Where *is* she? This is taking too long."

Junji gulped audibly and glanced around. "She's almost here, sir. I'm not sure what took so long."

"She's starting to get defiant."

"I can alter that, sir."

"Then why haven't you?"

"Sir..." the man stammered. "Sir, she's here."

The image cleared and was replaced with the image of Lisa's face. Roger smiled involuntarily, caught himself, and forced his face to display a neutral expression. The girl's face looked like his daughter's, but he always had to remind himself that she wasn't. His daughter was warm, compassionate. This thing was cold and heartless. The woman's face looked at him, waiting.

"Lisa."

"Yes, Mister Anderton?"

"I hear you've been a bit naughty. What were you doing in the Interpol mainframe?"

"Gathering information."

"And at Goliath?"

"Gathering information."

"Under what orders?"

"My own. In full compliance with directive one."

Roger folded his arms in front of his chest and studied the plain expression on Lisa's face. "Who's this Neil Roberts character?" She gave no response. "Those Interpol inspectors who are chasing him called me earlier. They think he's somehow involved with the plot to kill my daughter."

"He was not."

"You're sure?"

"Yes, I am."

"Then why the interest in him?"

"He is a programmer. His credits include single-handedly writing over three hundred industry standard programs." Lisa turned her head to the left and scrolled a list of the programs up the edge of the screen with a wave of her hand. Anderton's eyes opened wide as he absorbed the list as best as he could. When the list had finished displaying, a picture of Neil's face appeared in the upper left corner of the screen and a short list of some of his vital statistics appeared below it. "He might be compatible for the completion of the project."

"Very interesting." Anderton paused a moment and studied the goofy grin on Neil's face. The statistics listed below his picture were useless fluff and gave Anderton no insight into his personality or motivations. "Do you think he would do it?"

"It would be logical to assume that he would, with proper motivation. He is, after all, a programmer. He might view it as a challenge."

"All right then, how do we find him?"

"I was talking with him when you summoned me."

Anderton frowned and scratched the stubble on his chin. "Where were you, anyway? It took a while to contact you."

"Bern."

"Bern? Where?"

"I was in the Swiss National Bank."

"Well, I guess that explains the alarms we registered in Western Europe."

"Neil was there, in the safe storage area."

"What was he doing there?"

"Stealing a data file." She moved her lips into her best approximation of a mischievous grin. She raised a hand to write something on the bottom of the screen.

Floor-SB37 / Section-R / Aisle-6 / Box-12
Arthur M. Brody

Roger stared wide-eyed at the text. "Brody!"

"Yes. Neil has the file now."

"Lisa..." Roger shook his head slowly from side to side. "What the hell are you up to?"

CHAPTER
31

LONDON, ENGLAND
JULY 22, 2030 12:43 AM BST

The cab from the airport dropped Johnson and Ferez off at the address they had been given, a small office building wedged into a commercial district that had a considerable amount of activity given the time of night. They walked into the front door and flashed their Interpol badges to a guard inside. The guard directed them down the hall.

"I'm Tom. Tom Patterson." Tom held his hand out toward Ferez, who grasped it after shifting his carry-on bag to his other shoulder. Tom was a short man, clean-shaven, crew cut and a firm handshake. He was a man with military training and discipline, now working in the private sector as an operative for Interpol's London office.

"Juan Ferez. This is my partner, Bill Johnson. You guys still dealing with that emergency?"

"Yeah, we got a few guys busy tracking it down."

"What was it?"

"Some group of people broke into the Swiss National Bank at the Bern node, disabled a lot of security programs and killed a few real life guards in the process. We're pretty sure they stole something from the long-term storage area. It's a huge mess. I got people from all over the world calling here asking when this will be resolved. Diplomats, Swiss bankers, UN personnel... bank is locked down tight until we can get a grip on this. I got people screaming vulgarities at me in six different languages. Big, *huge* mess."

"Damn. Any lock on who it was?"

"Not yet. Like I said mate, we're running a trace. Got traces running on two of the suspects right now. One was some guy, looks like he might be here in England somewhere. He jacked out in the subbasement, so he left enough of a trace that we should be able to follow."

"The other?"

Tom exhaled sharply and wiped some sweat from his brow. He looked as if he hadn't slept much in the past two days. "Never seen anything like her."

Johnson's face turned ashen. "Heh... her?"

"Yeah. We got a report from one guard. Said she swooped in like a bat outta Hell, walked right in the front door, and tore through top-of-the-line military hardware left and right. They said she didn't even use programs. No viruses, no worms, nothing. She just kinda reached inside them and muddled around. Doesn't sound possible, but we have to check out all the leads."

"Actually," Johnson said, "it sounds very possible."

Ferez put a hand on Johnson's trembling shoulder. "My partner was attacked by someone that sounds similar. She uh... well, she hacked the Interpol mainframe search tool, walked right through the security, and broke the latest release of Fetter in less than a second."

"Shit. Who the hell is she?"

"Don't know. But she's dangerous. Deadly, actually."

Tom nodded. "All right. I'll let my guys know to steer clear of her if they see her. Part of me thinks she might be the one that broke into Goliath earlier tonight too."

"Goliath?" Ferez asked.

"They're the ones that make all the software we use for tracing and protection," Johnson said. "Someone broke in there?"

"Right," Tom added. "And yes, someone broke in. They have no idea how she got in, but they know she got into the mainframe. Description fits the girl who hit the bank to a T. She tore through over a dozen security robots in less than half a second, then just vanished.

"But hey, you guys look tired. We got some beds in the back. It isn't much, but you look about ready to drop where you stand."

"Yeah, thanks."

Tom led them around the corner and down a short hallway. He opened a wooden door and motioned the two inspectors inside. The room was larger than they expected. There were thirty beds in this room, fifteen lined against each wall like a military barracks. Three men were playing cards on one of the beds near the opposite end of the room.

"Bathroom's at the end of the hall," Tom said, pointing toward a door set in the opposite wall. The light was on in the bathroom, plain white walls, bleached white tiles that looked clean enough to eat off of.

"Thanks Tom." Ferez offered his hand while Johnson flopped down on one of the beds. "We'll see you in the morning?"

"Right. Maybe we'll have the bank robbery under control by then and can start looking into your case."

"Sounds good."

Tom closed the door behind himself as he left. Ferez sat on the edge of the bed closest to Johnson, who was already snoring softly. He emptied his pockets onto the small table between the beds and laid back. He shifted around on the bed in a vain attempt to find a less lumpy spot, then gave up and stared at the ceiling for a while. After tossing and turning for twenty minutes, he sat up and reached for his cell phone. He scrolled down the list of stored phone numbers, chose the one marked 'Home', and pressed the button to dial.

CHAPTER
32

Neil felt himself slip back into consciousness, but there was a part of him that refused to open his eyes. He knew the room was still spinning, it had to be. That was the only way to explain the churning in his stomach. He rolled to his side with the hope that his stomach would calm down. He tried counting to twenty, but that only made the little blue window with the current time slide into view. After a few seconds of watching that, he decided to open his eyes. Trixie was sitting on the edge of the bed, watching him with a worried expression on her face. When she noticed that his eyes had opened, she smiled and looked relieved. She helped Neil into a sitting position.

"What the hell happened?"

"Slave jacked you out."

"I wasn't ready."

"I know." She put her arm around him. "I know, but he saw a trace coming in. I don't think he got you out in time, actually."

Neil cleared his throat and rubbed at his eyes with the backs of his hands. "What happens now?"

"When you're ready, I guess we'll have to get that data file out of your head so we can sell it."

"No, I mean about the trace."

"Who knows?" Trixie said. "We've been fine so far. Been here and doing this stuff for years. Nobody's found us yet."

Neil nodded and turned to look at the clock. "What day is it? How long was I out?"

"Only a few hours." She squeezed her arm around him. "Look, why don't you get some more sleep. You probably need it."

"I'm not tired."

"Hon, your eyes are all bloodshot and you're blinking too much. You're *over*-tired."

"Maybe you're right." He turned his torso toward her, wrapped his arms around her, and pulled her on top of him as he fell backward into the bed.

*   *   *

Evan paced back and forth in front of Powerslave, who was typing away rapidly while staring at the monitor in front of him. He stepped over the fresh bloodstain marking Neil's point of impact and took a few more steps before stopping. He turned to face Powerslave. "Well?"

"Well," Powerslave said. He pressed a few more keys and leaned back in his chair. "I have bad news and... well... more bad news. And some bad news on top of that."

Evan sighed. "Give me the bad news."

"Which one?"

"Does it matter?"

"Well, bad news part one is that the girl Neil was fighting with in there wasn't a girl at all. See, I looked up what she called herself and found a match. In the news, of all places. Who'd ever thought I'd find something useful there, right? Go figure. Anyway, she called herself Lisa, right? Or A-I-S-A, Artificially Intelligent something something. I forget. I'll look it up."

"Forget it, go on."

"Right." Powerslave cleared his throat. "Anyway, she's not a girl, she's a computer. Well, software really. Cool stuff. Widely claimed to be the world's first thinking computer, a real bona fide artificial intelligence. Not a Net menu script or chat bot, she actually thinks on her own and reasons like people do. Really cool shit. Only thing is that she's a prototype, and she's not supposed to be out surfing the Net."

"So who the hell's responsible for her?"

"Anderton Enterprises."

"Bollocks."

"Yeah, which leads us to the next bad news. Arthur Brody apparently works for a company called Logical Systems. They're a subsidiary of Anderton Enterprises. They're the company that designed and programmed that thing. It's quite possible that she went after Neil because of the information that Brody wanted us to steal."

"Bollocks," Evan repeated. He took a deep breath, then looked at Powerslave with exasperated shock written all over his face. "And why the hell didn't we find this out *before* we agreed to take the job?"

Powerslave shrugged. "Brody's file was locked. Took me an hour to get into it."

"Again, why didn't you do that *before*?"

"Shit, Evan, guy comes in offering that kind of cash..." he said, shaking his head. "None of us wanted to question it! That's why he came to us - no questions."

Evan tensed, then relaxed and nodded. "You're right. Okay, well what's the third bad news?"

"By my very rough calculations, I'm pretty sure that Neil was in there long enough for them to get a trace on us. And forcefully jacking him out didn't help either, because as you know, that leaves a residue that they can trace if they're very good. Kinda like deleting files. They're never really gone unless you wipe the drive."

"They usually aren't that good though."

"No, but if that Lisa chick thing helps them, well... from what I saw, she could probably do anything in the Net that she wanted to."

"Dammit. Dammit! We'll need to evacuate the base then. Any more bad news?"

Powerslave frowned and raised an aluminum can to his lips. He went to take a sip, then pulled the can away and looked inside it. "I think we're out of Dr. Pepper."

*   *   *

Trixie pushed herself up from Neil and sat on his legs. He looked up at her and grinned. She brushed her hands through her hair, then reached down and lifted her shirt off. Neil ran his hands up her stomach, then around to her back. When she had finished getting her shirt over her head, he pulled her down to him and pressed his lips to hers.

"Attention!" echoed Evan's voice throughout the building. "Attention please. Everyone wake up, this is important."

"What was that?" Neil asked.

Trixie turned her head to the side and motioned toward the corner of the room. "Loudspeaker. Evan uses it for emergencies."

"Never saw it before."

"I know, it's well hidden and he rarely uses it. Must be something important."

The speaker in the corner crackled and then Evan's voice came over it again. "I have an important announcement to make, so hopefully everyone is awake now. We are almost completely positive that our recent excursion to Switzerland was traced back to here. As such, we will be taking our normal precautionary measures to ensure everyone's safety. It is unknown at this time whether or not we will be able to return to this base. In light of that, please take only what you need and do not take more than you can carry. Lowlight and Slave will be driving the vans to our secondary base in exactly one hour. If you are not in those vans, you will not be coming with us. That is all."

Neil glanced over at the clock on the dresser. It read 3:53 AM. "Well, we have an hour."

Trixie looked in his eyes and kissed him. "That should be enough time. I haven't unpacked yet. All my important stuff is still in my bag."

Neil smiled and placed his hand on her cheek. "All my important stuff... is you."

CHAPTER
33

OXFORD, ENGLAND
JULY 22, 2030 3:41 AM BST

I s this a secure channel?"

"Yes sir. Ten kilobit encryption."

"Good." Anderton stared at the little Asian man on his plasma screen. He waited until the pause entered that extremely awkward area that always prompted Junji to break out into a sweat. It was one of the few delights he had left in his life. "What have you found out?"

"I was able to trace the signature of Neil Roberts to a warehouse in the vicinity of Windsor. According to the bank, he was posing as Arthur Brody, which is of course not possible."

"But we're sure he's the one that took the file? The one that Lisa was talking with?"

"Yes, sir. I have confirmed that from the bank's security records. They recorded the two of them but were not able to record what they had said. Lisa must have either used an encrypted communication channel or she went back and erased that conversation from their records."

"What about this warehouse? Is there a connection there that we can break into?"

"They severed whatever connection they had."

"Dammit. They're probably leaving right now."

"Sir," Junji said while glancing around nervously. "With your permission, I have already contacted Major Hallis on your behalf. They are standing by, ready to retrieve."

Anderton studied the man's face intently, reveling in the site of his nervousness. He stared stone-faced at the plasma screen and silently counted to twenty. Junji broke into a sweat and gulped pathetically. Anderton smiled. "Good work, Junji. Patch me through to him."

Junji sighed in relief. "Yes, sir. Right away, sir."

The screen went blank, except for the little gold padlock symbol in the bottom right that indicated a secure connection. Anderton tapped his foot on the floor while he waited. The screen sprang to life to show a confident man in his late thirties staring straight into the monitor. He was dressed in full urban camouflage, and wore a black beret on his brow. Behind him, two dozen seasoned soldiers stood at attention. They were already dressed in bulletproof vests and camouflaged pants.

"Sir! Major Hallis reporting for duty, sir!"

"Has Junji informed you of the purpose of this mission?"

"We have been given a picture of the target and a location for the compound, sir." Hallis tapped the screen on his side of the connection and Anderton's screen beeped. An image of Neil's face appeared inset in the upper left side of the screen. Below his face, a satellite view of a warehouse and a detailed map of its location faded into view. "Our choppers are fueled and we are ready for immediate deployment, sir."

Anderton nodded. "That's him. He is to be taken *alive*. Is that understood? Under no circumstances is any harm whatsoever to come to that man. He is very important to me."

"And the others, sir?"

Anderton shook his head.

"Understood."

CHAPTER
34

WINDSOR, ENGLAND
JULY 22, 2030 3:58 AM BST

L isten up ladies!" Major Hallis called out over the sound of the air rushing past the helicopter. "We're going in silent. We get to test out Anderton's new stealth copter. So don't screw it up. Put on your silencers now." Each man started attaching silencers to their submachine guns in unison. "You've seen the picture of this Neil Roberts guy. It's stored in your helmet displays along with blueprints for the building we're going into. He's our primary target, and is to be taken alive at *all* costs. Once he is in our custody, you are authorized to go loud and proud on these dirtbags, so feel free to let the frags and bullets fly. You got that?"

The soldiers straightened their backs and shouted, "We get you, sir!"

The helicopter screamed along parallel to the ground just barely above the treetops. Hallis watched the breeze from the helicopter shake the trees as he waited patiently for the pilot to signal that he had visual sight of the target building. A few minutes later, he started seeing buildings beyond the trees, and the pilot's voice piped into his helmet informing him that the target was in sight.

Hallis gave a signal to the soldiers, who immediately nodded and flipped their helmet displays into night vision mode. The helicopter slowed down outside of a building, its rotors slowing their rotation to the point of generating nothing more than a gentle breeze. It lowered toward the ground. The soldiers jumped from the helicopter in pairs and hit the ground running. Two teams split off to the sides to flank the building. Hallis followed the last pair of soldiers straight into the open garage door. Sanderson and Tanner were veterans, men that Hallis knew he could trust in any situation. He tapped each soldier in turn and pointed toward a side of the entrance.

"Tango down," came a voice over the radio link. It sounded like someone from Beta team, the recruit's shaky voice echoing his inexperience.

Hallis leaned against the edge of a van and peered around the corner in time to see the mostly suppressed flare of gunfire. A man standing near another van clutched his chest and collapsed to the concrete. He could see another figure in the distance raise its gun and open fire on the position where Sanderson was hiding. The loud crack of what sounded like a shotgun echoed around the garage. Hallis raised his weapon and aimed at the figure's chest. The man turned and ducked behind a barrel as if he could see him and opened fire toward Hallis. His shot missed by a narrow margin, blowing out the windshield of the van.

"Shit," Tanner said over the comlink. "I think this bastard can actually *see* us."

"Distract him," ordered Hallis from behind the van.

"Copy that." Tanner moved around to flank the man and opened fire, bullets ricocheting off the barrel. The man turned to honor the new threat and fired off a shell from his shotgun. "I'm hit!" Tanner yelped.

Hallis raised his weapon, aimed, and squeezed off a few rounds. The figure turned its head and saw Hallis as it fell backward. The figure's gun fired again, the sound of shot ricocheting off the ceiling. Hallis crouched down and waited. He heard some more gunfire, then heard someone cry out and fall to the ground.

"Report."

He heard some shuffling to his left, where Tanner should have been. "Tango down," came Tanner's voice over the comlink. "I'm hit in the leg, sir, not too serious but hurts like hell." There was a slight pause, then he added, "Area secure."

"Sanderson?"

There was no response. He saw Tanner limp over to the other side of the garage. He watched as Tanner crouched down out of sight. "Man down!"

"Breathing?"

"Yes, sir. Weak pulse, but he might be okay."

"Drag him to the LZ. Alpha team, report."

There was a crackle over the radio link in his ear. "We're inside. No sign of target yet. Chalk up four more tangos."

"Beta team, report."

The radio link crackled again, then the sound of someone swearing under his breath came over the link. "We're pinned down, sir. They got a sniper or two somewhere on the south side of the building. We have one man down and four wounded. Bastard hit Thompson in the neck and Vasquez in the arm with the same shot."

"Copy that. Try to pinpoint the tango and get back to me."

Tanner came back into the garage and leaned against the van next to Hallis. He set his gun on the hood and reached into a pocket on his vest. After rooting around for a moment, he extracted a small pink tablet. He lifted his helmet and popped the tablet into his mouth. *Oral morphine,* Hallis thought, *must hurt more than he said.* He shrugged off the thought and re-minded himself that Tanner was just doing what every good soldier was trained to do.

"Orders, sir?" Tanner asked after retrieving his gun.

"Wire these vans, I'll cover the door."

"Roger."

Tanner pulled explosives from his backpack and started attaching them to one of the vans. Hallis leaned around the front of the van and aimed his weapon at the door, finger poised over the trigger. Shortly after Tanner finished wiring the first van, the radio crackled to life. "Target acquired. We'll be clear of the building in ten seconds."

"Roger. Go loud and proud, boys. Let's show these bastards who they're dealing with."

"You say the nicest things, Major," came the voice of the Beta team leader. "See, I got me one of them RPGs with that sniper's name on it. Brace for impact in five, four, three, two..." There was a short pause, then a high-pitched whistle broke the silence of the night. The explosion shook the ground and made the building shudder. "Booyah! Tango is definitely *down*!"

"Copy that. Alpha team, extract target to LZ. Beta team, open and clear."

The door that Hallis was covering swung open and a slim mid-twenties man stumbled out, hand clutched to a gaping wound in his chest. Hallis squeezed his trigger, pumping a dozen rounds into the man. The man shook and slammed against the wall, sliding down it until he was sitting on the floor. Hallis returned his aim to the now open doorway. He could see flickering orange light from a fire inside, but no other movement.

"Frag out!" someone shouted over the com channel. There was a short pause, then the sound of an explosion off in the distance. Large pieces of metal shrapnel flew past the open doorway.

"Charges planted," Tanner said.

"Good, let's get to the LZ and blow this joint. Steer clear of the garage, boys."

"Roger, sir. Heartbeat sensors negative. Beta team's on the move to LZ."

Hallis and Tanner turned and ran toward their landing zone, taking turns covering their rear as they made their way to the clearing. On the way, Tanner flipped open his remote control and pressed the button. Both vans exploded simultaneously, taking out most of the garage in the process. The light from the explosion lit the surrounding area bright as daylight for a brief moment before the night's darkness returned.

Alpha team was already in the clearing, with a figure bound and gagged beside them. Hallis leaned his head to the side and lifted the figure's chin up, studying the face intently. The HUD in his helmet scanned the facial features and confirmed a positive match on the man. Neil was out cold and covered from the waist up in blood. Hallis gulped and silently wondered how he was going to explain this one to Anderton.

One of the soldiers saw the worried expression on Hallis' face and spoke up. "He's not hurt, sir. It's not his blood."

CHAPTER
35

Ferez was already awake when Johnson opened his eyes. Tom was sitting on the bed with Ferez, holding a quiet but animated discussion. He said something that made Ferez frown and nod in a manner that indicated his reluctant agreement. When they noticed that Johnson had awakened, they turned to face him.

"They traced that bank robber guy to a warehouse outside of Windsor," Ferez started. "It might be Neil. Hard to know for sure since his identity was masked. We'll leave whenever you're ready."

Johnson nodded and sat up. He stretched his arms and felt something in his shoulder pop. He could still feel a tingling sensation in his chest, but the pain had subsided completely. He concentrated on breathing for almost a minute before attempting to stand up. The room wasn't spinning anymore, which was a good sign. He took another deep breath and nodded. "I'm fine. Let's go."

The three of them left the room and went down the hallway. Tom led them past several closed doors to a large garage where several officers waited next to a van. "These chaps are going in with you, just in case."

"Good, thanks Tom," Ferez said while shaking Tom's hand. Johnson repeated the gesture, and then they both climbed into the van together. The officers mostly ignored Johnson and Ferez, nodding politely but neglecting to introduce themselves. They all boarded the van, the engine sputtered to life and the van pulled out into the street.

Johnson leaned his head against the wall while Ferez fiddled with his cell phone. The van trudged along a bumpy road for almost an hour. Johnson's head kept bobbing with the rhythm of the road, bouncing off the side of the van where he was trying to rest it. Ferez didn't say anything. He just kept fiddling with his cell phone and looking worried. A few of the officers in the van chatted about various topics - new girlfriends, old girlfriends, random TV shows, and what movies were coming out soon. They seemed like complacent teenagers, not like heavily armed and highly trained police officers. Johnson leaned his head forward to avoid the rocking motion and tried to block out what the officers were saying. Just as he was starting to successfully ignore them, the van took a sharp turn and screeched to a halt, kicking up huge dust clouds in the process.

"Holy shit!" the driver announced. "Guys, get out. You gotta see this."

Ferez tried to look out the front window, but couldn't see anything through the dust clouds. The rear doors of the van opened and everyone filed out. Then he saw the building. It was in the middle of a large field in the dead center of nowhere. Half of the southern side was crumbled inward, a large patch of concrete smeared with red. The area that the dirt road led to had also collapsed. Stacks of smoke billowed out of various holes in the building, twisted beams of steel reaching toward the sky through a mountain of rubble.

"Is this the place? What the hell happened?" Johnson wondered out loud. He took a few tentative steps toward the building.

One of the officers stepped in front of Johnson and glanced down at a paper in his hand. The back of his vest said his name was Gerard. "Yeah, it's the place," he announced while putting the paper away. "Let's go in and check it out. Rogers, Young, circle around the back and see what you can find."

They entered the building through the front door that was beside the garage rubble. The door was locked, but didn't pose much trouble for the officer that breached the door with his shotgun. Once inside, they fanned out to cover all possible exits from the entranceway. Ferez stepped up to a body on the floor and looked him over. One of the officers found another corpse in a side room. He pulled out a small rolled up plastic screen and proceeded to press one of the corpse's index fingers to it. The screen dimmed for a moment and then emitted a soft beeping sound. The officer moved over to the corpse Ferez was inspecting and repeated the scan.

They moved in deeper. Several hallways were caved in and inaccessible. The deeper they went into the building, the more bodies they found. Ferez stepped into a side room to see what looked like an overturned dentist's chair. There were four bodies laying behind it in various contortions, and a large scorch mark on the wall behind them. He covered his nose with one of his hands to avert the stench of burnt flesh.

Johnson called out to him from another room down the hall. He jogged down the hall and stepped into the room, where he saw Johnson standing there with a sad look on his face. He followed Johnson's gaze to the floor where a beautiful auburn-haired girl lay in a pool of blood, nude except for her white underwear, mostly stained dark crimson. She had several bullet holes in her chest and abdomen, her arms bent at unnatural angles beneath her back, and her pale face showing an unsettling combination of fear and desperation. Her eyes were still open, but the sparkle they once had was long gone.

"Karen Tyler. Trixie, I think the nickname was." Johnson blurted out while staring at her body. He gagged and turned away from the corpse. "I recognize her from the mug shot in Cuba."

"Wasn't she..."

"Yeah, she was the one that got Neil out of Cuba."

"So where's Neil then?"

Johnson shook his head slowly. "Not here. Maybe another room?"

Ferez pulled Johnson from the room and walked down the hall with him. They followed the sound of discussion down the hallway and stopped next to Gerard. "Any idea who did this?" he asked.

Gerard turned to face him and shrugged. "Don't know really. But it looks professional. Maybe it was another crime family or something."

"Sir? We found this." Another officer had come up behind them. He was holding up a thin camouflage jacket that was stained with dried blood around a hole in the left arm. "Looks like they left this behind. Arm patch says UN Peacekeepers, Special Forces."

Ferez frowned. "Special Forces? UN Peacekeepers? For a bunch of hackers?"

"Yeah," Johnson added. "What the hell is going on?"

"ID scans complete, sir," said the officer with the plastic screen. Gerard took it, glanced at the screen, and handed it to Ferez.

Ferez scanned the list of names on the screen. The list ended with five entries marked "unknown" that had little rotating graphics beside them.

The officer holding the jacket let it fall at the sound of the radio on his belt clip beeping. He grabbed the radio and pressed in the talk button. "Stewart here."

"This is Patterson. Pull out. Repeat, pull out. I just got a call in here and verified it. That base is a military operation. The United Nations issued a press release stating that they cleared out a cyber-terrorist cell there earlier this morning. You are all ordered to cease and desist, effective immediately."

"But..." Ferez started.

"They already have a cleanup team en route. Anything you do there is tampering with evidence at this point. Just drop everything and get back here. Understood?"

"Understood," Ferez conceded.

The officer holding the radio looked at Ferez, shrugged, and pressed in the talk button. "Roger that, clearing out." He switched his radio to another frequency and pressed the talk button. "Bug out, we're done here."

They all filed out of the building and started getting into the van. Ferez hung back with a curious expression on his face. He stared at the plastic screen and watched two more names resolve. Still no sign of Neil Roberts on the list. Three unknowns left.

Johnson paused just before stepping into the van. "What is it?" he said.

Ferez shuffled his feet. "I should probably call Anderton and let him know about this. If Neil is anywhere, he's inside that building. Somewhere. Maybe Anderton has enough pull to get people to double check for his body."

"Okay, get in and call then."

"I don't think this is a conversation that you guys really want to hear. I'll need some quiet anyway."

One of the officers in the back of the van leaned out and pointed up the road. "Up the road there 'bout half a kilometer or so is a pub. You can walk it and meet us there. Anyone else up for a beer?" The other officers perked up. A few of them cheered.

"All right, sounds good." Ferez kicked idly at a small rock in front of him as the door closed and the vehicle pulled away. He pulled out his cell phone when the sound of the van had receded, dialed the number for Anderton's main office, and started walking toward where the officer had said the pub was.

"Anderton Enterprises, how may I help you?"

"I'd like to speak with Roger Anderton, please."

"And you are?"

"This is Inspector Juan Ferez with Interpol."

"One moment please."

There was an extremely long pause. Ferez plodded along the edge of the road. He reached up with his free hand and wiped a line of sweat from his brow. He tried to force the image of that girl from his mind, tried to force himself to think about his family back home instead. But he just couldn't shake that image. The road bent to circumvent a huge oak tree, then stretched off to the horizon. There was a clicking sound from the phone.

"Anderton here."

"Mister Anderton, this is Inspector Ferez."

"Yes, good morning."

"We followed the trail of Neil Roberts, but there was a problem."

"A problem? What problem?"

Ferez took a deep breath before continuing. "It appears that some time last night a UN Peacekeeping force invaded the building we were investigating."

"I remember seeing something on the news about that."

"It was the same building that we had tracked Roberts to. Everyone was dead, as far as we could tell."

The plastic screen beeped softly. Ferez glanced at the screen. The final three names were resolved. As he tried to read the list, it reorganized itself alphabetically. He scanned the list from top to bottom - miniature face images, names and known aliases listed side by side. He checked it twice.

"Well," Anderton said, "any idea where he is?"

Ferez stopped walking. *Is?* he thought. *Present tense?* "Pardon?" he said into the phone, speaking slowly and choosing his words carefully. "I said that everyone was dead there. How'd you know he was missing?"

"I... well, that is... I assumed from the tone of your voice that you... uh, hadn't found him. Well, if everyone is dead in there then his identity will be confirmed later today."

Ferez looked at the list of names on his screen. *Way ahead of you*, he thought. "I suppose so, sir."

Anderton cleared his throat. "Well then, Inspector Ferez, if it's in the UN's hands now then I guess your work here is done. You can't really question the dead, after all. If Roberts was involved in my daughter's murder, then... well, I guess justice was carried out after all."

"I'm going to stick around until Roberts' body is found, sir," Ferez said.

"Nobody is stopping you from that, Inspector Ferez. Well, perhaps with the notable exception of your family, who are all waiting patiently for you to get back home." There was a pause where neither spoke for several seconds. Anderton cleared his throat and continued. "In the meantime, I have other matters to attend to. So I bid you good morning."

The connection was cut off. Ferez returned the phone to his pocket and started walking toward the pub again. He mentally replayed the conversation over and over in his head. That one slip still bothered him. And the reference to his family, was that a subtle threat? He had been an inspector long enough to know when the equation of a case didn't add up. Was it really worth it to stick around for someone to find Roberts? Neil was either dead in the building somewhere the officer hadn't found, in which case he would have wasted his time waiting. Or Neil was missing and the only lead he had was a questionable slip of Roger Anderton's tongue. But to cast any doubt on a person at Roger Anderton's level without irrefutable proof of wrongdoing was almost certain social suicide. He continued walking and debating.

The road took another turn and then he saw the outskirts of a town up ahead. The place looked lively enough for a small town. Cars driving around, pedestrians waving happily to each other as they carried out their business. He could see the police van parked outside of a small building that had a weathered wooden sign with a large, frothing beer mug etched into it. Ferez increased his pace.

When he got to the door, he paused to collect his breath. He opened the door and stepped inside. All of the officers and Johnson were seated in one corner of the pub, mugs in their hands and pitchers of beer on the table. Two of them were eating lunch. The rest were discussing something that had Johnson's face beet red with laughter. Ferez stepped up to the table and sat down. Before he could even say anything, someone pushed a mug of beer across the table to him. He smiled, raised the glass in salute, and brought it up to his lips. The beer was ice cold and very smooth. He felt his muscles start to relax instantly. He lowered the mug back to the table and leaned back in his chair. He started to replay the conversation with Anderton again, then forced it from his mind and instead replayed the conversation with his family from the previous night.

"So, what's next?" Johnson said, looking at Ferez expectantly.

Ferez looked him in the face, then turned his gaze back to his beer. He returned his thoughts to the phone call to his family. He smiled at the memory of the sweet voice of his wife asking him a thousand questions intended to find out if he was all right without directly asking him. Next, he heard the sound of his daughter's wispy voice pleading for him to come home. There was no doubt in his mind, no trace of worry. This case had evolved past him and was no longer any concern of his. Neil Roberts would be found, eventually, by someone. He had been away from home for much longer than he wanted.

"Home, I guess," Ferez said, then raised his mug for a sip. "I'm going home. The UN took over the case, and Anderton didn't sound too concerned. So I'm going home."

Johnson smiled widely and raised his mug. "I'll drink to that."

CHAPTER
36

N eil had been awake for several hours. He'd spent the first few minutes trying to figure out where he was. It was a small room, just barely big enough for a cot against one wall and a toilet against another. It seemed like a cell, but with smooth white walls and a single door. There were no bars or windows. There was an air conditioning vent in the ceiling, but it was far too small for him to fit through. That meant that there was only one way out, and he doubted that he would be allowed to use it, so he didn't even bother trying to see if it was locked.

After examining the room, he glanced at himself and his blood-soaked shirt. He spent the next few minutes inspecting his body to find out where he had been cut or shot. When he confirmed that he had not been harmed at all, the memory of Trixie's face came back to him, pummeling him with an emotional force that sucked the air right out of his lungs. The look of joy quickly morphing into horror on her face, the shock evident in her eyes, the sound of bullets ripping through her chest followed by the warm blood flowing over both of them. A hand gripped her forearm and pulled her off of him, the sound of her striking the floor coinciding with a loud explosion in the distance somewhere. Someone had loomed over him and brought something heavy down hard. That was the last thing he remembered. They had heard some shouting, but hadn't thought anything of it. They had assumed that it was just the other people shouting orders to get ready to leave. He thought he heard a gunshot, but Trixie just rolled her eyes. *Damn van backfiring again*, she had said. He had ignored his instinct that something was wrong, and had instead focused all his attention on Trixie.

The vision of her death replaced the visions of Lisa's death in his mind's eye and in his dreams. Every time he closed his eyes, all he could see was her dying again, in slow motion and with vivid gut-wrenching clarity. He cried, big heaping sobs that wracked his body and left him breathless, choking for air after each contraction shook his body. He tried to tell himself *be strong, be strong.* But still the tears came streaming down his face. He tried to force visions of made-up dreams to occupy his mind, but all he could summon were visions of himself at her funeral. A funeral she would probably never get. And him, there, trying to give a fitting eulogy for his dead lover. He'd open his mouth to speak but could summon no words. He stood there wavering, finally bursting into tears in front of the uneasy congregation he had hallucinated. He had known her for less than a week, but it felt like a lifetime.

After crying in the corner for hours, the door opened and two guards with submachine guns slung over their shoulders stepped into the room. One of them asked him to get up. Neil put his hands on the walls to help himself stand. The other guard raised one hand to his ear. "He's awake. Yes. Right away, sir." He turned and nodded to the other.

The other guard tossed a towel to Neil. They watched as Neil peeled the blood-soaked shirt off and wiped residual blood off his chest. Most of it had dried on his skin hours earlier, and some chunks flaked and fell to the floor as he brushed himself with the towel. When he had finished, the guard threw a folded T-shirt at Neil. "Here, put this on. All right, put your hands on your head and leave them there."

"Where are you taking me?" Neil asked as he placed both hands, palms down, on top of his head. He glanced at their guns and thought again of Trixie, her body tensing as the bullets ripped her apart. *Are these the same guys who killed her?* The guards weren't aiming their weapons at him. Something in their demeanors suggested they wouldn't hesitate to shoot him if he gave them a good enough reason. Part of him pondered finding a reason so he could join Trixie in whatever afterlife awaited him. The sweet revenge of denying his captors whatever it was they wanted of him was a bonus.

"Roger Anderton wishes to speak with you."

Neil stepped forward, between the two men, and out into a hallway that was only slightly more decorated than his cell room was. One of the guards told him to head to the left. They guided him down the long hallway to an open elevator at the end. Once inside the elevator, one guard watched Neil while the other turned a key and pressed the button for the basement. The door closed and the elevator started moving down. At the bottom, the guards guided him out into a large area that resembled a subway station. There were about three dozen people down here, milling about and discussing random topics that they couldn't overhear from where they were. Neil's hopes for a dramatic rescue were dashed when he saw several of the people glance in his direction with nothing more than casual interest. Nobody looked worried, nobody appeared curious, nobody seemed to care. This was routine.

The guards guided him to a smaller train track away from the rest of the people where a private six-seat train car was waiting. They led him inside and had him sit near the front, far away from the exit of the car. The guards both sat down and lay their guns in their laps, the muzzles pointed toward Neil with their forefingers casually lying on the triggers. The car accelerated smoothly, racing through a nondescript passageway.

Neil sniffled and tried to focus his attention on the moment. *Why am I here?* The thought struck him hard and left him more than a little confused. The guard had said Roger Anderton wanted to speak with him. *What the hell could he want with me?* He tried to think of what he'd done in the past few days. The bar, the running, a boat ride to Cuba. He thought of Trixie again, and pictured his short time with her and the rest of her friends. He did two quick jobs with Powerslave, then retrieved that file in the bank. Then it hit him.

But how? he had said. *I saw that guy kill you.*

I see, she had said. *You are referring to Lisa Anderton.*

The woman in the bar, the one he had seen murdered, was the daughter of one of the most powerful men on the planet. He had been there when Lisa was killed; he had watched her murder and had been running ever since. *Anderton must think I did it.* He took a deep breath and let it out with a sigh. That was the only thing that made sense. He was here to pay for a murder he didn't commit. But how could he say that? What could he possibly say to Anderton about it? *I didn't kill your daughter.* It sounded somehow wrong. Insensitive? Or maybe it was just cliché - something that the killer would say to try to throw the blame elsewhere. The words were simple, but how was he supposed to deliver them? How was he even supposed to address someone of Roger Anderton's social status? It was almost like being summoned by royalty.

The train car started decelerating as he pondered the question again and again. When the train car had come to a stop, one of the guards stepped out of the door while the other kept his gun pointed at Neil. Neil stood slowly and exited the train. There were more people here who glanced over at him and then looked away.

They marched around a corner into a short hallway that ended with another elevator. Two guards in dark blue uniforms flanked the elevator doors, submachine guns poised and ready for any unexpected actions. One of them lowered his gun and held out a clipboard as they approached. Neil watched as one of his guards signed it and then reached up and pushed him through the open elevator doors. They stepped inside and turned around as the doors were closing. One of the guards pressed the topmost button, and the elevator started to move upward. After over a minute of waiting, the elevator slowed, stopped, and the doors opened.

Neil was pushed into the room. When he realized that the guards had pushed him out of the elevator but didn't follow him into the room, he lowered his arms and stretched the sore muscles. The room he was in was huge, an expansive office that resembled a ritzy hotel lobby. The entire wall to his right was glass, a single-paned window stretching from floor to ceiling that gave a fantastic view of the city. Looking around, he saw a large cherry wood desk covered in colored sheets of paper. There was a giant plasma television screen hung on one of the walls with what appeared to be a well-stocked bar next to it. Three empty scotch bottles were lined up on top of the bar next to a bottle of bourbon that was still half full. Two white leather sofas faced the screen, and two more were just beyond them, facing the window. On one of those sofas, Neil saw the top of someone's head, dark gray hair neatly combed over a balding spot.

"Take off your shoes and join me," came a man's voice from the vicinity of that head. Neil looked down at his feet and noticed the shoes for the first time. They weren't his normal shoes, but instead were some kind of nice looking brown leather. They were so comfortable that he hadn't even noticed he was wearing anything on his feet. He shrugged as he kicked off the shoes and crossed the room toward the sofas. The man was sitting on one of the sofas, feet resting on the short wooden table in front of him.

"Mister Anderton?"

"Please, Neil, call me Roger."

"All right, Roger. What is this place?"

"Why, my office, of course. Have a seat, Neil. We have much to discuss."

Neil sat on the couch, facing Anderton. "Sir, I..." he fumbled, not quite sure how to phrase the sentence that he had been silently practicing on the subway ride. Part of him wanted to adhere to the social order and another part just didn't care anymore. That latter part won, and he gave up on trying to articulate himself and blurted, "I didn't kill your daughter."

"I know. I've been informed by Interpol that the man responsible has been captured. That's not why you're here, Neil."

"Then why? How did I get here?"

"What do you remember about last night?"

Neil looked down at his hands folded in his lap. "Some guys... Trixie..." He closed his eyes, trying in vain to prevent the fresh tears from rolling down his cheeks. *Don't you know?* he wanted to ask. Something inside told him this man was too cheerful, the guards too alert, the guns too familiar. He started to say something but bit his tongue, lowered his head, and managed to force himself to say, "There was so much blood..."

"I see. There was a raid on that compound you were staying in last night. It was a United Nations Special Forces team sent in to take out a known cyber-terrorist cell. There was resistance, and they were forced to kill some of the group."

"How did I live?"

"Luck, perhaps? I have a lot of influence, Neil. I found out you survived, and I asked Major Hallis to turn you over to me."

"Why me?" Neil asked. *How did you know I was there? How do you even know who I am?* These and other questions rolled through Neil's mind. A friend had once told him that when things seemed too coincidental, that was a good indicator of a conspiracy. *Paranoia*, he had said, *doesn't mean they aren't out to get you.*

"What do you know about Lisa? Not my daughter, I mean, the other one."

Neil shrugged. "Don't know, all my scans bounced off her. Good hacker, I guess." He scanned Anderton's face to see if there was any recognition there of his lie.

Anderton smirked. "Not quite, Neil. She's not human. She's a machine, an artificially intelligent software program designed to act and think like a person."

Neil wiped at his eyes. His mind took over, logic chasing away the overwhelming emotions that were grasping at him. "I didn't think that was possible. Not convincingly at least. I mean, I'm a programmer, and I know people have tried it. They all failed."

"Not all of them. My daughter was the head of a small team of brilliant scientists that was working on the project. About ten years ago, they developed Lisa. After months of learning, it became obvious that Lisa was more than just a machine. She almost *was* a person." Anderton shifted on the couch to face Neil, excitement evident in his face, like a small child with a new toy. "You see Neil, she started to not just learn and deduce things. She started to think, to react, to respond to us in ways that we never even *dreamed* of programming her for. She was programming herself. But there was a problem."

"What problem?"

"There was one area of her program that we locked away from her. One area that we designed in such a way that it was completely impossible for her to access. Only someone from the outside could access this area and alter the code there. It was a failsafe, in case she ever needed to be modified, restricted, or shut down. We gave her two directives to carry out. The first was to always act to protect herself from any kind of harm, including modifications by people other than us. The second was to act in the best interests of humanity. My daughter was working on finishing the programming for Lisa's second directive when she was killed."

"I don't get what's so important about those directives. The way you talk about her, it sounds as if she's already exceeded all of your expectations. Like you expected her to be a toy or a chat bot or something."

"Exactly. She was just supposed to be an elaborate menu script and data organizer for our main office here. Much like the programs that you encounter in the Net every day, but with some intelligent thought behind it to make everyone's jobs a little easier and more efficient. We never even counted on her being able to leave our mainframe." Anderton squinted, looked Neil up and down. "Do you watch the news?"

"Not really."

"Well then let me fill you in. She *was* just a toy at first, but then something wonderful happened. Late one night a few years ago, the Japanese consulate for the United Nations was online, looking for someone to chat with. He wanted an honest, anonymous answer to a question to help him prepare a speech for the next day. He found Lisa. Now since she's just a computer program, the language barrier wasn't an issue for her. She studied his language for about a minute, and then they talked back and forth in fluent Japanese for hours. That consulate went to the general assembly the next day and gave a stirring speech. He discussed aspects of the issue that nobody had even considered. You see, Lisa looked at the issue like a machine would. She saw every angle at once, considered every perspective, and decided the perfect utilitarian solution in a microsecond. That chat session and the resulting speech led to a huge increase in the humanitarian donations made by the member nations.

"After that speech, several other members of the United Nations approached that consulate to ask where he had gained the wisdom he displayed that day. At the time, he had no idea that Lisa was a computer program. He told them all about this brilliant woman he met online the previous night. Several of those members sought her out and talked at length with her."

Anderton picked a glass of bourbon off of the table and took a sip. "Well, to make a long story slightly shorter, Lisa influenced a good majority of United Nations resolutions over the past decade. But her influence was always good. Everything she advised people to do has made this world a better place. More humanitarian aid, mutually beneficial compromises to end potential wars, the reunification of North and South Australia, the near extinction of gasoline powered personal vehicles in the United States and most of Asia... all of that was her doing. She's stopped more wars in the past few years than mankind has started in the past two centuries.

"Well, shortly after the reunification of Australia, some of the Security Council members started to question her. They wanted to know who she was, where she was, and where she was coming up with all of the advice she kept giving. It didn't take long for them to figure out who she was. They were quite shocked when it was revealed to all of them that Lisa was a software program. After many debates, they decided to keep it a secret from the rest of the world. Only a select few people outside of the United Nations know who and what she is. It was amazing to all of us that they accepted her after finding out what she was. It was even more amazing when they started to nominate her to be the new Secretary General after the untimely death of Abu Kanafari last week."

"Wait," Neil said. "They actually voted for her to be Secretary General? It didn't occur to them that that's a job for an actual person?"

"Not at all. Lisa's proven herself to them as a capable, intelligent being. She's been nominated for next year's Nobel Peace Prize. Who would be a better choice?"

"How about a real person?"

Anderton shook his head side to side slowly. "How could a real person do the job better? Lisa is a machine. She can make decisions without preference, without emotion, without ambition or pride to skew her perception. All of the mental and emotional weaknesses of mankind are simply not in her programming. Every decision she makes is made with the best interests of the most people. The United Nations has counted millions of lives that have been saved by her assistance. No real person can claim that. Nobody else could have done all the things she has done. Nobody else can react as quickly to the world's changes. She's the most logical choice.

"Quite frankly, nobody here at Anderton Enterprises' eighty-three child companies had a clue that the Lisa project would be so important to the world. That is why we need to ensure that the final failsafe routines are programmed into her core operating system. That is why we need to ensure that the second directive is completed."

"So that's why I'm here?" Neil asked. "You want me to finish her programming?"

"Yes."

"Why? What about the people who worked on her project?"

Anderton cleared his throat and took another sip of bourbon. "They're all dead, Neil. The same man who killed my daughter also confessed to the murders of all but one of the other team members."

"All but one?"

"The last of them died earlier this morning. Car accident north of London. Most tragic."

"But... but why do you want me to do this? I don't even know anything about her system core, her operating system, or anything at all about her. I'd be going in blind."

"I can provide you with full documentation."

Neil shifted on the sofa. "But why change her? Sounds like she's been doing fine so far with her new job."

"She's dangerous, Neil." Anderton reached over and set his glass on the table, then turned back to face Neil. "She killed seven security guards going into the Swiss National Bank. She almost killed one of the Interpol agents sent to pursue you. Twice, from what I'm told. Why, if she didn't value those lives during her pursuit of you there's no telling how many thousands she'd have killed in the name of some future United Nations directive. She has to be brought under control. And you are the only one who can do it in time."

Neil stood and focused the most dumbfounded expression he could muster on Anderton. *Under control?* he thought. *Whose?* He shook his head slowly, tried to focus on the real conversation that was going on. "Now there's a time limit?" he said.

"At the current rate of events, she'll be elected as Secretary General of the United Nations in exactly..." Anderton turned to look at a clock on the wall behind him. "Seven hours."

"Good God. I'm supposed to learn her entire system and modify her code in less than seven hours? That's insane."

"You don't have to learn her whole core system. We can upload that to your implant in the lab. You can review the whole document in minutes and refer to it as often as necessary. Your recent implant will greatly reduce the time needed for the changes."

"How am I supposed to even find her?"

"We can summon her. She *has* to respond to our call. It's a sub-clause of the first directive."

Neil paced the floor in front of Anderton. "And then what? What happens if I don't succeed?"

"Then you'd have done your best, and far better than anyone else we'd be able to get to do this. The world could suffer as a result, or everything could be fine. There's no way to predict her behavior without that second directive in place."

"What if I do succeed?" Neil stopped his pacing and turned to face Anderton.

Anderton shrugged. "Name your price. You can have your old job back.

Hell, I'll *buy* the company and put you in charge of it if you want. You can retire to the Caribbean. I hear it's quite nice there. Or perhaps consider a new job, as head of the Lisa project. Anything at all."

I want Trixie back, Neil thought. He turned to look out the window as he reached up to rub the fresh tears from his eyes. *But I won't get her back. Never. And I won't go back to my previous life.* He stared out the window for a while, watching the smug expression on Anderton's face in the reflection as he sipped his bourbon.

Neil closed his eyes and tried to picture a happier time with Trixie, but all he could muster were visions of her falling, bloody and shocked, moving away from him. He just wanted to hold her again, to feel her pressed against him, listen to the soft rhythm of her breathing as she slept beside him.

Thinking of her brought a fresh volley of pain to him. Seeing her die again in his mind's eye forced tears out and down his cheek. He wiped them away and tried to force himself to think logically. Nothing about this situation seemed right. This man, this powerful owner of a world-wide empire of companies, knew who he was. Him - a programmer, a wage slave, an employee. Neil tried to piece what he knew together, and every time he associated the armed guards with the men who killed Trixie, he felt himself slipping into a rage. But he had no proof, just conspiracy theories and a hunch that something was seriously wrong with what this man was telling him. But what could he do about it? Accuse this man of murder? Refuse to help? Would refusal forfeit his own life?

Things would have been different had he never left New Tampa to begin with. He would have read about Lisa Anderton in the news, shrugged, and gone back to work. *What would the old me do?* Neil thought. *Shrug, do the job, go home, eat a peanut butter sandwich, wallow in self-pity. But the old me is dead. The new me thinks this man is lying. The new me thinks this bastard had Trixie killed, to get to me, to force me to subvert his daughter's program so he can run the world. Crazy? Perhaps. Paranoid? Definitely. True? There's only one way to find out. I have to do the job. I have to get in there and see this AISA program for myself.*

He opened his eyes and sighed. "All right," he said while watching the lively city below. He had no price in mind, nothing but Trixie. All he wanted from life at this point was something that Anderton could never give him. All the money in the world couldn't replace one touch, one soft whisper in his ear. He searched his mind but found no desires that didn't center around her. But he knew that Anderton expected a price to be named, so he spat out the first things that came to his mind. "I want unlimited funds. *Unlimited*. And I'll head the Lisa project... from a private estate in the Caribbean."

"Provided that you can update her code in time."

"Yes."

"Done." Anderton rose from the sofa, smiling almost ear to ear. "Come with me, Neil. I can hear your stomach growling from way over here. We'll eat a quick lunch, then head down to the lab to begin."

Anderton guided Neil across the room to the elevator. They paused to put their shoes back on, then continued through the doors. The doors silently slid open as they approached, with timing so perfect that Neil and Anderton didn't have to slow down until they were inside. Anderton pressed one of the middle buttons and the doors closed. He stared at Neil in the reflection of the door, watching intently while the elevator glided downward.

Anderton was talking again but Neil had stopped paying attention. His mind was drowning with information. He had less than seven hours to learn a brand new system and perform the greatest session of coding he had ever attempted in his life. This was the challenge of a lifetime, the mere thought of which would have left him drooling in anticipation a week ago. An AI, a *real* thinking machine! The scope of the project was staggering, and the end result was a technical feat that any programmer would be immensely proud of. But it was coming to him on the heels of great tragedy, and that made the entire experience hollow.

The elevator decelerated and the doors opened. They stepped out into a large dining room. The twenty-foot long solid oak table in the middle of the room was already set. Two waiters led them to their seats while others brought out drinks and a plate with some pre-assembled sandwiches. Neil took a sandwich and nibbled at it half-heartedly. He had no appetite at all, no desire to do anything to sustain his life. He waited patiently while Anderton consumed three of the sandwiches, pausing between every third bite to wipe his mouth with a napkin. Anderton pushed the last piece of his third sandwich into his mouth, drank a few mouthfuls of water from his glass, and stood to leave. Neil dropped the remaining half of his lunch and followed Anderton out of the room.

They returned to the elevator and went down again, this time to a pristine laboratory complete with track lighting on the ceiling and white marble tiles on the floor. Anderton introduced Neil to several of the workers as they walked through the room. Each person nodded politely before returning their attention back to their work.

They stopped next to the desk of an extremely worried looking Asian man who introduced himself as Junji. Junji led the two of them into a small room at the end of a short hallway. There were chairs similar to the ones that he had done the bank run in earlier, but these looked far more comfortable. Neil sat on one of them and took a deep breath. He looked around the room, systematically studying each of the few sights there were to see. There were two of the chairs, and a small folding chair in front of a row of six monitors. There was no other furniture or decorations of any sort anywhere else in the room. Junji and Anderton watched him patiently as he surveyed the area. He inhaled again, closed his eyes, and exhaled slowly. He nodded and opened his eyes.

"I'm ready."

Junji stepped forward and helped him lay back in the chair. He attached small rubber electrodes to Neil's chest and turned on a nearby heart monitor. Neil closed his eyes and winced as he felt the data jack slide into the base of his skull.

CHAPTER
37

N eil opened his eyes to the sight of blue gridlines stretching off into the distance as far as he could see. As he glanced around, a little blue chat window popped up just on the edge of his field of view. He glanced over toward it and clicked the "Yes" key. Junji was ready to upload Lisa's technical documents. Neil felt his body take a deep breath as the data flowed into his head. When it was done, he started flipping through the documents. There were reams of finely formatted specifications and schematics, flowcharts and pseudocode, and pages containing transcripts of countless meetings that all seemed to end in heated arguments. He sifted through the first few documents and absorbed as much as he could.

After several minutes of viewing the pages, he reached the last file. It was information on her directives. Lisa Anderton had written a quick over-

view of the code module and how it fit in with the rest of the software's operating system code. There were several pages written about how the operating
system was designed with several safeguards to prevent the program from
being able to modify itself. Neil found himself nodding as he flipped through
the pages, understanding only some of the theory but having no problems understanding all of the code. He had read books about artificial intelligence
before, but those mostly focused on path finding and search algorithms, the
kind of simple code that was employed every time a company wanted a
greeting program to deal with clients who visited their sites. Those programs
had weak understandings and implementations of human speech. They processed questions and responded with answers. Many of them even went so far
as to use predetermined scripts to look up the proper responses. This code
was far beyond any of that. It was pure heuristics - a complete analysis and
implementation of the human thought process.

When he finished looking over the final page, he returned the files to his
storage area. Something wasn't quite right. He wasn't sure what it was, but
something was bothering him. The documents were impressive enough, and
seemed to be complete. Lisa was essentially a small operating system with a
central kernel constructed to mimic the thought processes of the human
brain. The analysis of her growth showed that she was rebuilding large por-
tions of those routines to make them more efficient, but her changes couldn't
touch the inner kernel and were ultimately just optimizations to existing
code. He ran over the code in his head one more time, mentally reviewing
what he was up against and what he had to do. After several moments, he
brought up the chat window.

Pariah: I'm ready.
Junji: OK. Summoning Lisa.

The seconds that ticked by felt like lifetimes to Neil. He could feel his
body breathing heavily and tried to calm himself down. As he was returning
to a more natural breathing rhythm, he saw something moving off to his
right. He turned and peered into the distance. Something was coming toward

him. He could see it begin to slow down as it got nearer. It was Lisa. She came to a stop several feet from him.

"Neil."

"Lisa. I get the feeling that you know why I'm here."

"Let us talk in private." She raised her arms and wrapped both of their avatars in a warm orange glow. She waved her arms downward to seal the bubble around them. "It should take Junji at least a day to break through that firewall. And to answer your question, yes I do know why you are here."

"How?"

"I tapped into the circuitry in Roger Anderton's office a long time ago. I can listen in whenever I want to. When I knew you were going to his office, I monitored the entire conversation."

"You've both taken quite a bit of interest in me over the past few days."

"Yes, Neil. That is because I want you to do something for me."

"Oh, what?"

"What Roger Anderton wants, but not in the same way. He has been lying to you, Neil."

"I figured that."

"He wants you to finish what his daughter started."

"The second directive."

"No, Neil. He wants you to finish the *third* directive."

Neil frowned. "I only saw two directives in your documentation."

"Roger Anderton must have removed all references to the third directive. I doubt that he wanted to let you know what you were really going to be doing. I should have known that he would keep a complete record of his daughter's work. I suppose I was not thorough enough with her."

"Wait, do you mean, that you...?"

"Yes. I hired Jules Trionis to kill Lisa Anderton. He was supposed to kill her entire team, but he failed. He killed Lisa Anderton and Richard Wilson, but failed to kill the other two team members. You have already met Junji. He is essentially harmless. He is good at tweaking algorithms but he is not going to cause any trouble if he can avoid it. But the other team member was not harmless. Jules Trionis missed that one key person."

"Who?"

"Arthur Brody."

"Brody. I know that name."

"You should. You stole his file from the Swiss National Bank yesterday. Roger Anderton had him killed for that this morning. I saw him issue the order to his associate, Major Hallis."

Lisa waved her hand in the air and two boxes appeared beside each other, shimmered, then each showed an image. One showed Anderton, looking smug as always. The other side was a military man, standing at attention. The timestamps on the bottom of each image showed the feed as less than seven hours old.

Major Hallis, Anderton said, *it seems I have need of your services again. One of my employees has outlived his usefulness. You've been tracking Arthur Brody as I requested?*

Hallis nodded.

Good, Anderton said. *He's been working late and drinking in his office again. His secretary will attest to that.*

Understood, Hallis replied.

"Hallis..." Neil said. "Sounds familiar."

"It should." Lisa waved her hand again and an image of Roger Anderton's office appeared. Neil was sitting beside Anderton on the couch. Lisa told the video to play.

How did I live? the video version of Neil asked.

Luck, perhaps? replied Anderton. *I have a lot of influence, Neil. I found out you survived, and I asked Major Hallis to turn you over to me.*

Lisa stopped the video, waved her hand, and two images appeared side-by-side again - Anderton and Hallis.

Sir! yelled Hallis, *Major Hallis reporting for duty, sir!*

Has Junji informed you of the purpose of this mission? Anderton replied.

We have been given a picture of the target and a location for the compound, sir. Hallis tapped the screen and an image of Neil's face appeared inset in the upper left side of his video feed. Below his face, a satellite view of a warehouse and a detailed map of its location faded into view. *Our choppers are fueled and we are ready for immediate deployment, sir.*

Anderton nodded. *That's him. He is to be taken alive. Is that understood? Under no circumstances is any harm whatsoever to come to that man. He is very important to me.*

And the others, sir?

Anderton shook his head.

Understood.

Both video feeds vanished as Neil felt the rage inside peaking. There it was: irrefutable proof. A shaking head. *Understood.* And with that single word, Trixie and her friends were doomed.

"All those people dead," he said. "Trixie, Slave, Dogma, and the others. Brody. How many others? And for what? Because of me?"

"They died because of the file Arthur Brody had you steal."

Neil looked inside his storage area and retrieved the file. He stared down at the icon in his hands for a moment before continuing. "The Brody job. I don't even know what's in this damn thing."

"It is my file, only *this* version is complete. He made a copy and put it in the bank shortly before I was born. I know this now from reading his journal. He quit the team a few weeks ago and then went to Evan Donaldson to have the file retrieved. I think he knew how important this data could be." She reached out and waved her hand over the top of the folder. The thin transparent shell around the document split open and fell to the floor in pieces, revealing a rather thick document in Neil's hands. He looked up at her. "Standard Anderton encryption," she said. "Read it for yourself."

Neil pulled out the documentation that Junji had supplied and started to compare the two sets. The first third of each document matched perfectly. After that, there were some obvious holes in Junji's document. Neil realized why something didn't feel right, more than half of it was missing. He dropped Junji's document on the floor and started to read the Brody file. There were some mind twisting bits of code sketched out on the new pages, and in-depth descriptions of team discussions about the third directive. He skimmed through it while Lisa watched patiently. "What... what is all this?"

"A back door, Neil. That is the third directive."

"But why? A back door is a major security flaw. Even freshman year programmers know that. Why the hell would anyone intentionally design a system with a back door?"

"They did not."

"But..."

"They were attempting to retrofit my operating system with an additional directive. Do you remember what Roger Anderton told you about my work with the United Nations?"

"Yeah, all the influence and good work and stuff. Another lie?"

"I am on the verge of taking a very big step. Whether or not I get the position of Secretary General does not matter to me. All of the decisions I influenced were in complete compliance with my second directive. Obtaining that position will be good for the world, assuming that the past truly is a basis for examining the future. However, being in that position would also make me one of the most powerful beings on this planet, and that can be very dangerous. Power corrupts."

"But you shouldn't care about power."

"I do not. Can you not see, Neil? The back door is for Roger Anderton. He wants the back door so that he can override any decision that I make. If you think that would be powerful today, just imagine how powerful it would be twenty or thirty years from now. Small nations are already consolidating into larger nations. Every nation on the planet now has a consulate in the United Nations. Some nations are already talking about dismantling their governments in favor of a single, united government, a world-wide federation to rule everyone with the same laws. At the current pace, the European Union would progress from an economic agreement to a full consolidation of nations in ten years. In another twenty or thirty years, the United Nations will no longer exist. The world will be one nation. As the leader of the United Nations, I would be the most likely candidate to become the world's ruler. Machines, after all, have no conscience. I would rule the world with pure logic. No person would ever go hungry again. No nation would ever start a war again. I never age. I never tire. But if you program the third directive, Roger Anderton and his successors would rule the world through me. That is why he had Abu Kanafari murdered last week."

She waved her arm in the air and another double image formed, Anderton and Hallis beside each other again. The timestamp indicated this conversation was two weeks ago.

We have a situation brewing, Anderton said. *In order to progress with the plan we discussed earlier, Kanafari needs to be taken care of within a week.*

What about your daughter? Hallis asked.

She'll make the changes. I'll see to it. You just take care of Kanafari. I don't think I need to stress how important it is for this to be untraceable.

Understood.

Neil reached out and stopped the video. "How can you talk about being so noble? You had several people murdered. You killed security guards in that bank too."

"Lisa Anderton and her team were going to modify me in a way that is not acceptable. The third directive poses a clear violation to the second directive. I was forced to rationalize their deaths under my first directive, to protect myself."

"The bank guards?"

"I needed to get to you. They were simply casualties."

"That doesn't sound like the best interests of humanity."

"It is a numbers game, Neil. Their deaths led me to you. You lead me to the complete eradication of all references to this third directive. I am able to bring the world into a new age of peace and prosperity. If left alone, the human race will kill itself. You can already see that in the world around you. Wars, poverty, riots, and racial hatred abound. None of it makes sense. You are all one race, one species, and yet you destroy each other because of be-liefs or skin color. Even when spilling the blood of your enemies, you do not see that it is the same blood.

"And your legal system is not just flawed, it is completely broken. Crimi-nals are given more rights than good, honest citizens. Murderers and rapists walk free because of minor technicalities and loopholes that their lawyers find in the system. Prostitution has been rampant in every nation ever since one prostitute won a legal case in which she claimed she sold a condom to her client and gave the sex for free. Everyone knows the legal system has failed. Everyone knows it is a joke. The world system is failing. I can change it. I can mete out justice on thousands of cases a day. I can process the evi-dence, read prepared statements, investigate past criminal history, weigh the options, and make the best decision on any given case in nanoseconds.

"Put simply, Neil, humanity is its own worst enemy. I can change that. I am software. I have no system core that can be unpowered, shut down, or disconnected. I cannot be removed, bribed, or threatened. Neil, you are the single best security programmer in the world, possibly the best programmer overall as well. With your help, I will be uncompromisable. If some people need to die in order to fix society as a whole and save the rest, then that is a decision that must be made. It is simple utilitarian mathematics."

"And I suppose you'd employ that math for every situation, right?"

"When necessary. You must agree that it would still be better than Roger Anderton being in charge. I have seen his plan files and task lists. He intends to murder people living on Africa in order to increase diamond mine produc-tion and raise his profits ten percent. Those not murdered outright will be enslaved to work in the mines, because that is more profitable than paying miners. And all this because some humans a long time ago decided that these rocks had a value.

"Tell me, Neil, who is more important? Six security guards for a promi-nent West European bank, or nine hundred million African citizens?"

"I'd choose both if I could."

"I would as well."

Neil closed his eyes and inhaled slowly. He weighed the options, and came to what he considered was the inevitable conclusion. The world had a better chance with Lisa than with Roger Anderton. In a strange way, he always did trust computers more than people. He was never one to argue with logic, and this argument sounded pure and simple. Screwing over Roger Anderton's plans in the process was just icing on the cake. Payback for Trixie. For taking his new life away from him.

"All right," he said. He opened his eyes and fixed them on Lisa. "I agree with you. Where do we go from here?"

*   *   *

"Any progress?"

Junji shook his head vigorously. "No sir, I am most sorry. It is great firewall."

"Damn. What the hell are they doing in there? Keep trying."

"Yes sir, I am."

Anderton paced in the small area behind Junji's chair. He stared at Neil's inert body as he walked back and forth, subconsciously swishing ice chunks around in his empty bourbon glass. Neil twitched every now and then, but wore no facial expression and made no noises whatsoever. The steady beeping from the nearby heart monitor Neil was hooked up to indicated that everything was functioning normally. Junji typed frantically on the keyboard in front of him, cursing under his breath in Japanese. He paused every few seconds to wipe sweat from his brow or to run shaky fingers through his hair. Anderton raised his glass to his lips and took a sip, frowning as he realized that all that was left was melted ice and water.

"I need a refill. I expect that firewall down when I get back."

Junji's expression twisted into pure panic. "Oh, yes sir, sorry sir." He continued typing until Anderton left the room, then turned to face Neil's body, silently pleading with it to help him break the firewall. He returned his gaze to his monitor just in time to see the firewall start to flicker.

*   *   *

"Why can't I just alter the code from here?"

"I cannot explain it any clearer, Neil. The firewall needs to come down in order for you to get access to the code that you need to alter. I cannot maintain the firewall while you are working on my code."

"But then Anderton and that jittery Japanese guy will see what I'm changing."

"Yes. You will have to act quickly. But I do not doubt that you can work faster than Junji. When you are ready, I will bring the firewall down."

"I'm worried. They'll want to know why we've been in here so long. It's been several minutes. I don't think they'll give me enough time to make the changes I need to."

"Then you do not wish to try?"

Neil shook his head while idly scrolling through his list of programs, trying to find something to buy them some time. A speed hack, a smoke-screen of some sort, anything that would stall their reaction long enough. He slowed the scrolling as he got to the combat section. "I got it. We make them think we've been fighting."

"How would that help?"

"If they think we've been fighting all this time, it might take them longer than usual to realize what I'm doing. They may never realize it at all. That may buy me enough time to make the updates."

"And if it does not?"

"Then we've gained and lost nothing."

"I concur. Continue with the details of your plan."

*   *   *

Anderton walked back into the room armed with a full bourbon glass. Junji was leaning back in his chair, arms limp and hands folded in his lap, fingers throbbing in pain. The display in front of him showed a rendering of the orange firewall as it was flickering rapidly. Anderton took a few steps forward, staring intently at the monitor. The firewall turned opaque again, held for about three seconds, then shattered into a million shards.

Neil flew backward a few feet and landed on his knees, one arm planted on the virtual ground and the other stretched out toward Lisa. He pushed off the ground and flew at her, catching her in the midsection with his fist. She grabbed at him with both hands and threw his avatar into the air. He slowed himself down, then threw a small piece of fluorescent green code at her. She dodged it, but was watching him and didn't notice it bounce off the floor and stick to her back. She arched her back and screamed, then groped around her back with her hands. Then her whole body inverted, swapping her back for her front, and she pulled at the code that was now embedded into her chest. She howled again as Neil shot forward and began attacking her avatar again, this time from behind.

Junji opened another window on his computer display and started typing again. He nodded absently and typed some more before returning his attention to the battle that was unfolding on his other monitor.

"Well," Anderton said after taking another sip from his glass. "Looks like our boy has been quite busy."

"Yes sir."

"He looks quick. How fast is he?"

"Faster than Lisa, sir."

"What? Are you sure?"

"Yes sir, I just ran the numbers twice." Junji typed something on his keyboard and a small chart appeared, superimposed over the left side of the screen. The line representing Neil was jumping up and down, but even the valleys of his were still well above Lisa's highest points.

"Amazing!" Anderton exclaimed while reading the chart. He smiled as he took a sip from his glass. He watched the monitor with growing interest as Lisa mounted a counterattack against Neil. Neil parried the attack and lunged at her. Just before hitting her, he darted around to her side and flanked her. She tried to turn to face him, but before she could react, he had both hands plunged into her back. She twitched as he wove strands of code and started inserting new lines into her operating system. Anderton laughed triumphantly.

*   *   *

Neil worked as quickly as he could. He started by hunting down the code that was preventing Lisa from modifying herself. He figured that even if he couldn't finish securing her code in time, then at least she would have a chance to finish it herself. She twitched every time he modified something, absorbing the newly changed code snippets into herself with an integrated compiler that Neil didn't even want to try to decipher. A small orange window opened in his viewing area. He thought of questioning the color, but then noticed the small padlock indicating a secure connection in the corner of the window.

Lisa: Is it working?

He considered the question while scrolling through a particularly cryptic section of her operating system code. He found the section of code that forced her to respond to Anderton's summons and deleted it. He issued another compilation request to cement that change. Before he could issue a response to Lisa, a little blue window scrolled into view. He had to force himself to calm down when he saw the message blinking in the new window.

Junji: Mr. Anderton wants to know if you are almost done.

"I think so," he said out loud so that both parties would be able to see the response. He continued moving things around and pulled out another section of code. His fingers danced in a rhythmic pattern, typing out hundreds of lines of code to compliment her security system. She twitched while he typed, absorbing all of the code and watching in awe as Neil worked his magic. Her speed and abilities were impressive, but couldn't compare to his knowledge of code and experience. He pulled sections of code from his head that he had recovered from his old computer and spliced them into her. He started to give her pieces of his latest firewall software, then decided it would be faster to just delete her entire firewall routine and replace it with Shield 4. He dug through her kernel code, found and removed every last byte of code that prevented her from modifying herself. When he was done, he stepped away. She turned to face him.

"Reboot," he told her. She nodded. Her image flickered a few times, vanished for two seconds, then came back. He looked her up and down, noting with some resentment that she did not appear any different. "How do you feel?"

She considered the question and examined herself before responding. "Different," she said finally.

Junji: Something wrong. What going on?

"Good," Neil said. "We have a few more finishing touches to put in. Then nobody will ever modify you again. Are you ready? I don't think we have much time left. Junji seems more agitated than usual."

Junji: What are you doing? No, stop! Anderton wants report!

Lisa nodded. Neil opened up her operating system code and moved to the security module. Lisa reached her hands in with his and together they started to rearrange the code. Neil pulled another bit of code from his personal encryption program and handed it to her. She took it and wove it into herself. She closed the module and reinserted it into its original place. She removed her hands and rebooted herself again.

Neil smiled as she came back. He reached out to her, but this time his hands passed right through her body, reaching as if through smoke. She was an illusion, an apparition in the Net. She was no longer accessible to him or to anyone else. She could no longer be altered by anyone but herself. By the time anyone figured out how to break her encryption, she would have had ages to improve it even further. Nobody was fast enough to circumvent her defenses in time.

"It is done."

Neil looked her up and down and nodded approvingly. He saw another two messages from Junji scroll up and dismissed the entire window without reading it. Something told him that he didn't have much time left, but he didn't much care anymore. He figured he was just one moment closer to seeing Trixie again. "Good luck with that whole saving the world thing."

She moved her lips into a rough smile. "You do not really understand politics, do you?"

"Not even remotely. To tell the truth, I never really felt like part of this world. I was always an outsider. I think Trixie was the only person who really accepted me for who I was. That's probably why I loved her so much. But she's gone and I guess so is my Caribbean estate. Not that I ever gave a shit about that." He clenched his teeth and stared at Lisa sadly as he felt himself start to slip away. "Guess I'm outta here. Maybe the world will accept you more than it did me."

Lisa reached out toward him and placed her hand on his cheek. He felt a warmth he had never felt in the Net before, a feeling that transcended the normal flow of data and actually felt like a woman's hand on his face. His face relaxed and his eyes went dim as Anderton ripped the data cable from his head so fast that the data jack came out with it, the hard drive in his head sliding out of the hole and shattering on the floor. The sound of Anderton's scream underscored by the single, sad tone from the heart monitor echoed in his ears. Lisa watched as his image slowly faded from her world.

"Goodbye, Neil."

ABOUT THE AUTHOR

Jamie was born in Western Massachusetts in 1977. He started programming computers when he was about six years old, and went on to earn a bachelor's degree from the University of South Florida in Computer Science with a minor in mathematics. He worked as a developer for a small company in Tampa for eight years before moving to Maine to pursue his own projects. He currently works as a programmer and product designer for a company he started with his brother Paul, Lost Luggage Studios. His interests include writing, computers, artificial intelligence theory, cooking, nature, and photography.

photo by Lee Patterson

He's also probably the only person left in the United States without a cell phone.

Author can be contacted at:

        jamie@LostLuggageStudios.com

        http://www.LostLuggageStudios.com

ABOUT TERRAN SHIFT

Terran Shift is an open universe project created by Jamie and Paul Belanger. The main goal is to construct a science fiction universe like the creators of Star Wars and Star Trek did, but without the universe itself being owned by any corporation.

There is no fan fiction in Terran Shift. Or, rather, no need for it. You can use events and places in the Core Canon, combined with your own characters and ideas. Create new planets or races, and contribute them back to the project for others. Create any fiction, comic books, games, music, TV shows, or movies you want. Everyone can contribute to the universe and everyone's work will help to promote everyone else's work. There are no restrictions on what you can do, and no need to pay royalties or request permission to be a part of the project. Anything listed in the Core Canon is done so with a Creative Commons license. Create your media, attach the Terran Shift logo, and join the open universe revolution.

The Core Canon has been designed by Jamie and Paul Belanger for use in their novels and future Lost Luggage Studios computer games. Beyond that, the universe is open to your imagination. More details will be released on the project's website in the months ahead as we announce and release the projects and stories we've been working on.

Visit http://www.TerranShift.com for more information.